THE HOPE CHEST

Charleston, SC
www.PalmettoPublishing.com

The Hope Chest
Copyright © 2022 by Anne Yorke

Hardcover ISBN: 979-8-8229-0810-9
Paperback ISBN: 979-8-8229-0811-6
eBook ISBN: 979-8-8229-0812-3

THE HOPE CHEST

ANNE YORKE

DEDICATION

This book, a labor of love, is dedicated to my two sons.
One whose spirit lives on in my memories and is present
with me always.
The other son whose spirit embellishes my existence
and offers me the
promise of good things yet to come.
I could not have been prouder of, or more in love with,
you both.

Perhaps we are not meant to know somethings, for that is life too. A seeking. It may be our only purpose here.

–Gabriel Byrne

PART I

REMEMBERANCES
AND
REMINISCENES

CHAPTER

1

The girl sat with her legs folded beneath her, facing a large unremarkable, wooden chest. Her mother called this "the hope chest". The child, who was learning to read, had read of fairies and genies, offering magic lamps and wish fulfillment. She had been told about the leprechauns in her grandparents' home country of Ireland, promising unending pots of gold and riches. She could only imagine what assurances of treasure the hope chest might hold. Daddy had been in the war so there must be many medals attesting to his bravery. She was sure she would find photographs of all the strange and distant places he had been. There had to also be pictures and trinkets belonging to the four grandparents she had never met. She sat silently as usual, twisting her braids and gazing in wonder at this monument to her past, present and future that she had by now entrusted with all her hopes and dreams.

Maybe it was the stark surroundings of that one room in a boarding house that inspired her to dream of more. Grace would speak often, and descriptively, throughout her life of this early home she shared with her parents and baby sister. The bed where all four of them slept, the wooden sled that served as a table for meals for the younger ones and Daddy's stiff, uncomfortable wooden "easy chair". There was no stove, no refrigerator and no toilet. A hot plate, a box in the window and a porcelain pot in one corner of the room substituted for these amenities. Mom and Daddy of course could go upstairs to the communal bathroom in the boarding housed but it had been declared too unsafe and nasty for the girls. But bleak as this might sound to others it was a warm and loving home where she learned to love, read, write and dream. Even during the great Christmas blizzard of 1947, the dining sled did double duty providing some wonderful memories of those snowy days in New York City.

She had her family and her mysterious, compelling hope chest. Her imagination and inquisitiveness were also being forged in the cauldron of an Irish Catholic home. There would be gatherings, celebrations, storytelling, music, the brilliance of Christmas and the offering of redemption and life ever after. Yet her formative years would also be tainted with the weight of the guilt, fear and secrets that were the holy trinity of Irish existence. These would become spirit numbing to a child such as Gracie, impelling her to thoughts of escapism and discovery. Thus, forging her destiny with the contents of the hope chest.

Gracie rose and stood over the chest. Mom had gone downstairs to speak to the landlord bringing little Clare with her.

Finding herself alone she had been magnetically drawn to this treasure trove again even though she had been admonished so many times about staying away from it. Jiggling the latch in the front, she was lost again in her daydreams of possibilities. It was then that she heard her mother's voice, shouting angrily, "Haven't you been told not to touch that box?" She was confused by the sternness in her mother's usually, mild and forgiving voice. She realized that her mother had just called this precious hope chest a "box" as if it too were being degraded by the girl's audacity. This was indefensible! It would not be the last time Grace stood her ground and questioned the judiciousness of this ban. "Why mom, why can't I look in the chest?" "Because you were told not to" came the reflexive response, still not answering her five-year old's question. And so, the years would continue like this.

CHAPTER

2

Gracie was a very bright little girl but boredom and poverty can be a soul killing combination. Right behind their house, in the adjacent small backyard, common in row houses, a man was teaching neighborhood kids to walk on stilts. She was drawn to the window often by their laughter and squeals of achievement. She imagined the man to be part of a circus troupe. He seemed to love children, as any circus performer she could conjure up must. Being Grace, she began fantasizing about learning how to walk on stilts as her inroad to a life in the circus. She was entranced by the thought of traveling all over the country and maybe even the world if she joined a circus. Surely, she could be a trampoline artist or one of the bejeweled ladies that rode the elephants. Mostly she wanted to be a clown who would make children and sad adults laugh! When she asked her parents if they could take her around the corner to meet the stilt-walker and start her lessons, they just looked at her in fear. Mom finally responded by telling her father that the man was "too friendly" with the children and with his high stilts she thought he may be looking in the window. That put the kibosh on her circus career. Ironically enough, as Grace grew into woman-hood she would encounter many other "too friendly" men in the NYC subways system. Her parents of course could not protect her then. For now, however, besides the chest she was told to stay away from the window and that first little seed of fear and uncertainty was planted.

CHAPTER

3

Through the years Gracie's fears were propagated and nurtured at home. If she wanted to ride a rollercoaster the story of the boy who stood up in the coaster and had his head severed on a turn by a low hanging beam, was told and retold, eventually even to Grace and Clare's own children. They were warned of the miscreants and child predators stalking the children of the neighborhood only to snatch them away to sell to people worse than themselves - the Gypsies! Surely her stilt-walker must be one! As she grew and wanted to go on car rides with family members, since her dad didn't have a car, she was treated to, and was terrified by, stories of tragic and terrible car wrecks. Her personally most frightening tale was of the arms that were severed by passing trucks of careless children who stuck them out the car windows after being warned. It was many years later that she pondered the irony that this never seemed to happen to dogs, who were the happiest with their whole heads sticking out the window of a car, catching the wind as the vehicle sped along. Clearly, they were never subject to the same laws of the universe as the children in Grace's family. Then of course there was the gratuitous story of the child's head rolling down the street under the elevated subway because, of course, he stood too close to the platform edge with the train pulling into the station. Mom would always offer the trilogy of the Holy Family, "Jesus Mary and Joseph" and bless herself after telling this little tale. Throughout her life her mother made every car ride an ordeal by threatening to jump out of the auto if the speed unnerved her, citing of course one of several stories that she could call on to convey this lesson. There were always limitless tales of selfish children who had their scars and injuries to prove that they did not listen to the warnings of their adoring and selfless parents. They fell and had head injuries and broken bones because they stood on swings or climbed fences or didn't keep their hands on the handlebars of their bikes. Incorrigible children with no fear of God, because disobedience to parents was disobedience to God and that was a mortal sin as noted in the ten commandments. These and many more became an indelible part of her oral family history. Like the generations before in the old country who heard stories of banshees and dullahans to frighten the young, this was the way of teaching Irish children the fear of living before they had even begun their journey of life. No surprise that the Irish became such gifted story tellers and eventually writers. It was a tool of social order and conformity applied beautifully through the ages by both family and church.

CHAPTER

4

Far more frightening and lethal were the weapons of fear invoked by the priests and nuns, at mass and during religious instruction. The demons and curses at the disposal of the Church were shattering to the minions of little ones struggling with their catechism classes and preparation for their first CONFESSION! There was the tale of young Saint Agnes, who was beheaded for not renouncing her faith and defiled first, a fate never explained to, nor understood by, the children. Grace would choose Agnes as her confirmation name however, because the nuns made little maid Agnes exceptionally honorable. The case of her suffering was rendered in gruesome detail. Grace knew from the nuns that this teenager had really suffered before death. It was almost as if she were one of theirs in a very tangible way. Let's not forget those poor put upon Portuguese shepherd children who were threatened with being boiled in oil for refusing to recant their claim that Mary, the mother of Jesus no less, had appeared to them. Of course, there were always the omnipresent fiends and devils, sent by Satan himself, hurling temptations that would of course secure your one-way ticket to hell. Martyrs and saints were the good guys in this epic struggle for the souls of the young. Stories of their sacrifice and demise were told regularly to reinforce the control of little minds. Shrines were erected to honor and perpetuate their faith and fortitude such as Our Lady of Fatima in Portugal, Basilica of Saint Frances in France and our lady of Knock in Ireland.

She also learned of Limbo during her religious upbringing. Limbo was taught to be an alternative to heaven and hell. A lonely place where unbaptized infants and children who were not conceived in grace were exiled forever. What a terrible image limbo conjured in her fertile young mind. A barren and cold place, lacking both love and laughter. Grace would make sure the children she looked forward to mothering would be well protected from yet another peril resulting from lack of faith. The Church had promised her that her children would be born without original sin if they were baptized. It would insure their eternal residency in Heaven. Grace vowed to obey this rule for the consequences of her resistance were too, too, terrible to consider.

Of all the tools and weapons at the Church's discretion to enforce compliance, the power of the confessional was possibly its most sinister. It elevated fear to the level of the atomic bomb to 1950's Catholic children. It ranked up there with school shelter drills. But instead of the "commies" they were dealing with the fear of not receiving absolution for the trivial little "sinful" actions that youngsters invariable perform. Cheating at a board game, answering back your parents, not saying your prayers or having impure thoughts. Grace, who could be very literal, eventually confessed to this major sin. She had found a copy of Lady Chatterley's Lover in the depth of the clothes hamper of all places. After a quick perusal of the text, she was sure she had done a very bad thing. First there was the question of permission from her parents which of course had not been sought or given. Then there was the lure of the very descriptive text which she did not understand, but knew was not to be read by her. This she concluded could lead to impure thoughts although, like the term "defilement", had been left broad and undefined. The fact that the book was hidden from her clearly meant it contained words not suitable for a young mind and the thoughts it might generate. Her next confession found her in the confessional box with Father Wilson eager to confront her sin and willing to do her penance. She was ashamed when he told her she was a very disobedient child but felt she deserved that depiction. However, she did not expect to be told at seven years old that she was already living with one foot in hell! Of course, she could not share this rebuke by the priest with her parents. Their physical retribution would be far more painful. From that day forward she hated the concept of confession. Her useful gift of a fertile imagination provided many great, if contrived, stories to share with Father Wilson in the years to follow. He would smile as he blessed her chaste little soul at the communion rail. She knew however, she had earned her place there at the altar by meeting fear with fire.

CHAPTER
5

On a particularly brisk Sunday in December, after having attended mass together, Grace found her mother in a very light hearted mood on their long walk home. She was singing as she often did during her moments of happiness. The child loved the little rhyming melodies her mother made up at these times. "Mom", she said, "Can I ask you a question?" "Of course, Gracie" came the quick and artless response. "Why do you call my treasure chest a hope chest?" Mare replied, "Oh that's an easy one love. Proper young ladies acquire and accumulate items and mementos that they save to help begin their married life. They keep them in a chest which they call their hope chest. Things and necessities they hope will help set the tone of a happy home." There was a note of wistfulness in her mother's voice that Gracie attributed to the realization that the home she had been dreaming of as a younger girl was not exactly the one-room they all lived in now. Gracie decided to use her mother's obviously distracted state to her own advantage. Pushing the issue, Grace dared to ask, "Is that what you keep in the chest?" Now on alert, and no longer singing or even humming, her mother responded. "Of course not! Not at all. I am already a married lady and have used the things I had once kept there. Now Daddy and I use it to keep important papers and the like. Although, come to think about it, I do have something still in it I will show you when we get home, OK?" Grace wondered if she had heard correctly. Was she actually going to be treated to a look inside the chest? Gracie was now on what felt like the longest walk ever home from church. Not being able to believe her good fortune she was consumed with anticipation. But when they arrived home, to her disappointment, she was told to stand on the other side of the room, turn her back to mommy and close her eyes tightly. She heard her mother unlatch the lock, raise the old protesting lid and rustle within its sacred contents. When her mother was satisfied and had closed the chest again, Gracie was told she could turn around. In her mother's hands rested a beautiful, though old, crackled cup, a teacup actually. Her mother explained this had been her mother's and she used it to read tea leaves for the family and neighbors back in her hometown of Cavan, in Ireland. Grace discovered that day that her grandmother had the "gift of sight". She would learn later that this was not the rarest of talents amongst the ladies of the Emerald Isle. Given the influence of the Irish gypsies, or tinkers, the Irish propensity for "tea" drinking, and the wonderful, colorful "gift of gab" that was part of their culture, Grace concluded, that there must have been many an Irish woman who could prophesize thru the placement of leaves at the bottom of a cup. But on this day, in this room, from the depths of her beautiful chest, Grace had learned a wondrous thing about her grandma. Though they had never met she now knew she was magical, capable of magical things. The energy of the cup resonated in Gracie's hands and heart. Grace would grow to accumulate her own collection of teapots and teacups but her grandmother's cup, cracked and chipped as time passed, would always be her favorite. Throughout her life there would be many events that would confirm for her that she, as well, was "fey touched".

CHAPTER
6

Gracie began to think more now of her mother's parents. She found it easier for her own mother to be open about this topic than anything pertaining to the chest. She entertained her daughters desire for insights into her own childhood. The child learned that her grandparents had traveled years apart as teenagers on big ships from their home country to America. Coming from large and economically insecure families, they would make the Atlantic crossing in "steerage" sharing their deck space with as many as a thousand fellow travelers and all manner of livestock being shipped abroad. The steerage area was smelly, dank and noisy and certainly a very risky environment, especially for a young woman. Their price of passage had to paid for well in advance and secured with the promise of employment upon arrival. Generally, a prepaid ticket would be purchased by a relative who had already established themselves in this new country. This same family member would pledge and present proof of employment secured for the new arrival. In the case of her grandmother, Maggie, she was grateful to secure a position as a maid and nanny in the home of a wealthy NYC family. Grandpa, who had been a civil engineer in the old country was fortunate to gain work with the Con Edison company of New York, arranged by his family with his passage money. She was told that despite the homesickness and fear of the unknown they had been welcomed by generous and joyful relatives who did their best to make their transitions as easy as possible. Both her grandparents' hopes were high for a bright future and grew brighter still when they met, and danced, at an Irish social organized by a local parish. Their courtship played out, it was revealed, in an area known as Hell's Kitchen. To her young ears this did not sound like the Garden of Eden that Adam and Eve had lived in! Over the years she would discover she was right. Hell's Kitchen, home to thousands of Irish immigrants and a lesser number of violent gangs, was a notorious and frightening place close to the waterfront on the westside of Manhattan. It was rife with crime, poverty, disease and despair. Some of Mom's relatives still lived in a building at "666" 10th Avenue. Gracie and her mom had visited them once.

CHAPTER

7

She was filled with trepidation as she approached a building with the sign of the devil, 666, in the middle of a neighborhood called Hell. Gracie knew about the pucas, dark, hairy looking spirit creatures with Satan like ears. She knew they could be riotous pranksters capable of both good and evil things. She had been imagining her relatives as these impish fairy beings living in this dark and violent world since she first was made aware of their existence.

As her mother rang the door buzzer, she tensed knowing the moment of reckoning had arrived! The still pretty older lady with the warm smile and musical voice (later to be recognized by Grace as the Irish lilt) was not who Gracie had been expecting. She welcomed them with a passel of warm hugs and directed them into the kitchen, situated further into the interior of her railroad flat. The layout was aptly name because of the narrow walk thru nature of the rooms. After cups of tea, and delightful little shortbread biscuits, Grace's great-aunt Cecilia, or Sissy, as she was affectionately known, began to tell family stories the child had been longing to hear. Grace learned that as newlyweds, Aunt Sissy and her husband James had sponsored her grandmother's relocation to America as well as other brothers and sisters adventurous and desperate enough to make the crossing. Her grandparents, Maggie and Daniel, took residency here with her growing family when they were wed. They would eventually move to the Bronx where they would have four children themselves and her grandpa she learned, became a superintendent of a large Bronx tenement. This insured his growing family free rent if not the spacious apartment her grandma would have appreciated. It was during this revelation that Grace learned of the death of the grandfather she had never met. A young, hard worker and relentless provider with three young children and a wife expecting their fourth, he succumbed to the Great Spanish flu epidemic of 1918. Many, many years later during the Covid 19 killer flu of 2019 she'd reflect on this period of her mother's life and grieve the grandfather she had never met. He was only 32 years old when he died. His sister, through tears still, extolled his handsomeness and great wit. His sense of duty to family and the church were not forgotten. Gracie felt her own eyes well up as sister, child and grandchild mourned together the loss, too early, of young Daniel.

At this point in the telling of her grandparents' story, a bellowing and boisterous force entered the room. When Grace looked up, she could not make the connection between the image invoked by the bellicose noise and the thin, frail near-man before her. He was a cyclone of motion though, reaching with one hand for a beer while laying a gun atop the icebox with the other. "Wanna see my gat Mare?" he offered Grace's mother in the lingo of the neighborhood. "No thanks Gerry" she responded. "We were just getting ready to leave. We have a bit of a journey ahead but it was good to see you." Ignoring the protestations of his first cousin, Gerry continued to regale his guests with the escapades of "his boys". Grace laughed at his demonstrations of the skills of Seamus McFisticuffs, a local boxer and neighborhood hero. Gerry of course was home, unemployed, where he lived with his poor put upon elderly widowed mom. The gift of an audience for his lurid stories was not something he would easily relinquish. His pals had names such as Spider McGee, Rat-faced Reilly, Declan Roach and Bugsy Murphy. Whether or not these were really his friends or just men in the neighborhood Gracie now realized that, among its other problems, Hell's Kitchen had a frightening bug and vermin problem. This little miss, who longed to see the world outside her lonely and restricted quarters was, for the first time, happy to be going home to the sanctity and relative safety of her one room residence. She very gratefully placed her hand in Mom's and held tight as they left.

CHAPTER
8

They were not home long when her mother, after rustling around in the hope chest, emerged with several old photos. One was a picture of Grandma that she had actually seen before. The other a mesmerizing sepia colored photo of a young man with a magnetic gaze. He was not tall it seemed, but dressed quite nicely in, what would have been called at that time, his Sunday best. He had very dark hair and eyes and a prominent nose. To Grace he resembled any one of the Italian men who lived in her neighborhood. She took the photo and after examining it turned it over. To her surprise it was a postcard. She did not feel the same instantaneous connection she did when holding her grandma's teacup for the first time. Her mother had no other photos to show to confirm the authenticity of this picture. She herself was only 2 years old when he died. Therefore, she had no memories or other evidence to offer as proof of his existence or his place in Grace's young life. While this saddened the girl who longed for grandparents like the other girls who paraded theirs in front of her, she was not one to readily accept things just told to her. Realizing that her mother seemed to treasure this photo Grace thanked her for letting her see it. Grandpa Daniel was returned to the hope chest where he remained throughout much of Gracie's life.

On days that Gracie thought of the few remembrances in the chest that she had been treated to, she realized her mother had certainly had a difficult and sad childhood. With the father she couldn't remember deceased, and her mother alone with four children, it was not an easy life for her growing up. Her grandmother took on the duties of her deceased husband, hauling tenant's garbage and mopping hallways in their tenement building. Eventually, with her children growing and the need to supplement this meager income, she went off to Manhattan to clean business offices at night. Later she would switch to being a maid in one of the more prestigious hotels in New York City. Eventually two of her daughters would follow her into the hotel industry, a job haven for Irish women and many other immigrant groups, throughout the city's history. Mare would be one of them. Eventually she would meet Clare's father, a head houseman at the Essex House Hotel where she worked. Grace believed already, that her mother's work experience could not have promoted a positive self-image or engender self-worth in a young woman. Grace was happy to know it was her birth that caused her mother to stop working in the hotels. In years to come Grace would find herself in the middle of the social revolution brought on by the women's rights movement. She was passionate about the idea of women having the same opportunities as men. It also made her painfully aware of the limited choices afforded to her grandmother, mother and aunts when they sought employment with no degrees, diplomas or skills to recommend them. This combined with gender bias must have been crippling to their life chances. She knew it would not be allowed to happen to her.

CHAPTER

9

While her grandmother worked, the younger siblings were left in the care of the oldest daughter, Margaret, or Marge, herself only a pre-teen. Mom told her once how she was almost kidnapped from their apartment by a man who had entered through the fire escape window. Encountering young Mare, he told her he was there to take her to dance school. Knowing her mother could never help fulfill the dream she had of being a dancer, Mare was willing to go with him but first needed help fastening her high button shoes. Calling out to Marge loudly and shrilly, she caused the man to quickly exit through the same window. Mare was safe due to the presence and vigilance of her sister. Gracie who loved her Aunt Marge, recognized early her authority in the family. She spent years of her younger life as a surrogate parent and cook for the younger ones. Gracie loved the story of how she cooked tapioca pudding for the children one night offering them a treat for their good behavior. However, she had accidently substituted salt for sugar in the recipe. Though the kids were gagging and pleading when she served this, she stood over them until each one had finished their bowl. "Mom, works too hard for us to be wasting food" she berated her brother and sisters. "So, eat up!", she threatened which, unsurprisingly they did. This parable served as an example to Grace of the love, respect and obedience of these young, second-generation Irish children for their elders. These, and other disarmingly humorous stories of sadness, mixed with dedication were told over and over at baptisms, weddings, funerals and family gatherings. The resilience of the grandmother she never knew, who would feed the soccer player friends of her daughters with platters of food and three roasts every week, spoke to her generosity and kindliness. The young widow who pledged a payment for a stained-glass window to honor her deceased husband during her Church's renovation taught her much about her family's magnanimity. Unfortunately, as an adult, remembering this particular story of her grandmother's gift to her parish church, Grace was bothered more by the Church's greed at accepting this humble woman's gift. It tarnished, for her, the beauty of her grandmother's gesture. It spotlighted the Church's desire to control, not only help, its intelligent but ignorant newcomers to our shores.

Gracie's Mom would emerge from this childhood of life in a strict devout Irish Catholic family as a lovely, graceful, and generous woman who might be found singing and dancing around in a simple cotton housedress decorated with safety pins picked up and saved. Grace found her mother beautiful with her thick, dark brown braids criss-crossed on the top of her head. They resembled a tiara and lent a regal air to her mother. However, she was self-deprecating to a fault and appreciative of any kindness shown to her or her children. It was always painfully obvious to Grace that her mother had her secrets and fears to contend with. Fear of heights, bridges, elevators, even escalators. In addition to the usual warnings and admonishments of talking to strangers, she would add her restrictions on what you could reveal to landlords, neighbors, teachers or friends and their parents. Her constant remonstrations included, "Never tell anyone about the family." "Don't call attention to yourself'." "Never become a blot on the family reputation." "People will talk. They have nothing better to do!" To Grace her mother's greatest fear seemed to be her fear of moving up, over or forward socially.

CHAPTER
10

Despite her disabling phobias though, she was a patient and artful teacher. She invented endless games with the simplest of materials, often just pencil and paper, to teach her daughter, and the grandchildren yet to come, to read and write. It was the ideal of fun and learning combined. She had an innate gift for nurturing the intellect and imagination of children. As a wonderful story teller she would often do her children's creative writing homework eager to hear the grade and any comments she would earn. Her style of writing was imaginative and beautiful which Gracie would soon skillfully adopt since it was modeled so brilliantly for her. She was probably the reason Gracie would pick English in college as her field of study.

When Gracie was 9 her mother became the vice president of her grammar school's PTA. This was done at the behest of Father Wilson who was seeking to expand the church's sphere of influence in the local public school. Grace would look back at her mother's decision to do this as a good thing for her mother, who began to explore the world beyond her nuclear family. It was, however, a terrible manipulation of her mother, and a method of circumventing the First Amendment to our constitution Grace thought. Shame on you again, Father Wilson!

In the most tangible way, it was her mother who eventually enabled Grace to attend her university classes and secure her degree. Grace would grow up to marry and divorce young, with two little boys to raise. By agreeing to babysit her grandsons, she gave Grace the greatest gift of all - loving and protective grandparents to help raise them and transmit the values and culture of her own youth. Of course, she would also be the transmitter of the same fears, guilt and regrets that had shaped Grace's inner world and nourished her suspicions of the plausibility of events in her life as they were being revealed.

CHAPTER

11

Growing up, her mother would proclaim, her greatest love of all was Jesus and her family, though Grace could not tell you in which order they were ranked. There was her sister Irene, the youngest who would never be held by her father but quickly became her mother's favorite. This fact Gracie heard Irene hurl maliciously at her sisters whenever there was tension between them. The verbal onslaught against her would always abate, and all invectives cease when she resorted to this weapon, only she could wield. She was the secret alcoholic aunt whose sisters, and husband unfortunately, enabled her self-destructive behavior. She was the most religious of all her siblings and attended mass daily.

On Sundays these acts of faith and fidelity earned her a spot on one of the bar stools in a favorite pub. Aunt Irene and her Uncle Aloysius often took Grace to church on Sunday, to save her soul she guessed, but also, so she could ride in their car. Afterwards, she would accompany them on their tour of their favorite beer-gardens and watering holes. Gracie loved the atmosphere of the pubs with the gaiety, singing and boisterousness of the clientele. She was treated to unlimited glasses of coca cola and pretzels, even games of shuffleboard or bocce. On special occasions they would go to a big beer hall in Rockaway, Queens with an impressive open-air veranda. What made it even more special for Grace was the amusement park near this bar. Her uncle would give her some coins and she was off to play the games of chance hoping to win a big stuffed animal. Most often she would return to her aunt and uncle empty handed but with a smile on her face. The Rockaways had long been a summer enclave of the Irish-Americans in the city. Hard-working parents, such as her grandmother, would save all year to give their children the opportunity for the benefits of the safety, sun, sand and surf of this special place. If they could afford it, they would rent small, dank bungalows close to the ocean for a week or two.

After a Sunday out at the beer joints, Uncle Aloysius would drive home under the elevated subway ensured of their safety because he had made them all bless themselves before they departed. He also had the protection afforded by his statue of Saint Christopher, saint of travelers, on his dashboard paying homage to his personal navigator. These would all become fond memories for Grace until she was able to see later how early she was exposed to the acceptance of such destructive behavior wrapped in the religious rituals of a Sunday afternoon.

Later in her life, during the 1960s and 70s Irene could be seen around the neighborhood wearing her signature hat and gloves. She always wore big gaudy pearl earrings and "poppit" plastic pearl necklaces and carried her pocketbook in the bend of her elbow. The hat was probable because she still went to mass every morning followed by her daily visits to the three funeral parlors in the area. She would bypass the Jewish funeral parlor of course. She was particularly drawn to the wakes of soldiers killed in combat. She would enter the parlor, sign the guest book, say a prayer and offer condolences to the grieving family. On Sundays, at the pub, she would denounce the horror of war and the sorrow of these broken families. Her compassion was acknowledged and her comrades at the bar would raise a toast to the deceased and recite a mournful poem or Irish blessing. Only her narration of a mass of the angels, she had attended during the week, for a child, who had passed away by illness or accident, brought her more attention and more rounds of her favorite beverage. It was the adult Grace that would look back on this aunt she truly loved and mourn for her. She'd remember the Easter clothes she would purchase for Clare and her when money was tight. She would recall the trips to amusement parks and movie theaters. Her illness had gone unacknowledged and tacitly accepted by everyone hiding this sorrowful family secret. Grace was embittered by what she perceived to be a failure of the family culture and her Irish Catholic faith to save Irene from herself.

CHAPTER

12

Marge was her mother's oldest sister. "Marge the matriarch" she would become with the passing of Grace's maternal grandma at 59. Kidney failure she was always told but Grace would one day come to believe she had suffered from the same family curse as dear Aunt Irene. Marge was only 33 at the time but fell easily into the role that had been set for her many years earlier. Marge was high strung and nervous throughout her life. The family believed it was because the four year old child had walked into the room during her father's embalming. In those days it was not unusual to hold Irish wakes in the parlor of the home.

She was also the renegade who married a Protestant without the blessing of her mother. She could not even get married in a church at the time but was married instead in the rectory of the parish priest. Ironically it was her and her heathen husband,

Artie, who gave shelter and comfort to Grace's grandmother during WWII. Irene and Mare would move in, as well, not long after her grandmother's death. Very pregnant with Grace, and Eddie in Europe with the army, Mare moved in with her family. Marge was both brash and nurturing, cherished and respected for her important role in the family's survival. Hers was Grace's first real home. How sad her grandmother had died right before her birth and not been there to welcome her daughter and grandchild home. It was during this time, though very, very young that she would hear stories of her grandmother and grandfather and their lives in Ireland. She would be shown pictures of her daddy now overseas so she would recognize him when he returned to them. It was also Marge who would teach her to say "bastard" while showing her his picture.

Marge had a bit of a gambling problem. Her afternoons were spent primarily in bingo parlors and her weekends with Artie at the racetrack. With four state tracks in close proximity to their home this was easy enough. Friday nights were couples' poker nights. Sunday family meals in her house would end with games of poker and pokeno for the adults, the children looking on waiting to be treated at the end with a few coins from the winners. Grace was told by her mother that Marge had called one afternoon threatening to jump off a roof because the bookies were after her. Never having a bank account or discretionary funds, my mother called Irene pleading for help for Marge. The money delivered, and her deathly plunged averted, Marge continued with her lifestyle often including Gracie on her gambling escapades. Of course, no one ever told Artie about the bookies or the threats on her life, and life returned to normal.

It was all fine with a naïve Grace until, about to get married, she was told by her aunt to please thank Uncle Artie for the generous wedding gift she had not received because Aunt Marge had spent the money. Though her first reaction was anger and resentment for being asked to participate in this lie, Grace forgave her eventually. Predictably Marge outlived her siblings. Really, hadn't Marge gone to Catholic school and been exposed to such vices because of the wanton gambling supported by the Church, bingo, bazaars and raffles. It was getting harder for a young woman, about to become a newlywed to ignore, the often, negative impact, of her religion on the people she loved. Secrets were piling up.

CHAPTER

13

Her mind drifted to thoughts of her Uncle Barney. Extremely handsome, tall, dark-haired and loved to the point of obsession by his three younger sisters, he could more aptly be seen as the thorn among the roses! He was an unabashed member of that Irish American subculture known as "the Shanty Irish". He and his English wife, with what her sister-in-law's described as her "airs" and her lace curtain ways, had four children. The two boys, neighborhood trouble makers and the two daughters, neighborhood tarts. They all attended parochial school though which raised their social currency in the family. In fact, it was only Grace and her sister that went to public school. The teasing was relentless from Barneys brood that this fact made the girls stupid. It most certainly insured that they wouldn't be going to Heaven either because of their pagan education. Grace longed to tell them that they in fact were already paving their own path in the opposite direction. She would always refrain, however, because of her mother's great love for Barney, who she always called her favorite. Clearly it was Barneys drinking that was the catalyst for the chaos in his family. He had been a big beer drinker since his youth often accompanying his mother to the tavern. By adulthood he had an obvious problem that no one talked about except his overburdened wife. Her complaints fell on the deaf and adoring ears of his sisters. Grace could remember a visit from her uncle one week night late into the evening. When the door was opened, he stood there with a pot on his head and mashed potatoes cascading down his forehead and cheeks. "Mare, she threw me out", he sobbed. "God love you Barney", mom replied and helped him to the day bed my parents had just purchased. "You'll stay with us. No trouble. She'll take you back tomorrow". And she did. After all he had a job with the government and had served with distinction in WWII with the Navy. My mother was left to clean the urine stains he had left behind on her new daybed.

His wife had inherited a ramshackle house on a corner plot in a still semi-rural area of the Bronx and there they raised their hellions. On the corner was a public bus stop where the passengers could see over the hedges right into the backyard belonging to her aunt and uncle. There he could be seen in the summer sitting in a kiddie pool, watching tv on a precariously set up receiver with its electrical cord, and several extensions cords, running through the open kitchen window. Cans of Schafer beer would be floating around him. This second-generation son had achieved the American dream. Yes indeed, God love you, Barney!

CHAPTER

14

MOVING TO THE BRONX

On a beautiful day in May, Grace's mom announced to her that they were finally moving. It was after a meeting at her cherished PS1 that the plans began to form. Grace recalled the conference with her teacher, her mother and herself, convened by the school nurse. Given her age though, Grace only partially understood the purpose of the session. It seemed to have something to do with some kind of tests that Grace had done very well on. Her teacher, to her dismay, was explaining that the school could not offer Grace what she needed to thrive. Even skipping her ahead two years was not an option since she was really small and all things had to be considered when taking this route. The intellectual, emotional, social and physical size of a child were all evaluated. The teacher and nurse had reservations about placing little Grace in an environment where her school peers might take advantage of her and her academic success would be hindered. The teacher suggested that the family should move to a neighborhood with "smarter" children and more involved parents. A Jewish neighborhood was her recommendation. For a youngster preparing for her First Holy Communion, she was bewildered by why they would send her to a Jewish school. She was always asking her mother if she could go to Catholic school like her cousins but that never happened. Mainly she wanted to March in the St. Patrick's Day parade but that would never happen in a Jewish school!

When her teacher left the room, the nurse revealed herself as a bigger problem. She began telling her mother about this fine, wealthy, cultured couple that were looking to adopt a bright, healthy, white child, just like Grace. They were willing to pay well for this opportunity and she could facilitate a meeting with them. This would work to her financial gain as well, Mare was sure. To Grace's relief, her mother rose abruptly, took her hand and they left the nurse's office with hardly a goodbye.

She listened closely that night while her parents discussed that frightening consultation unaware that she had understood the gist of it. She, of course, was not included in the discussion or the decision to come. Fortunately, her parents were affronted, outraged and disgusted by the nurse's proposal. But they did agree to think about moving. The nurse never knew how fortunate she was that the child's parents either didn't know how to or didn't care to report her. They feared it might lead to a confrontation with authorities. Since a big household caution was not to discuss personal business, especially publicly, this would not be allowed. She went to bed happy knowing they must love her.

CHAPTER

15

Her mother had enlisted the help of her sister Irene in finding a new place to move the family to. Her Aunt Irene located them a suitable, one bedroom, apartment in the building in which she and her husband lived. Though the rent was somewhat more expensive, her father had just attained a full-time job with the U.S. Postal Service in Manhattan and so the relocation was "do-able". He had been working as a sub for the post office since his return from the war in Europe. He was spending time and money traveling every day to a different postal station. Often, he would be told upon arrival at the location that there was not enough work and be sent right back home disappointed. On those days he would either be quiet or argumentative but always discouraged by his inability to obtain full-time work and provide better for his family. Grace knew all this because hurt, or hot, feelings were hard to conceal in a one room home.

As moving day approached, Grace became more withdrawn, even sullen. She spent time thinking of her life now and what she would miss from it in the future. She would surely miss dipping her arm past the elbow in Mr. Kaufman's big pickle barrel in front of his store. Grace would never forget the fragrance of that experience and the luscious taste of those pickles. It would set her upon a life-long quest for the perfect pickle. Inside the store she would be treated to a chocolate-covered jelly ring or a sliver of halvah by Mrs. Kaufman as mom paid the five cents for the pickle and the other goodies offered for sale in their appetizing store.

Grace thought of the man she knew only as Vinnie. He was a cemetery worker at Calvary Cemetery and would stop every day to bring beautiful flowers to his elderly mother who lived across the street. If Grace was sitting on the stoop of her building, he would cross the street and make a small bouquet which he would present to her as though she was a princess. Years later Grace would realize those beautiful flowers had been removed from the graves of other neighbors to brighten the day of his own beloved mom. She would deduce that he had fostered a productive, symbiotic relationship between the living and the dead. Vinnie's stature would be elevated in her mind forever.

Grace then thought how she would miss the playground right down the street. It was on the corner of a very busy truck route through the area. Thinking back, after she had become a mother, she would question the location of such a park for the neighborhood children. However, it was a wonderful place to play at the time and she looked forward to seeing the ever-vigilant park attendant almost daily. Miss Johnson, who looked over the children and supervised their play, was a lovely black, cherubic looking woman. Miss Johnson would often sit with Mare in conversation while they both monitored the children. It was not surprising that one day she would invite Mare and her children to lunch at her house nearby. She had the first, and most beautiful, grand piano Grace had ever seen, sitting in the parlor. She played and Mare and her girls sang along together. It was a thrilling experience and permitted Grace a glimpse into another world peopled by individuals who appreciated more than a kazoo! She had heard the Irish loved the fiddle and the harp but, sadly, not a single person in her family showed any musical inclination whatsoever. Grace vowed that day that her own children would be given music lessons and have experiences like she did that afternoon.

On her "things to mourn" list in her mind, was the Silvercup Bread factory. It would be the odor of fresh bread baking that emanated from this busy, huge building that would stay with her for life. Trucks would be continuously coming and going with the bright logo painted on their sides. The logo reflected the huge "Silvercup" sign that graced the top of the structure and could be seen from anywhere Grace believed. Besides the heavenly aromas, there were the miniature wrapped loves of Silvercup bread a child only had to ask for from the employee posted at the entrance to the plant. This same worker surprised her one day with a promotional small milk pitcher. Shirley Temple's image was painted on the front of this lovely, little cobalt blue depression glass keepsake. Grace would keep this forever in her collection of teacups and teapots that grew over the years.

Grace would surely miss her first "puppy love", Billy. She made her First Holy Communion with Billy who looked so handsome in his navy suit, holding his catechism and rosary beads that day. This snapshot would remain in her photo album always. Mare was good friends with his mother so they played together often in the playground or his apartment. His parents had actually purchased a television set. This one fact alone convinced young Gracie that they must be very rich.

One night Eddie alerted Mare that there were light trucks outside Billy's apartment building. The lights were trained on the windows of the third-floor apartment occupied by Billy, his two brothers and their parents. There was also a sound truck with a voice emanating from it stating, "This is the FBI. Come out with your hands up". Grace and Clare were put to bed while their parents monitored the activity from the stoop of the boarding house. Questions were discouraged the next morning with the usual warning from her father that, "Children should be seen but not heard". Even her mother, who had appeared unnerved by the events of the previous evening, would not entertain her inquiries. Grace never heard of, or saw, the family again. If her parents knew what became of them, she was never told. It was about this time that Eddie and Mare would talk about a politician named McCarthy who was waging a war against the "commies". Grace could only pray that it was not these commies that had abducted her friend and his family.

Most of all Grace knew she would miss the diner Mom would bring her to for pancakes after mass on Sunday. It was a time to talk, laugh and giggle just the two of them, since her dad would be home watching her little sister. It was a social time as well since they would encounter other children and their parents following the same Sunday morning routine. Most of these children went to catholic school. Grace knew them, tangentially, from practice in church for their shared, upcoming Holy Communion. Her own religious instruction came from the "release time" classes she attended every Wednesday at St. Mary's. She always thought that term mysterious. It sounded like it was for prisoners rewarded for their good behavior, "He has been given early release time for his fine progress making license plates". Or perhaps, it referred to a reward for a catholic, but public school child, suffering from the scourge of their pagan, public education, "The seven year old benefitted from release time so she could be with her own kind".

Though she embraced her religious instruction and the prayers she was learning, liking the nuns who taught these was quite another story. To begin with, they had dark, flowing and colorless garments unlike her teachers at P.S.1. Many seemed quick to embarrass a child who could not recite, from memory, whole passages from the Baltimore Catechism. Reprimands were often accompanied by scorn at a child's lack of familiarity with the religious material. Clearly not a problem for the parochial school students who found themselves continuously exposed to the material. When it was not disdain it was frequently pity, she detected emanating from the nuns. This made her perhaps more uncomfortable than the verbal scolding.

Nonetheless, she embraced her lessons, learned her prayers and looked forward to the day of her Communion.

Though the Church was selling special tiaras, with tiered veils attached for the girls and beautiful knee length white, silk stockings, Grace learned at one diner breakfast over her pancakes, that this would not be an option for her. She was fortunate, she was told, to be given a lovely, dotted-swiss garment that had been worn by the daughter of Aunt Irene's employer for that child's own communion. The wealthy parents had also donated the girl's simple headband, with a single layer of tulle attached, to Grace. Mare had spent whatever small amount she had on a prayerbook and rosary beads that the nuns at St. Mary's were also hawking. Aunt Marge, her godmother-to-be, had purchased her little white patent shoes and cotton white anklets. There was nothing more to be said. Grace would walk down the center aisle of St. Mary's with a long line of other little female communicants. They would be dressed in layered dresses of nylon and lace, hem length tiered veils and silk stockings that would evoke the envy of a bride. Grace, embarrassed at the time, would realize eventually that she had been dressed more appropriately for a seven year old girl, with the gift of her simple cotton white frock and her little flowered headband and veil. After pictures in the playground taken by Aunt Irene, undoubtedly to share with her generous employer, they were driven to a party at Aunt Marge's in her honor, celebrating this important rite of passage in her faith. And it was wonderful and boisterous as all such occasions are in an Irish-American home. The laughter, storytelling and jokes recited were limitless. The beer and drinks being served were also.

Guests were served all kinds of cold cut, rolls and condiments to accompany the store-bought salads, such as macaroni, potato and coleslaw. The menu was a testament to the refined cooking skills of her female relatives.

Most importantly, it was her day and family and friends found time to come and celebrate her alone. She happily received little gifts or envelopes with a small amount of cash inside. When she had the time, she sidled off to the spare bedroom in her aunt's home and counted her cash gifts. Grace was excited to realize these amounted to a total of $28! The joy of her new fortune had hardly settled in before Aunt Marge approached her when everyone had departed the festivities. Her aunt advised her that she had to give her the $28 to pay for the beer. The arrangement had been made between her mother and Marge. Grace, remembering the nuns and their stories of miracles to watch out for, concluded she was witnessing one of those miracles now. She had $28 and the beer bill was $28. Wow! That night she went home feeling full of the warmth of family and friends. She said a prayer to Jesus before falling asleep. She thanked him for the wonderful day but not for her communion dress or the cost of the beer."

CHAPTER
16

M om began to notice Grace's obvious withdrawal. The child seemed nervous about the impending move. The usually inquisitive little girl had become sullen, not barraging her mother with as many questions as was her usual nature. Mare decided to try something she knew would lift Grace's spirits. "Grace, would you like to see some things daddy brought home from Europe?" she asked as she motioned towards the hope chest. Grace could not believe what she was hearing and just nodded rather than have her words break the spell and change her mother's intentions. With Grace safely ensconced on the far side of the room, Mare opened the chest and after a bit of burrowing around came out with a manila envelope. Closing the chest and opening the envelope she displayed the contents on the closed lid of the vessel. She summoned her daughter over to view the small array she had created. Here the girl beheld a collection of beautiful postcards. Each card revealed another wondrous photo of France. She knew her daddy had been there during his time in the army. There were pictures of large and ornate cathedrals which her mother told her the names of, reading the back of the cards. Fountains, gardens, statues and wide boulevards of houses and shops allowed her to feel she was on a visit to this beautiful place. Her father had spoken often of the friendliness and gratitude of the French people. Grace made a promise to herself that day that she would someday go and visit this fairyland that she envisioned. Surreptitiously, while Grace was caught up in her reveries, Mare removed a tiny statue from her apron pocket and showed it to the girl. It was a small replica of a much bigger and famous statue located in Belgium. This too had been carried home from the war zone by her father. Her mother called it "the Prince" and offering it to her, placed it in her hands. Grace turned it over and over trying to imagine its larger version sitting in a park in Europe. Grace rushed to place it with her religious statues on the one dresser they all shared. These statues were like her dolls and in the way of poor children she imputed to them whole background stories and adventures. At night she would say her prays with them, and after kissing them all she put them to sleep on the dresser. As she placed the prince with his new friends her mother silently closed and locked the hope chest. Her eyes brimmed with tears seeing the absolute joy these small treasures had bestowed on her child. The "Prince" would remain on Grace's dresser forever. The religious statues were not so lucky!

CHAPTER
17

Time was drawing closer to the move to their new home in the Bronx. Grace had always lived in New York City. Both daughters had been born in Manhattan. The small apartment they were now in was situated in an industrial section of Queens. Soon they would be moving to Hunt's Point, a peninsula in the southeastern part of the borough. The hope chest, she was assured would be making the trip with them. Hunt's Point was also a manufacturing area, but without the small homes and townhouses of their previous neighborhood. It was instead an area of tall multi-family apartment buildings, with steep streets and factories. She remembered most in later years the smell of the Bustelo coffee being roasted everyday down the block on Oak Point Boulevard. It would soon be joined by a delicious Puerto Rican bakery on Hunts Point Avenue that would open to the public at 10pm for bread and rolls as they prepared the deliveries of their product for restaurants. Hot fresh rolls with butter before bed was an incomparable treat to Gracie and Clare! Bustelo was left to her parents.

Thinking back Grace would remember that Hunts Point was indeed a culinary delight. Mother's Pie Company sold to the public along with its prolific wholesale trade. A visit to Mother's for some dinner dessert was like walking onto the stage of the Lucille Ball show that she would watch at Aunt Irene's house. Her own family did not yet have a television set. Long convey-or belts would send the pies forward for ladies in hair nets to box and prepare for the trucks. It was a face paced operation that absolutely enthralled her! Combine that with the Jewish appetizing stores and bakeries, the Greek diner and the Italian pizzeria and you were in gastronomic paradise. This was when pizza was only sold as a full pie, in sit-down restaurants, with tablecloths and Chianti bottle candles on the table. Pizza by the slice was still years into the future.

On the other hand, there was a huge garbage treatment plant situated on the river just several streets down. It was here as a teenager that she and her friends would swim in the East River. They ignored the outpourings of human waste from the facility as they swam. Occasionally the older boys would attempt to swim to Riker's Island, a city jail located directly across the river from this spot. Before anyone ever reached the island a patrol boat with armed correction officers would be dispatched to intercept them. They would be advised to turn around and swim back. This was a perilous task, given the fatigue they must have experienced and the treacherous tides of the confluence of rivers at that spot. They would all return safely, thankfully, but unfortunately some would eventually return, to this "island paradise" as guests of the city.

There was a monastery inhabited by cloistered nuns up the block on Manida Street. Mare, Grace and Clare would visit there on special holy days. They enjoyed the lovely choral voices of seemingly faceless and bodyless nuns that floated to them from behind a large metal grate. They strolled the grounds and see the fields of vegetables these isolated spirits would grow their own food upon. Her mother would remark, "aren't they brave to take their vow of silence?" "Isn't it beautiful that they spend their life in the glory of God".? Grace did not respond but feigned interest in some plant or insect of the moment. Best not to question Mom's perception of the situation. Though the grounds of the monastery were beautiful and peaceful the life of the nuns was frightening to Gracie. The degree of their commitment was beyond reason or necessity. It was also a degree of control even a young Grace was disturbed by. She was not yet old enough to articulate her discomfort. It was also an irony that right down the street and almost contiguous to the monastery was the NYC youth house for incarcerated boys. Yet interaction between the two groups, she believed, was never achieved. Now that did seem like a positive idea to Grace's young mind. Perhaps nuns and novitiates could help in counselling or comforting these youngsters. Or make them pies or take them some goodies from the garden. Or sing to them. This she felt would have accomplished more than singing in the dark to no one in particular. But a niggling thought told her she was somehow being blasphemous or having impure thoughts again, so she kept these, her first thoughts of social criticism of the Church, to herself. However, the ideas would take hold and germinate in her mind. But, in spite of obvious human short-comings, the monastery and its grounds remained an oasis for thought that Grace would seek out as she grew.

CHAPTER
18

The neighborhood was in a time of economic transition but the school system was still regarded very positively. And of course, Mare would be moving closer to her sisters. This move would be especially hard on their Boston born father a Red Sox loyalist who would now be forced to contend with those obnoxious Bronx Yankee fans and a longstanding baseball rivalry. Gracie, always seeking her father's favor, was gently molded into the fanatical Red Sox fan his first born was ordained to be. He failed miserably with the second child who over the years became an ardent Bronx Bomber fan which she remained until her death. She was of course forgiven at that point. Though on opposite sides of this greatest of all time sports hostilities, he would be smiling broadly as he sparred with Clare about the omnipotence of each other's team. The back-and forth-banter elicited howls of delight from him. On the rarest of occasions when Grace would attempt such an interchange during a game, he would tell her to "Shhh" while scowling. Her mother said it was because it was difficult for him to listen to the radio and concentrate with her asking too many questions. Grace knew it was this way with many things she approached him about. Clare, it seemed to her young mind, always got the pass. This only compounded her suspicions of being less loved than Clare by her father. Strangely enough, it was surrounding this rivalry, baseball not sibling, that further suspicions of what unwelcome revelations the chest might hold were formed.

The latest offerings from the chest had kindled an interest in her father's life much like the photos of her mother's parents had stoked an interest in hers. Her father was a remote presence in Grace's life. For the first 2 ½ years he had been physically absent in the most literal way serving as he was in the military. For many, many years after his return he was a presence without a defined persona in her life. He was imposing though at six feet and certainly handsome with beautiful, piercing gray eyes. Many years later he would develop eye diseases that he contributed to his combat service but he never pursued any form of compensation for this disability. Chronic infections led to several operations and finally the removal of his left eye. Miraculously the beauty of his eyes was preserved in the perfectly matched glass eye he was fitted for. It would be Clare over the rest of his life who could take out this glass orb to wash it and return it to its place as necessary for Mare could never do it. He was a very pensive man who Grace would recall from her young life as a White Owl smoker, a Schaffer beer drinker and had a fondness for baked beans. She also wondered why he never went to church with them but would abide no excuse for their absence. His only explanation when asked by the child was, "Don't do as I do, just do as I say". She had become used to his curt slogan-like answers to her questions. He also had an air of remoteness which can be misconstrued by a young child as rejection or lack of affection. As she would witness later, not all fathers were so stoic with their daughters. Her friend MaryAnn's father was very warm to his daughter hugging her with open displays of affection even when her friends were present. In her own home this would be an anomaly. Grace had learned "the hard way" not to trouble her father with the desire for such reassuring gestures. Since all communication in the family went through her mother Grace asked her one day, "Mom, why doesn't Daddy love me?" Her mother actually was stunned. "Why Grace, of course he loves both you and Clare very, very much." "Well, I know he loves Clare" Grace countered "but does he love me?" "Why would you even have such a thought Gracie" her mom responded. The child explained how, while he seemed relaxed, even playful with her younger sister, tickling her from time to time, so he could see her beautiful dimples, he was different with his older daughter.

Grace had seen his sternness. It was on display if she spilled milk at the kitchen table or was found to be answering back either of her parents. It was in the snap of his belt that he cracked as a warning to her when she misbehaved. She told her mom how she hated when he made her the "soldier" to his officer, in his olive-green pie cutter hat, putting her through her drills. "At ease soldier," he would command as she stood before him, "A-ten- hut" he would bellow and she sprang to rigid attention as she saluted him. Then he would keep up the cadence as she marched around the tiny living room. Though she couldn't express it at the time due to her age and behavioral conditioning, she could sense a palpable disappointment in her dad towards his job, his surroundings, her mother and herself. Only, it seemed, Clare did not disappoint him. He would openly express his despair in his inability to return to his roots in New England. He would sometimes utter some vague political ideas that he had. But for the most part he was silently political. He saved his real emotions for a couple of beers and a Red Sox victory. It would be many, many years later that the world would learn of PTSD and its effect on our military, particularly our frontline soldiers, and their families. But not in time for her dad and her.

After this conversation with her mom, Gracie though only 8, would realize how much she relied on her loving and comforting mother for feedback and information about the family, the neighborhood, even the world, spiritual and tangible. She also provided the positive feedback for the identity and self-image she was developing. And Mom loved to talk to Grace who was her only companion besides the toddler Clare. As mom brought her into her confidence offering details of someone's life or shared secrets she was trusted with, Grace would respond with an inevitable "Really?" Her mother always responded "Would I lie to you?" Grace often opted not to answer this simple query.

CHAPTER
19

It was from her mother that Grace learned about her father's life. His own father, a plumber, had died at the age of 42. His name was Bernard and he was the second grandfather Grace had never met. Mother said he was a plumber who had stepped on a rusty nail and become infected with gangrene of the leg. An operation to remove his limb had failed and he had passed on. Her father, the second oldest boy, unable to find work in his hometown in Massachusetts, had headed to NYC with a friend to find employment. His goal was to send money home to his widowed mother so that she could provide for the seven siblings still living with her. Grace never knew this grandmother her father seemed to adore. When he referred to her it was clear to see how respected she was by her children. Grace heard of the sorrows she had endured and the beautiful singing voice she had that enriched the choir at their local catholic church. When the little girl would sing in her dad's presence he would request his favorite song, "So low and far away." It was when she realized the implication of this, she became embarrassed and far less musically adventurous. It was made clear to her that she did not have his mother's beautiful gift of song. She had, however, been given her name. What confused the girl was the absence of visits, cards, letters or gifts from such a wonderful, talented grandma who was, in fact, her namesake. Mare rounded out the description of her paternal grandmother by telling Grace she was a chain smoker, liked a drink, loved the Red Sox and lived in a nursing home because she was difficult to get along with. Her fears and suspicions were piling up and she felt the hope chest had more revelations for her beyond pretty pictures and delightful little statues.

Her Dad though did share highlights of his life with her if the mood hit him right and the game had gone his way. It became known that his first residence in the city had been in Harlem, at the time a lively and busy place in the northern part of Manhattan. His landlord it turned out was a bookie and bootlegger and offered her father employment in this lucrative industry. He became a runner for the man. He did not have the thin frame, though, she felt would befit this job. She asked him about this and wanted to know if he became tired from all the running. She remembered the kind laughter and beautiful smile on his face as he replied, "No little girl. I was more a delivery man than an actual runner, but thank you for being concerned about your old dad". Grace was just happy she had pleased him that day. Her interaction with Dad, too often, seemed to provoke his anger. Her attempts to engage him at these times were usually unsuccessful and led to a scolding. It was not this way with Clare who always could get his attention and elicit that lovely smile from him.

Over the passing of time Mom would feed her more information about Dad's first family. The oldest son William, who would marry and eventually divorce, was kicked out by his spouse because of his excessive drinking. When his daughter, who he was not allowed contact with during her growing years, was married her mother told her Uncle Bill stood in the rear of the church, unrecognized by the bride, and cried. He eventually wound up in a home for the destitute and would end up burning down the facility and dying in the fire. Authorities declared him an arsonist and by extension a murderer, for others had perished as well. The family blamed the drink and of course not the man. He was a lost soul, but a good Catholic. Clearly the divorce had caused his downfall. To Grace, and the catechism as she understood it, his fate had been sealed by the method of his demise. It surely indicated in who's kingdom he would ultimately reside despite the prayers and sympathy of his family.

Uncle Joe was one of her father's younger brothers. He lived in a state hospital due, she was told, to his hypochondria. She was also told he didn't serve in the military because someone had to stay behind to take care of the much, adored mother. Grace tried to imagine how he accomplished this from his hospital room. Unable to solve this conundrum, she eventually lost interest in his plight. She did, however, enjoy shopping with her mother for gifts to put in the big Christmas package her parents sent him every year. Included would be socks, t-shirts, and a nice flannel shirt for the holiday parties they must have had at the state hospital. Mare would also include all kinds of candy, gum, nuts and several magazines for his enjoyment. A nice greeting card with all their signatures, even Clare's and Gracie's, would be placed in the carton. Weeks later she would receive notification from the staff at the facility letting her parents know the package had been received, examined and forwarded to Uncle Joe. Grace never did see the Christmas card her mother confirmed had been received every year from Uncle Joe overflowing with his gratitude. Maybe they too were kept in the hope chest beyond her perusal.

Although her mother had no more information to share on Uncle Joe's life (had he ever worked? been engaged? etc.) she did have a most remarkable revelation for Grace. It seems, a young Uncle Joe, had entered a country wide contest to name a new pudding due to be introduced to the market. Joe submitted his suggestion and My-T-Fine pudding was born! It was the only one Mare would cook, she explained, due to family loyalty. Grace would recall this account every time she ate pudding for the rest of her life. As more time passed, she hoped the story was true, though she could never find research to confirm this. She would learn, as the years went by, that her imaginative, creative mother had the ability to fashion wonderful, yet fanciful facts, for the people she loved. This ability often brought beauty and brightness, to the, sometimes bleak, existence they shared.

There were three other brothers. Uncle John was tall, 6'7", and hilariously zany. He did come to Hunts Point to visit one time with his wife, Grace's Aunt Loretta. He arrived wearing a big, round silk hat with a pom-pom, the size of a large pizza tray. He called it his bebop hat that he had purchased for his trip to the city. He said this indicated he "was a cool cat" and therefore he would fit in easily on his tours of the area. Eddie convinced him to leave the hat behind on their outings together. He was particularly attentive to Clare and Grace, making them laugh with his silly jokes and tricks. They all went to the Bronx Zoo one afternoon where he rewarded his nieces with souvenirs and treats to eat. It saddened Grace that he and his wife had no children of their own. He seemed like the perfect father, talkative, funny and patient. She even fantasized what it would be like for her if he could only change places with his brother. In the end she felt guilty for these thoughts. Were these the impure thoughts she had been warned against? Were they worthy of confession she wondered? In the end she decided instead to pray for God to send her aunt and uncle a baby of their own to love and be loved by them. It was not long after that her mother shared the shocking news that Uncle John had died suddenly. There would be no answer to her pray.

Phil and Paul were the youngest boys. The unique thing about them was that they, had indeed, married two sisters. Phil was married to Kay and Paul to Sally. Phil and Sally had one child named Cherie. She was a tiny, delicate beautiful little child who reminded Grace of the little souvenir dolls that were sold in Chinatown. They too had come to visit her family in the Bronx on one occasion. He seemed more like her father than Uncle John. They seemed more comfortable with each other. In a stroke of irony, her father had purchased tickets for them to enjoy a Yankee/Red Sox match together, not aware of Phil's conversion to the Yankees during her father's absence from their hometown. They did have a wonderful day however but she was sure it was because you can guess which team was victorious! Grace was sad when this visit ended. She enjoyed spending time with her father's family. Through the years the visits would be few and far between and eventually cease. One day Grace would be ashamed to admit how she envied the adorable little Cherie and the way her parents, particularly her father, doted on her.

Paul and Sally had three boys at this time. The oldest one only one month older than Grace. Since they never made the trek to New York she would never really get to know them well. A disturbing thing she did know, however, came from her mother. Mare who had been praying for a boy during her pregnancy with Grace had accumulated a lovely layette of baby boy necessities and little blue outfits she would use to dress her new baby. When Grace turned up female, and her mother couldn't, in her delirium, convince the medical staff to take her away, she shipped all these things to her sister-in-law who had been lucky enough to have a son. (Not to mention the two more sons she had in quick succession). For years Gracie would listen to her mother's lamentations about having a daughter and the clothes she had shipped away having been denied the opportunity to use them for her own child. It was always her mother's mantra that, "I always wanted a son" whenever she learned of an impending birth. She would offer her prays to the new mother and pray for her that she would bear a boy. The gesture would be accompanied by the story of how she walked to the middle of the Whitestone Bridge, Grace an infant in the carriage, with the aim of flinging the child into the river in an act of suicide/infanticide. Her sadness of having a boy was compounded by Eddie receiving his induction papers on the day they brought their newborn home. Standing in the middle of the bridge, in a torrential rain storm, as she created the setting, she suddenly realized little Grace would never have to join the military like her dad. This realization she would always claim had save Grace's life. How much of it had destroyed it Grace would often contemplate. Even though she would hear this story repeatedly throughout her life it would sometimes change to add the fact that because Grace had entered her life, she was afraid to go on without her husband. Apparently, the thought of the infant's existence was more frightening than bridges, the church or the axis powers.

Her dad also had two sisters, Mary and Anna. Grace had never met either one. Mary was married to a milky eyed man who had ensconced her in a trailer much like some Irish tinkers might inhabit. They had not been blessed with any wee ones as Mare would say and bless herself. On the other hand, very little was known about Anna by her mother except to say she never married and was Eddie's favorite sibling of all.

CHAPTER

20

At the time of the move to Hunts Point Grace was eight years old, Clare was four. It was an important year in her life. She would be entering the third grade in her new school. It was also the year she would begin studying for the sacrament of Confirmation during release time. This was an important religious transition. Now being seen as mature enough to declare her faith in God and the Church, she would be formally confirmed in the faith. So important an event was it, that a bishop would be sent by the Chancery to administer the oath to each child. It was a scary compilation of words and intentions that absolutely frightened the young Gracie.

I renounce Satan and all his work and ways, and surrender myself to You,

O triune God, Father, Son and Holy Spirit, in belief, obedience,

And the earnest resolution to remain faithful to You until my end. Amen

After her sponsor had recited her confirmation name (Agnes) and the bishop had reminded her of her duty to defend the faith as a soldier of God, the rite was concluded with a light slap on the face to "seal the deal" as it were. The coming years would prove that Clare would need more than a love tap to keep her faith in that which the Church would require of its followers. Thankfully though, when the day of the event arrived, she was happy to learn there would be no party at Aunt Marge's. How could Clare have afforded the liquor bill anyway? This time her family would go to the local photography studio where Mare had made an appointment for a portrait sitting of her daughter to memorialize this day. This made Clare ecstatic since she had been given the most beautiful white, tiered nylon dress with little white satin rosettes to wear on this occasion. Surveying the girls in church there was one thing she absolutely believed that day. She had the prettiest dress of all! And the picture to prove it!

CHAPTER

21

Gracie adjusted well to her new school, PS48. The school was situated directly across the street from their apartment building. Her mother could be seen most days leaning on her fifth-floor kitchen windowsill looking into the school classroom windows. By the time Grace reached sixth grade her classroom windows were right across the street in full view of her mother. It was like being a frog sitting in a terrarium on many days that school year! Her mother always wanted to be a teacher so she would be full of questions when the girl arrived home. "How was school? Did the girls like your dress? Mrs. Newman looked lovely today, didn't she? Did she like the book report I helped you write?".

One afternoon, when Grace was in fourth grade, she sat telling her mom they were learning about Holland. Since the class would be performing a play in the auditorium in a month,

Grace, who always loved to act out little stories she wrote at family gatherings, was hoping to get a part in the play. Grace knew from her classroom studies that Holland had much to do with the development of NYC's history. In fact, it was a Dutch settlement, New Amsterdam, that would become New York City after the arrival of an English fleet took control of the colony. She went on to tell her mother of the clogs, or wooden shoes she saw pictures of Dutch children wearing. Unexpectedly, her mother became very animated and left Grace to go into the bedroom where the hope chest had been settled. She returned with the sweetest little pair of wooden shoes in her hands. Grace was so excited! Her mother confirmed that they had been in the hope chest since Dad brought them back from Europe. In France and Belgium, they were known as sabots. He had brought these home for Mare as a souvenir but she wanted her daughter to have them now. Grace was so touched by her mother's beautiful gift she asked her if she could bring them to school for show and tell. Mare was delighted by her daughter's reaction and readily agreed. Grace went to bed with her little wooden shoes, even too small for her by this point. She prayed that night that they would guarantee her a part in the class play. They would always remain on display in her own home. Another wonderous treasure brought forth from the chest. How many more could there be?

The sabots became instrumental in developing Grace's life long, passion to travel. She would begin with a hobby inspired by their surprise revelation. She wanted to learn more about the world and its people and began writing for brochures and information to satisfy this curiosity. Hours in the library would help determine destinations to read about while hoping to one day visit. Magazine tear-out forms from Redbook or Ladies Home journal requesting brochures were perused and often pilfered from the homes of Aunt Irene and Aunt Marge. Scrapbooks were filled with her research. Photos and pamphlets sent directly to her upon her request from embassies and travel agents accumulated as her interest grew. One day her mother gave her a small packing box with a lid that she had procured from a local merchant. She suggested Grace decorate it with pictures and some glue. As she presented this very utilitarian cardboard box to her daughter she said, "Grace, I wish it was fancier but this is your first hope chest. I know how much you hope to travel someday and this is to keep your dreams alive." As her collection grew, so did her desire to see the world. She shared her prized possession with friends and family too. Her Uncle Albee began jokingly calling her "the wacky professor" since she had so much information to impart. The nickname seemed appropriate actually, because during this period the child had begun wearing glasses for eyestrain and they seemed enormous on her tiny head with tiny features. Grace cherished this box until it ultimately fell apart with the weight of her treasures. She never forgot the beauty of her mother's gesture nor the encouragement she offered. But it did temper her curiosity about the "real" hope chest for a while and perhaps this was part of Mare's motivation as well.

CHAPTER
22

During this time, early on in their arrival in Hunts Point, her dad decided to take the family on an adventure. This appealed to Grace's vagabond streak and she was overjoyed! However, when she was informed they were going to Manhattan, she was surprisingly apprehensive about this. The year before Aunt Marge had taken her to Rockefeller Center in Manhattan. Mare felt the need to alert Grace to the fact that since Manhattan was indeed an island, they would have to travel on the subway. The subway would have to pass beneath the East River on their way to the city and she hoped the evil Irish leprechauns that lived in these tunnels would let them pass safely. Mind you, these were not the impish little mischievous characters given to mendacity and associated with rainbows and pots of gold. These were depicted more like the tommyknockers of England, dreadful looking and dangerous creatures who lived underground in mines and the like. She was petrified on this trip, that would feel like crossing the river Styx, to a nervous young girl with an overactive imagination. However, they were granted a safe passage allowing her to view the mesmerizing spectacle of the Rockettes performing onstage at Radio City Musical Hall! She decided that day to become a Rockette and would practice their graceful synchronized leg kicks until then. She arrived home eager to share the experience with her mother and beseech her for dancing lessons. Unfortunately, that idea joined the others in the funeral pyre of unfilled dreams she could not pursue; stilt walking, girl scouts, puppies, camp, parochial school, marching in parades and others that had been forgotten already. Same disappointment, same reason, the lack of money. When she was older and read Vanity Fair by William Thackeray, she would relate to Rebecca Sharp and how the "precocity of poverty" affected the course of her life. But for now, she felt only sadness and anger.

As the family set out together on the trip Dad had promised, Grace tried to guess where they were all going. She was so happy to be experiencing a family outing like the ones the kids in school talked about on Mondays. The tales of menacing leprechauns barely entered her mind as they ploughed underwater through the tunnel to New York. Afterall her father was there to confront these little miscreants now. It was Mare who seemed tense and uncomfortable until they emerged above ground in Times Square. The place was a riot of color, sound, humanity, neon lights and traffic. Grace thought to herself she had never seen something so spectacular! Nothing in her travel brochures prepared her for the spectacle of sight and sound she was experiencing. The sensations intensified as they approached an arcade in the middle of Times Square. Bells ringing and lights flashing beckoned her in. Clare and Grace were cautioned to stay close to their parents. This would be easy for Clare who was always close to Mom, hanging on and clutching her dress if anyone was nearby. For Grace it was agonizing. She wanted to be set free to explore this riotous place. Dad shepherded his brood to the inner reaches of the arcade to a small area with a showcase. Inside was a profusion of tiny turtles, of all colors, climbing and crawling over each other. It was painful to witness this for Grace, who was feeling so restricted of movement herself at the moment. To her surprise her father told the turtle torturer he wanted to purchase a turtle for each of his daughters. The girls, were instructed by the salesman, to each pick the one she wanted. Grace quickly picked the smallest one hoping to save this little turtle tot. Eddie directed that the names of each of his daughters be painted on their respective turtles so there would be no arguing at home over which belonged to who. They would leave the arcade two turtles richer than when their journey began. Mom was glowing. She said, "Girls did you thank Daddy for this outing? Did you thank him for your new pets?" Mare was so happy and pleased by this action on the part of their father that Grace complied. She was already in deep thought, however, about naming her turtle. Even though she had always asked for a dog she knew the name Fido wouldn't work. In the end she named him Anthony to honor the saint who watched over animals. Although she took care of him carefully Anthony met an unfortunate end.

He was stoned to death. Clare accidently dropped a rock on his back. Grace had let him out of confinement to crawl around the living room while the turtle bowl was being cleaned. Just then Clare came running into the room carrying the large turtle basking rock her mother had just scrubbed. The poor child stumbled and tripped sending the rock she was carrying onto little fragile Anthony's shell. His shell had been weakened by the paint and decoration it was subjected to. Everyone comforted poor Clare who was crying profusely about this tragedy. Grace however received no sympathy for the loss of her first pet. She was deemed responsible for the turtle's demise and poor Clare's unrelenting sorrow. After all Grace had been irresponsible to let the turtle out of his bowl. He would now join Clare's turtle, Cutie, who had passed before him, in the big arcade in the sky.

CHAPTER
23

Grace was first beginning to take serious notice of Clare at this time. Prior to her fourth year in the family Clare had been just a baby to Grace. She had chubby little arms and beautiful dimples to match a beautiful smile. She clung to her little rubber doll "Rennie" and would care for it like a little mother. "Pock-a-book" was her first word, a difficult word for a new speaker which gave insight to the intelligence that would emerge as she grew. She was, however, a fearful, timid child who would cower behind her mother when other, older children would approach.

Grace could recall her sister's crippling fear of Santa. Although she loved Christmas and the beautiful carols Grace had taught her in preparation for their Christmas spectacular in the living room, Santa remained a fearsome character. She would NEVER visit Santa or sit on his lap and confide her wishes for gifts he might reward her with. She took her chances every year that he would just know what she wanted. She was a very good girl after all. Grace however, was given to teasing her sister. Every Christmas eve when they were put to bed in anticipation of the big guy's visit, Grace would point out the red and green landing lights of approaching planes and tell Clare they were the lights on Santa's sleigh. They lived across the East River from LaGuardia airport and planes would fly over frequently and at low altitude as they made their approach for landing. Poor Clare, believing everything Grace told her, was terrified he would see they were awake and add them to his naughty list. She feared there would be no presents for them. As much as she implored, Grace would continue talking and singing. Clare of course would eventually fall asleep only to be woken up to the beauty of the Christmas tree and the bounty of gifts beneath it. Grace was just happy she had made the good list.

Through much of Clare's young life, Grace would be her protector in a neighborhood that was rapidly changing and falling into decline. Gradually she became an important part of Grace's life. She enjoyed playing, and singing along to her little plastic records on the tiny kiddy phonograph record player she had gotten for Christmas. She would walk back and forth through the apartment singing her favorite song by cowboy star, Tex Ritter, "I'll be a sunbeam for Jesus", while Mom and Dad beamed at their little sunbeam, Clare. Grace thought she was the sweetest little child in the whole world with a sweet little voice to match. As with most baby sisters, Clare would do anything if Grace would give her attention. She was Grace's student when they played school, and her theatrical protégé when Grace directed little variety shows for the family. She could impeccably recite the words to Grace's original poetry that they spent endless hours in their own imaginative world rehearsing. They had two uncles that worked in the photoengraving industry who supplied Grace with the most garish orange paper to write her poetry on. This resulted in the garish orange poetry book Grace had fashioned from it. She carried it everywhere always ready to do a reading if requested. It would become worn and dog-eared eventually from the many shows and recitals it formed the basis for. Mare had complained that Grace was pushing Clare too hard and would make her anxious but Clare couldn't get enough of this big girl play, as she called it, with her big sister.

Clare must have been born with a thrifty nature. As a little child she would separate two ply tissues into two separate parts rather than waste. When her mother gave Clare her first black marble notebook to practice her letters she began writing on the last page, last line of the book. The next day she would erase what she had written and write her new letters in that space. She would do this until she wore a hole in the paper and only then would she move up a line. However, she could be easily tricked by Grace into sharing her little bounty of coins she had accumulated. All Grace had to do was say, "Let's play, one for you and one for me" and Clare would run to get her coins and drop them in a pile, with the paltry few, Grace would contribute. Then to her great excitement, her older sister would appoint her in charge of distributing the coins equally to each of them as she recited, 'one for you and one for me". Grace had convinced the poor child she was teaching her math. This "game" soon became known to her parents and was not played again. Grace was given her first lesson in how she was pursuing a criminal life and where it would take her. "Grace", her mother would intone "do you realize you are lying to Clare and stealing from her? Do you know that a liar turns into a thief, a thief turns into a murderer and a murderer gets the electric chair?" Stunned and worried about the reprisals for such a horrible act, Grace vowed to go to confession and add the sin of thievery to her repertoire of offenses. Only little Clare felt sorry for her that day.

Grace had to admit as a youngster she was jealous of the comfortable, cheerful way her dad interacted with Clare. When she was still tiny he would toss her in the air and catch her, only to do it again as the little one filled the room with giggling laughter and shouts of "Again!". Mare would even caution him about over-exciting the child. His way of interacting with Grace was different, more serious, less jovial. For this reason, she often felt she was a disappointment to him. But certainly not to her adoring sister Clare. It was Clare who, as she got older, would challenge their father if she thought Grace had been unfairly or unnecessarily punished. The girls became best friends and confidantes for life. They kept for each other, the deepest secrets with the same silence and taciturnity that their mutual heritage had honed.

CHAPTER

24

As spring returned Mare announced another family adventure. Beyond Grace's wildest expectations, they were going to the Ringling Bros., Barnum and Bailey circus. Recalling her earlier musings of joining the circus, thoughts of this adventure thrilled her. As the big day neared, her and Clare would draw circus pictures. Clare's were of animals and Graces' were of colorful, expressive faces of clowns. They would be traveling further into Manhattan this time to Madison Square Garden known as a popular venue for sporting events, the Ice Capades, rodeos, and now the circus. The circus would be inside the arena on 8th avenue between 49th and 50th streets. At the time it was surely the most famous arena in the world hosting the best-known traveling circus in the USA! As they emerged from the subway at Penn Station it was only a brief walk to the Garden. Before them loomed the spectacle of a beautiful, arched, lighted marquee over the main entrance to this historic building. Vendors were hawking their wares outside and giant posters and more vendors were in the tunnel leading to the interior. They passed animals in cages and men on stilts as they hurried along the corridor eager to get to their seats before the ringmaster appeared and the show began. The total experience consisted of the actual circus, a freak show combining some sad reality with fanciful creations and the clowns. Thankfully their experience with the freak show never went beyond the viewing of the predictably disturbing posters hanging along the passageway. The corridor was rank with the stench of caged animals mixed with the sickening sweet odor of cotton candy and caramel popcorn being sold on the way to the arena. Grace was virtually gagging as they reached their coveted seats.

The ringmaster entered, the crowd cheered, the performers demonstrated their prowess on trapeze, trampoline, and high wire. The animals roared while following the commands of their handlers, the huge, wrinkled elephants paraded around the ring, the crowd roared again and again and finally the clowns appeared in all three rings. They were hilarious! Their energy was palpable. She was amazed how many clowns jumped out of their colorful little clown car. Their silly skits drew her in. They made quite an impression on Grace. She could not wait to go home to begin drawing her clowns again. This time she did not have to be coached by Mare to thank her father for this amazing day. She did ask her mother, though, if she felt all the professional stilt walkers meandering around the tunnel entrance were bad people. That defiant little question earned her the Mare stare!

At school the next day the teacher asked if anyone had yet been to the circus. Grace almost shook her arm off trying to get Miss Cohen's attention, hoping to be called on. She was eager to share her experience with the class. The teacher announced that the Ringling and Bros., Barnum and Bailey circus was sponsoring an art contest for NYC students to paint a picture of what they most loved about the circus. The teacher pointed to an easel in the rear of the classroom that she had set up earlier. Unbelievably she called on Grace and asked if she would like to paint first? The girl was elated by the opportunity to paint but also the attention she received from Miss Cohen as she spent two days of classroom free time sketching the funny faces of four imaginary clowns she had chosen as her subject. When she added the paint colors to their jovial countenances and the complementary background of bursting confetti and streamers, she was finished. Only then did she become aware of Miss Cohen's presence at her side and the silence of her classmates. "That is so beautiful", said the teacher and the children began clapping. "I am definitely submitting this lovely artistic work to the contest headquarters." She was still feeling the afterglow of her success when Miss Cohen announced to the class the following month that Grace had won the city-wide contest sponsored by the circus. The teacher then produced her painting, now matted and framed, and advised her to tell her parents that a photograph of the painting would be in Sunday's centerfold of the Daily News.

When she reached home, before she could even share her happiness, her dad sitting very erect in his chair by the window, said he had something to speak to her about. He motioned her forward. Clearly, he was holding something behind his back and she could only hope for the best. He then produced a pink box, and kissing her, told her how proud he was of her. She opened the box to find a pretty Cinderella caricature watch with a sweet little pink band. Her Mom emerged from the bedroom holding the now precious painting. The school had sent an aide on a home visit to notify her parents of the award and to deliver the painting personally.

As she stood in the living room with Clare and Mare, Grace's father hung her prized possession on the wall behind the sofa. He then taped to the wall around it, some of young Clare's representations of circus animals. Grace could never remember if there was a tangible prize she received for being the contest winner. Her clowns' painting and the photo of it in the Sunday paper was all she needed to feel like a winner. The praise of her parents and teacher was its own reward. The painting remained on the wall until Grace eventually married and her parents moved. It was lost by her parents in transit. She was always grateful she had taken a picture of it with a brownie camera borrowed from Aunt Irene. The picture, never lost in her many moves, would stay in her photo album the rest of her life.

CHAPTER

25

A wonderful thing about her school was that on Mondays, for only 10 cents, you could return to the school auditorium where movies and cartoons were being shown. It was called Movie Mondays. Grace would see the heart wrenching story of Old Yeller in this venue and cry from the end of the film all the way home that day. When she was in the fifth grade, with Clare now in first, she would take her sister with her to the show. On a day in fall as they sat waiting for the teacher/projectionist to begin the films, Grace overheard some older girls from the 6th grade chatting. One said to the other "I know where babies come from. A husband and wife lay down on a bed, back to back, and 9 months later a baby is born." To this insight her friend rejoined, "No, they do not. They lay face to face. My mother explained it all to me when I asked her where I came from." She quickly changed seats to shield

Clare from any further commentary lest her mother believe she was teaching her bad things if she repeated the conversation. Thankfully Clare seemed completely unaware and unconcerned by the youngster's repartee. Grace, however, had had her interest piqued and decided she would ask her mother about details of her own birth. From Aunt Irene she had heard about storks delivering babies. Aunt Marge contended parents picked them out of cabbage patches. Now she was at the age that she doubted these could be true. She was sure Mare would clear this all up for her.

She never imagined the story of her beginning would be so gruesome. Mare told her a story the Grimm brothers could not have topped. It seemed that on her way home from work one windy, rainy evening she was passing an alley behind a restaurant in Manhattan. Mare thought she heard a cat shrieking. Thinking the animal might need some attention, she headed to the large trash bin the mournful sounds were emanating from. Looking inside Mare did not see a cat but a baby. The pitiful little creature was swaddled in a filthy, bloody pink blanket with a nametag pinned to it that read, "My name is Helen Kilroy". As she retrieved the infant from the trash, she realized it was not blood on the blanket but ketchup instead, probably thrown in the can with the trash like the child. At this point her mother reminded her how lucky she was that it was her that had found her in that filthy, disgusting place. Since her and her husband did not have any children yet, she took the baby home with her. She realized this baby must be a gift from God. Grace could not understand why she did not feel grateful. She would wonder for years why God chose this delivery method for gift-giving. It also troubled her that she was not called Helen as obviously God had wanted. Many years late she would learn of the psychological destructiveness of this birth story told to a little girl. At the time it only compounded her suspicions of secrets in the family. She was certain now she would learn more from the contents of the hope chest.

She did not have to wait too long for the hope chest to spew out more of its treasures. One day in an attempt to atone perhaps for the obvious distress shown by Clare to her birth story, Mare presented the youngster with a delicate gold bangle bracelet which was a gift her dad had brought to her from overseas. Mare also shared with her, a beautiful mothers' day card she had received from Paris from her husband. The delicacy of the bracelet and the inscription on the card revealed a different side, a softer more romantic side of her father. Clare had caught glimpses of this "other father". He never forgot Valentine's Day and brought home heart boxes filled with candy for his "three girls" as he called them. Loft candies nougat bars were a payday treat they all looked forward to. He was a postal worker, working in Manhattan and never left for work without giving three "pecks" to each of his daughters who were always asleep when he bestowed them. Every night before work he would be sick. Mom explained he had a nervous stomach and for that reason, although he was evidently very bright, he would not seek a promotion. He shunned the responsibility of being a supervisor or foreman on the job. Grace was old enough now to feel sympathy for her dad. He was stuck in a job he did not enjoy because he had a family to provide for. She would not let this happen to her.

CHAPTER
26

Grace enjoyed listening to the radio with her dad. She felt closest to him when they sat in silence hovering in front of the large radio in the living room. Her imagination was ignited by the programming of The Shadow or Gangbusters. Eddie enjoyed This Is Your FBI and anything to do with WWII. One Sunday night, alone with him in the apartment since Mare had taken Clare across the hall to visit Aunt Irene, Grace decided to risk asking him about the name Helen Kilroy. "Nope. Never heard it ", he said without hesitation. You must mean "Kilroy was here". He then began to explain the WWII legend of the anonymous soldier who taunted the Nazi soldiers by writing "Kilroy was here", accompanied by a cartoon picture of the author, on fences, buildings, tanks and airplanes throughout the European theater during the war. Dad, who served in the army under General Patton, at that time, was animated while sharing this tale with her. Grace feigned interest in the story because Dad clearly enjoyed his memory of this time in his life and was willing to share this with her. She was extremely disappointed, however, that his explanation led her no closer to her birth story. Since she could gain no ground on this matter with either parent, Grace ultimately put the issue to rest for many years. She was hoping her treasured chest would be more forthcoming in the future than her own her parents. She lived with the certitude that it would.

Mare returned from her sister's later that evening with a sleepy-eyed Clare in tow. Grace's gaze quickly focused on the delicious looking, homemade cake, in her mothers' hands. Since her mother never baked, she could rightfully assume it had been made by her aunt. Mare blamed this inability to bake on the landlord. The oven knob on the stove had been broken long ago and never replaced therefore she was forced to do all cooking on the stove top. Nothing could be baked, roasted or broiled in their home. She was continuously lamenting her limited options for food preparation. It also explained the lack of homemade birthday cakes. However, when asked if she had notified the landlord of the situation, she had to confess that she had not. She would become defensive when asked, "why not?" "I'll tell you why not. We don't need the landlord in here snooping around in our business." Did she think he was a thief who might want to sneak off with their plastic drapes or worn linoleum in the living room? Yet again, it fortified the notion that there were big things to hide from the world and its agents. Ironically, the oven knob would be found in Mare's sewing box after her passing much later. It had been hidden there all those years. She had forbidden the girls to go in her sewing box because of her fear they may get stabbed by a needle or cut by the small set of scissors it contained. Mare could fabricate the most altruistic and compelling reasons for their obedience! Lucky for her she had two daughters who loved her too much to ever doubt her.

CHAPTER
27

That summer found Grace on the threshold of one of the most consequential years of her life. She would be going into the sixth grade in September. Since she would be matriculating into junior high school next year, she was given more freedom that summer and allowed to go downstairs and play with other children without being accompanied by her mother. The caveat was of course that she had to remain in front of the school building directly across the street from her apartment house. As she emerged from the building on that first day of summer vacation, she looked up and saw Mare stationed at the window ledge in her kitchen on the fifth floor. Though this at first intimidated and disappointed Grace she would learn to be thankful for her mother's vigilance. Besides hopscotch and giant steps, the youngsters would often jump rope and play hide-an-seek. One afternoon it was Grace's turn to be "it". She turned her face towards the school building and was about to cover her eyes when she saw a man approaching swiftly in her peripheral vision. Something about him alarmed her and she was immediately immersed in an aura of danger. The man reached for her, put his hand beneath her dress and tried to drag her away. Had it not been for Mare's wariness he may have been successful. Instead, her mother's screaming and calls for help alerted the teenage boys who congregated outside the candy store on the opposite corner. They pursued, caught and took the man back to the store until the police arrived. Her parents appeared and went with Clare to the police station where the man was charged with molesting and attempting to kidnap her. Due to her age her testimony was ultimately given in the judge's chambers. He was subsequently convicted and last she knew, sent to Riker's Island prison in NYC. Clare learned from her mother that the man had a child, a girl, the same age as herself. This, more than the whole experience, saddened her and she would pray for the little girl she called Erin because the family were Irish Americans like hers. On the way home the day of the incident, her parents stopped at the candy store to thank the owner and the heroic young men who just last week had been referred to in her home as young thugs. They would watch over Grace for a long time after that and Mare could rest easy at her perch. These same young men began calling her mom, Paula Revere, in deference to her ability to alert them to danger approaching, as her namesake in Boston once did. Way to go Paula!

This time was also her introduction into the world of politics. Senator Joe McCarthy had started congressional hearings attempting to rout commies from all arenas including school. At the same time NYC schools had begun shelter drills. The goal was to have children, when at school, take practical steps to survive an atomic bomb attack. Huddled under her small desk with images of the disaster at Hiroshima playing on a reel in her mind, Grace never believed this procedure could ever possibly save her. She did however spend her time during the exercise mentally reciting the Act of Contrition in case Joe McCarthy and his adherents were right about the communist threat. If the attack ever happened, while she might not survive, she at least wanted to insure her place in heaven.

The first television her family owned, purchased at this time, allowed Bishop Fulton J. Sheen to become a frequent visitor to her home as well. His television sermons, presented as classroom lectures with his blackboard omnipresent on the set, clearly impressed her parents. She found them long and boring and the bishop himself, more than a little frightening. However, on the good side, this meant Dad could watch his favorite sport, baseball, comforted by the fact that McCarthy and Sheen were keeping the world safe and religion intact. For Grace it meant a growing anxiety about the threats that exist in the world, both spiritually and physically. Given her experience with the molester, and now the knowledge of the potential threats to her soul and body, she developed a vigilance in her about her environment that would stay with her forever. Dad, she was relieved, could now focus on the real enemies, Mel Allen and the New York Yankees. The baseball rivalry at home heated up. Dad and Clare, when watching a Yankee/Red Sox game would engage in a little banter. She was still quite young but knew the anti-Red Sox teasing would get his attention. He would smile back at her and her interest in the game would wane She was off to play with her dolls. Grace, a true fellow Boston enthusiast, would sit through most of the game with him asking questions in her attempt to learn the sport for real and gain his respect. He would generally just "shush" her. She was always surprised when, in defeat he was sullen and petulant, not just towards the victors, but to her as well. Her mother tried to explain away this reaction by pointing out that dad had been drinking his beers as this would happen only on his days off. She recommended that the youngster steer clear of him at such times. Grace, who knew better than to be insolent to her father, never questioned his difference in treatment of his two daughters on these days. She just registered it as favoritism and, in her mind, she was on the losing end of this issue. It fueled her feelings of somehow being an outsider in this, her little nuclear family.

CHAPTER
28

Starting sixth grade she was overjoyed to find out she, as a school senior now, was being appointed to a special position in the school as a lower grade, student monitor. This honor, it was explained, was given on merit as a reward to those students who showed leadership, academic ability, and helpfulness to others, especially teachers, at school. The position came with a shiny, white patent strap that diagonally crossed her chest, identifying her as one of this elite squad. The duties included meeting your assigned class in the schoolyard, taking attendance and escorting them safely up the stairwells to class. When a monitor was needed in the main office one of this squad would be enlisted to help. It was a prestigious appointment and she was eager to share her good news at home. She hoped the fact that she took Clare to school daily would not impede her ability to perform her duties. They only lived across a one way, street from the school so Grace did not anticipate a problem. Unfortunately, she had forgotten that Clare shared Daddy's tribulations with a nervous stomach. She would throw up every school morning. She would sob unconsolably, as well, hoping she would be allowed to stay home and play with her mother instead. Ultimately this condition was determined to be school phobia but not before it had caused Grace to lose her coveted position at school. She was repeatedly late in the morning, due to be her obligation to poor sick, suffering Clare. She was, therefore unable to fulfill her responsibility to arrive before the younger students in the class she attended to. It was her duty to greet them upon their arrival. Sadly, she was dismissed at great embarrassment and humiliation to herself. At home her distress over this loss was not formally acknowledged to her satisfaction. She was given some perfunctory sympathy but told not to fret too much. She was reminded that her real responsibility was to the family and her sister. That was more important than any silly belt she had been given by the school.

Grace had become by this time, an avid reader. She read every Nancy Drew book she could find. She loved the girl detective's ability to solve difficult cases she was confronted with. To Grace it seemed much like her own life and her never ending attempts to learn the real mysteries she was sure existed in her own family. The keys to these mysteries she knew would be found in the hope chest. She fancied herself as a main character in a best-selling novel, entitled, "The Secret of the Hope Chest". Her daydreams made her feel encouraged that she would uncover these secrets eventually.

The local library became a place Mare would take her to once a week to satisfy her unending need for new reading material. While Mare supervised Clare in the toddler section, or stood by while the librarian conducted a story telling session for the littlest visitors, Grace would browse the shelves mesmerized by the abundance of books. She would leave the library each time with as many books as she was allowed to lend and Mare cautioning that she was going to ruin her eyesight. One day she began reading a new book that she had not seen in the library before and promptly used her library card to secure. It was entitled, "The Diary of Anne Frank".

It was an autobiography written by a young girl in Holland during WWII. As a Jewish family, her family was forced to hide in an attic over a factory hoping always they would not be detected and brought to the attention of the Nazis. Such discovery would lead ultimately to the concentration camps for the family and almost assuredly death. The story both frightened and saddened Grace. She admired Anne and her ability to deal with the fearful, restricted life she was forced to endure. That Anne could do this, while still sharing what little joy she had, was inspiring. Grace felt disappointed in herself that she complained about the very close quarters of her family's first, one room home. Suddenly the things she could not do at that time became frivolous and unnecessary. Grace shared these feelings with her mother. She read sections of the book to her that especially moved or impressed Grace. Ultimately, she used this book as the basis for a book report in class. Her teacher, Mrs. Newman, told Anne she had also read the book. Her teacher was impressed by Grace's ability to understand

and relate to the young protagonists struggles. She gave Grace an A+ on her report written in bright red ink across the top of the first page of her report. Excitedly Grace rushed home that day to share such good news with her mother. Mare was very proud of Grace's grade on the report and hugged her tightly. Then all of a sudden, and completely unexpected by Grace, Mare approached the beloved chest. When she turned back around, she had several items in her hands that she displayed in front of her daughter. Grace had no idea what any of them were!

Mare held the first item out to Grace. It appeared to be a very shiny chrome pipe, with a large embellished chrome ball at the top. When Grace was unable to identify what it was, Mare volunteered that it was the top of a Nazi flagpole. Grace recoiled, feeling she was witnessing an evil artifact. She could not understand its presence in her wonderful treasure chest. It was accompanied by the next item in Mare's hands, an armband with a Nazi swastika embroidered on it. Witnessing her daughter's severe negative reaction to these things Mare, quickly explained how they came to be in the chest.

At one time during the war, her father had been put in charge of the POW camp in an area of Belgium. Those young, frightened and desperate German soldiers, would offer things in exchange for cigarettes or small favors. This was how her father, who apparently treated even prisoners kindly, came to possess these things. Also included in this new trove of surprises were two language handbooks, one in German and the other in French. While shunning the German one, Grace took the French manual to peruse. She would have to select a language this year, to begin studying during junior high. She had already decided it would be French over Spanish or German, the only choices being offered. This would give her a good jump on learning conversational phrases at least. It would also give her an opportunity to share something new with her father who frequently spoke of his love of France and the French people. It would turn out he was very proud of this decision she would make and happy to discuss some of his war time experiences with her. This bonding time with her dad would be remembered fondly later in life. The little Prince would play his part as well.

The school year ended on a very positive note for Grace. She was invited to sign the school Honor Roll, a big leather tome that was dragged out yearly during each subsequent graduation. The principal invited all signees to come back at any time to revisit the school and look once more inside the lofty ledger. Grace ascended the steps to the stage filled with gratitude for the recognition of her achievements during these formative years. She proudly entered her well-practiced signature in the book. She felt as if she was signing an important historical document and was channeling John Hancock for this occasion. However, it was the pride of her parents seated in that uncomfortable and aging auditorium that she remembered through most of her life. Clare clapped the loudest of everyone when Grace came off the stage. Her reaction of pride in her older sister almost erased the embarrassment of Grace being ejected from the elite, school monitorial squad.

CHAPTER

29

The preteen years are crucial for the development of all youngsters and the events that follow in their lives. For Grace it was a time of broad self-discovery and social awareness. With new freedom and growing knowledge of the world she was forming new friendships and having new experiences outside the boundaries of her family. She could go to the movies with friends and browse along the broad and busy, Southern Boulevard where three movie theaters were located. Buying records and listening to music with friends was a new happy and liberating pastime. The early throes of rock and roll, and adult reaction to this new music form, was part of these experiences. Her and her contemporaries felt that this was their music, separating them further from the parental controls of the age. She became close friends with Daisy and Holly, during this sixth year of elementary school.

One lazy summer afternoon as they sat in Holly's house sharing expectations of junior high school that was only weeks away, she confided to them that she thought she was adopted. It was the first time she had ever articulated this idea aloud. When she saw the incredulous looks on their faces, followed by silly offers of sympathy expressing their sorrow at this news, Grace knew she had made a mistake. She quickly said she was only fooling with them. Their anger at her playing with their feelings in spite of their friendship, was far easier for Grace to handle than their original reaction to her announcement. She realized then, that this was a big deal, if true, and that knowledge made her terrified!

September came suddenly. That first summer of adolescence behind them, Grace and her friends headed off to JHS 60, filled with excitement, hope but mostly trepidation. They would be attending an all-girls school. Located over a mile away from her home, Grace would be traveling on the bus for the first time without her mother. There would be no parents to monitor her, but also, no parents to protect her. She had been told this was a dangerous neighborhood located squarely in the middle of the 41st precinct, as the Simpson Street police station was known. This area would go on to be called Fort Apache, as the precinct was eventually rechristened in the press. What confused Grace the most was why had the wizards at the Board of Education, elected to keep her male 6th grade classmates in the present school for 7th and 8th grade while sending her and her female classmates off to the hinterland and on their perilous daily journey. Her parents, however, were just grateful the girls were being separated from the boys. That would not be true for long!

The junior high years were truly Grace's "coming out years". She would interact almost exclusively with girls from different races and cultures, primarily black and Hispanic, with the exception of May Wong. May was a very intelligent, sweet young girl who was in Grace's class throughout junior high school. Eddie was always referring to this classmate as Anna Wong, the name of a famous actress of his era. He laughed heartily when Grace explained her family owned a laundry shop that they lived behind. Although she did not get the reason for the amusement, she joined in.

She was infatuated initially by the music that was pumping out from the bodegas on her daily ride to school. She quickly learned, her new classmate's interests, were the same as her own. Their world was about family, clothes, girlfriends, music and boys! They included studious youngsters like herself and some less serious about school and schoolwork. At no time did Grace ever feel threatened or intimidated by anyone. Probably because she was quickly gaining acceptance by her peers and acquiring her street sense. She was comfortable in this ambiance and her sense of humor and her verbosity served her well. Being short of stature at the time, she found it easy to extricate herself from any situation she perceived as menacing. Whether it was dealing with a teacher or a pugnacious student Grace always acted and felt self-confident. The foundation of tolerance, acceptance and compassion was being laid for the rest of her life's journey. She was one with her community and that felt so right for her. Her memories in time would include, the street vendors selling coconut slices, candied apples and candied marshmallows at lunchtime. The delicious French fries sold in the back of the corner pharmacy to waiting, throngs of girls cramming the store during lunchtime. The shaved ice merchants and their colorful carts competing with the homemade ice cream produced in the shop around the corner. All these treats to be sampled after a lunch of spiced ham and cheese on a roll, a bag of Tom's potato chips and a pineapple-orange soda. The sandwich, which she could never replicate exactly, was only 15 cents! What a bargain, especially when accompanied by some lively merengue music playing on a speaker in the store. She loved her school and its lively neighborhood denizens!

During the three years Grace spent in junior high school her life changed significantly. Besides her own personal metamorphosis, things were developing at home as well. Her mother, with much more time on her hands, and her creative mind needing stimulation, began watching the children of other occupants in their building. Hers was a hard fought, and eventually won, battle with Eddie. He was old-fashioned in this area and did not want Mare to work, even though she would be at home, and they could definitely use the extra income. He worried it reflected poorly on him. He cited the fact that her sisters were housewives and unemployed, hoping to sway Mare to his side on the issue. Mare who would not be deterred suggested perhaps she should then drink or gamble and follow their lead. After realizing she would not abandon her plans, even when confronted with his reminder that he slept during the day because of his night hours, Eddie conceded. Grace could not believe Mare's triumph! She was extremely proud of her mother and promised to help when she could with the children.

The building in which they lived was now occupied by many immigrant families. They had come primarily from Cuba and other Caribbean nations. There were others from Puerto Rico and, although they arrived as citizens, they too were confronted by racism and were limited in their career choices. These industrious people usually could be found working in hotel kitchens and as maids. Their story mirrored her own maternal grandparents' saga. Clearly, Mare identified with their plight and that of the children. She was welcoming to the parents and nurturing to the little ones. There were generally four youngsters she would be caring for at a time. The parents of two toddler daughters from Spain and a family from Cuba with a small son and baby girl were her longest clients.

The family of Arturo and Angela were fleeing the corrupt, brutal regime of General Batista, the Cuban military dictator supported by the USA. Hunts Point, being a heavily industrialized area with many factories, all four adult parents pursued employment in these plants. Naturally their pay was a subsistence one and these tireless workers were frequently unknown to the authorities. That negated any extra assistance for them. Although she was supposed to be making $10 a week for the care of each child, in truth, with her good Irish heart and love of children, she was often spending more than that satisfying their needs (and most of their wants). She indulged them at Christmas, hosted all their birthday parties and taught them their alphabets and numbers. She was the primary English speaker in their lives and they all learned quickly to speak their new language. The parents were eternally grateful for her devotion to their youngsters. Angela and Arturo, also Catholic, asked Mare if she would be their little girl's godmother. Of course, she accepted. Both children already called her "Ma" and now she was given the respectful title "madrina", or god-mother. Grace would recall how moved her mother, and father as well, were when such a beautiful honor was bestowed on her.

Mare's two sisters, however, reacted in a manner totally un-expected by Grace. Aunt Marge thought it blasphemous for some reason. Apparently, her Catholic Church was different from the one in Cuba although both were recognized by the papacy under Pope Pius the II at the time. In fact, to Mare, Spanish seemed closer to Latin, which was the official tongue of the Church. Aunt Irene told her mother not to visit if she was bringing any of her little wards with her. It embarrassed her she said when the children called Mare, "Ma" in public. Grace was sure it also offended her good Catholic neighbors who she prayed with every Sunday at her parish. Mare, to the delight of her daughter, called her sister a bigot on that occa-sion and suggested she go to confession at church and seek forgiveness. This also insured that Angela's delicious chicken soup and black beans and rice would continue to grace her mother's kitchen table.

On the night Castro entered Havana, Grace's family sat watching the televised event alongside Angela's extended fam-ily of brother in laws, their wives and children. There was Latin music being played by a trio of Cuban musicians, friends of the family, in the corner of the small living room of the tiny apartment. There was dancing, singing and celebration for these newcomers and freedom for their country. And Grace, at fourteen, danced her first meringue with Roberto, the seventeen year old nephew of Arturo. Viva la Revolucion!

CHAPTER
30

By the end of 9th grade Hunts Point had become Fort Apache, once desirable apartment buildings had become tenements and crime had become an epidemic in the community. In an attempt to create outlets for teenagers, and in response to the emergence of teenage gang culture, public school night centers became a feature in the neighborhood. They were designed to provide positive social and sport outlets to compensate for the lack of such facilities in the community. Basketball, ping pong, knock hockey and badminton were offered as diversions to the attractiveness of the street. There were opportunities for some arts and crafts as well as listening and dancing to the popular tunes of the time. There was ample potential for social interaction. Cliques formed, disbanded and reformed as new entities, given the fickleness of teenage friendships. What did not seem to occur to the well-meaning designers of these refuges, was that the problems plaquing the larger community would soon become endemic in the microcosm of the night center. Fights were common amongst different groups of boys as well as girls. Younger boys hitting puberty were given to teasing and obnoxious comments to the young ladies. Girls responded in kind. Older teenagers, and their "guests" were accused of being pushy, even coercive with the girls, especially when dancing. Drugs were making their way into the bathrooms and stairwells of the school at night. A new term, overdose, was becoming part of the teenage lexicon. It reached the point that many youngsters, recognizing that the thugs had inherited the kingdom, abandoned the centers. Whether this was commonplace throughout the city, it certainly was on the Hunts Point peninsula.

One night, before the deterioration began, Grace brought Clare to the center for the evening, at the request of her mother. Though Grace felt embarrassed dragging her younger sister along, she was not prepared for what would greet her at home. Mare was in the kitchen preparing hot chocolate for the girls when Clare blurted out the word "fuck" repeatedly. Stunned by her daughter's new speech pattern Mare demanded an explanation. Clare confessed, of course, that it was not her fault. She was only imitating Grace and her friends. Mare cautioned Grace that if these behaviors continued, she would not allow her to attend the center. Grace's visits to the night center would not go on much longer at any rate. The new menacing atmosphere at the center would take over in spite of the best efforts of the staff. Grace made the decision to stop participating in any activities there. Strangely, she felt relieved even if she was giving up some of her new found freedom.

Their small apartment soon became the new "hangout". Her long-suffering Dad, having adjusted somewhat to Mare's "nursery", would now be confronted by a group of teenagers every evening playing the relentless strains of Elvis Presley, and other memorable teenage idols and groups, on Grace's new hi-fi record player. Again, Mare stood her ground on this issue declaring, "I want to know who my daughter's friends are and this way I will". Her father conceded to her wisdom on raising girls.

Grace and her friends loved that Mare was such a generous hostess. How well liked her mother was by her friends made the girl proud. Her mother quickly learned each teenager's soda preference and always had that available in addition to potato chips and bags of candy. She was easy to talk to and soon she was learning about each young person's life, their interests, families and their aspirations. She never acted judgmental or austere. Her personal goal with this interplay was to gently steer Grace away from potential troublemakers she identified. She had always cautioned her daughter about choosing friends wisely. Her oft repeated warning to Grace was, "birds of a feather flock together", a subtle execution of her control over her daughter's friendships. Grace was witnessing the effects of the naivete of her friends. She was remembering her mother's remonstrations about offering too much information to adults. Clearly Mare was well aware of the pitfalls of this for the youngsters but subtlety plied the teens and built their trust and her "dossiers".

Grace had mixed emotions about this technique. She was angry that her mother would deceive her friends at times. She could, however, see the value of the lesson she had been taught in her home regarding being too revealing. This proved very effective with Grace despite the fact that she felt there was more to her parent's social reticence than they had yet to reveal to her. Grace trusted her mother, and therefore always took her direction. Grace rarely lied to her parents. Her openness, however, often led to conflict in the home. The Church's position was considered by Grace in such situations. There was the threat of venial sins for lying and mortal sins for being insolent to one's parents. Rather than risking the wrath of God and banishment in the afterlife she erred on the side of honesty with her parents. Her friends frankly found this much transparency strange.

Eventually as young girls do, they each decided to assume new identities within the group. They accomplished this, as generations before them, with the help of nicknames. The monikers chosen were usually coy or cutesy names, deemed apt for each personality, (i.e. Penny, Kitten, Candy). When it came to Grace they were stumped! Grace didn't standout because of her beautiful clothing or lustrous head of hair. Though of course she longed for both of these attributes. What defined her was her honesty and genuineness. She was candid with her feelings and generous with opinions when requested. She was a good listener and her friends treasured her for this. Grace gave advise that was truthful even when someone would rather hear her reinforce and support their own ideas. So, there it was! Her candidness and realistic approach to everything earned her the nickname "Frank". Not exactly the name she was hoping for as a young girl becoming aware of boys and her own feelings toward that awkward group of humanity. The more she thought about it, however, the more she realized it was exactly the nickname she should have. To her it was far better than the non-descript, hopelessly silly pseudonyms of her girlfriends.

Several things brought this clubhouse at her apartment to its demise. The new linoleum Dad had purchased for the living room was worn out from the vigorous dancing that it was subjected to. Dad finally declared his "castle" as he called the apartment, off-limits to marathon dancing. He placed a decibel level on the music as well. Mom was in accord because, by then, she had weeded out who were, to her thinking, the worst and most dangerous of the boys and girls Grace associated with. Time would prove her correct on all but a few of her predictions. One day Mare decided to shame Grace publicly for her untidy habits. She walked into the living room with Grace's panties and bras draped over her extended arms. There were several friends in the room and Grace was absolutely mortified. In Grace's defense there was no room in the one dresser the family shared nor was there room in the hamper that was perpetually overflowing because there was no laundromat close by. The one in the basement of the building had been robbed and broken for quite a while. Besides, it was not safe for her mother to be down there alone. After this humiliating experience Grace was happy to call the party over.

What actually brought the party to an end was life outside the apartment. With economic problems facing too many families, a lot of her friends began to look for part-time jobs at grocery stores as stock boys while the girls sought babysitting opportunities after school helping working mothers. Also, many friends were pairing off as couples and going "steady". The worse the neighborhood became for a young women's safety the more parents turned a blind eye to the practice. They felt their daughters were safer in the company of a young man than dealing with the perils of "the point" alone.

Grace and Clare had dealt with such hazards walking up the staircase of their building. They were accosted by some brutish men they had to fight off together. Only because both men began laughing and continued on their way did Grace determine they were just being intimidated. After that incident the girls would be watched coming upstairs by their mother peering down over the fifth-floor banister and calling their names repeatedly till they were safely within her sight. The street was filled with many insolent men who would catcall and suck their teeth when girls or women passed them. The fact that Mare would be with her daughters did not impede their harassment in the least.

There was also the violence. Teenage gangs were becoming endemic to the area. The newspapers reported more and more on the painful aftermath of clashes between these groups. Grace and her friends were stopped by the police one late summer evening and questioned because of a shooting outside PS48. Parties in apartment building basements would end up, too often, with a dead, overdosed teenager. Police were handing out juvenile delinquent summonses to the children of parents too ineffective and overwhelmed to address the needs of their offspring.

Grace recalled the day the Fordham Baldies, a notorious Bronx street gang, were rumored to be coming to her school. Fears of impending rape and kidnapping were rampant throughout the classrooms and hallways. The school office was over-run by girls calling home, hoping to be picked up by their parents. At dismissal, Grace and several of her friends that lived close by, walked home together. It was a mile and a half walk that led them right past St. Athanasius, their local parish. The girls stopped to offer a quick pray of thanks that they had evaded the Baldies that day. Thriving, even coping, in an environment such as this was not an easy task for any teen-ager. Those that contributed most to the violence and decline of the area, were, in truth, its biggest victims. Nevertheless, it was becoming more and more dangerous to be a teenager in Hunts Point.

CHAPTER
31

Grace's response to the changes she was experiencing, both internally and externally, was to grow ever brasher. Always outspoken at home, she was now beginning to be impudent, even insolent. Nowhere was this more manifest than at school. After completing two very successful academic years of junior high, Grace moved on to her 9th grade. This would be her final year before moving on to high school. She showed up that first day of 9th grade to find herself surrounded by former classmates, but many new students as well.

After introducing himself, the teacher began calling the role. When her name was called, the teacher asked her to stand. Since he had not requested this of anyone else, she rose confused and embarrassed. He then directed the entire class to look at Grace. "This girl here is going to win all the medals at graduation," he announced. Grace quickly plopped back into her seat feeling all eyes on her. Happily, he continued taking attendance and eventually that school day would end. Later, after class, he would explain to her that his remarks were prompted by her IQ as noted in her school record. He intended this as a compliment but since it was obvious his remark caused her distress he apologized. Grace was unable to articulate how defensive his comment had made her. She knew instinctively she would now have to prove she was just like the other girls to continue to be accepted. She could not explain to him how his declaration had reminded her of the conversation between her mother and the school nurse way back when she was just beginning her education. The confusion and suspicions generated that day were back and she would have to find ways to deal with them. Years, later when she was in therapy and told her therapist about this incident, he concluded that this had indeed been a hostile remark. In attempting to impress his new class with his proclamation of clairvoyance, he had most unwisely used her as a foil. This was most unprofessional and harmful on the part of that individual. Grace was most thankful for this assessment, but that would come later. She would begin that day to rebel in new ways that school year. Thinking again of her hope chest and the revelations she knew it portended, she prayed again its contents would soon lift the veil of obscurity that engulfed her.

Though she continued to do excellently academically, Grace was developing a belligerent attitude in school. Her keen sense of humor was being used by her to be disruptive too often during lessons, though it gained her many admirers among her classmates. It was more important to her to be seen, at that time by her peers, as one of the "gang". She eschewed the role of bright, cooperative, future medal winner! When Mr. Cantor took the class to the Museum of Natural History on one occasion, Grace arranged for her neighborhood friends, that did not attend her school, to meet her there. She seized her first opportunity to sneak away with them.

They were having a wonderful day in Central Park when her teacher and the rest of the class appeared! After some impudent verbal back and forth with Mr. Cantor, who was trying to convince Grace to return to school with her class, she walked off with her friends. She surely expected to arrive home to her parents being fully aware of her transgressions that day. All evening she continued to wait for the parental harangue that, to her amazement, never occurred. It dawned on her that the teacher did not report the incident to the school lest he be held accountable for some form of dereliction. Therefore, her parents were unaware of what had transpired. She declared a silent victory for herself.

The next day, however, her teacher arranged to meet with Grace privately. With no friends or classmates around, she was able to listen to his concerns about her poor decisions of the previous day. She sensed he was genuinely concerned about her safety and the consequences that might have followed her rash choices. He also explained the untenable situation she had put him in. First by so blatantly being disrespectful to him in public. Secondly, by jeopardizing his career because of his failure to return with the entire group he started out with that day. Even though it had been his remarks that first day of class that had been the catalyst for her subsequent downward spiral that school year, she forgave him completely in her heart. He could not know of all the forces at work in her life to bring her to that point, nor could he be responsible for them. She was able to share much with him that day and was inspired herself to become a teacher someday. She wanted to be able to accept students for who they were and motivate them to move forward in life. He had done that for her. She would think of him often as she eventually pursued a career in education.

Grace loved French class and her teacher. Mrs. DuVal was a very short, stocky woman and already well into her later middle-ages. With her curly, salt and pepper hair fastened wildly on the top of her head she led the class with vigor. Her French was beautiful to listen to and her love of all things French obvious. Her animated lectures brought the customs and culture of France to that south Bronx classroom. Already a Francophile, Grace was her best student and was called upon often in class. She could never imagine being insolent to Mrs. Duval.

One day, however, Grace arrived to French class late. Mrs. DuVal requested an explanation. When Grace did not reply, she became more demanding of a reason for her tardiness. Grace, embarrassed before the class, lashed out, using a terrible, derogatory term to describe, a shocked, Mrs. Duval. She then ran from the room. Not much later she was summoned to the guidance counselor's office where Mrs. Duval was waiting. Since she had always liked Grace, and it was obvious Grace was successful in her class, Mrs. Duval had suggested the counselor act as mediator in her discussion with the girl. Grace was totally ashamed of herself. She apologized to her teacher, profusely, through real tears of remorse. She admitted not knowing why she had acted in such a manner and Mrs. Duval, content with this explanation, accepted her apology. The guidance counselor set up a few appointments with Grace to follow up on her progress at school. Grace was pleased by this outcome and happy to have an outlet to discuss her feelings and fears going forward. The meeting ended with the decision on the part of the professionals not to involve her parents at that time. Since she was only months from graduation now, she was glad her parents would not be troubled with this incident. Graduation loomed before her beckoning with wonderful opportunities for the future. She promised secretly that a trip to Paris would surely be hers one day!

CHAPTER

32

A wonderful tradition of graduation was the purchase of autograph books to be signed by a student's family, teachers, relatives and friends. The first sighting of an autograph book clearly signaled the ending of the junior high experience. Students rushed to get their own memory books, with their names proclaimed in gold glitter. Pages designated for family members, as well as special friends and favorite teachers, were also similarly adorned. Each page, when completed, would contain a special wish, memory or saying by another person. The rush to get your book completed, cover to cover, was fun yet competitive. The completeness of your autograph book became the real indicator of how well you did in junior high school!

Mare took Grace to buy her treasured memento. It was pristine white vinyl with a gold-tone clasp. The pages inside were of several pastel colors. On select pages, and given certain names to include, the shop owner created a masterpiece with glue and glitter. Grace felt she had never owned something so special and personal. She hurried home, where Clare, Dad and Mom would become her first signees. When her father signed her book, he addressed his words, "To my doll". With those three simple words the event became one of the happiest in her life to date. Her mother wished her immortality just so she could reap the benefit of all the good wishes she had for her. Clare, now in 4th grade, eagerly added her sincere, little girl thought, "2good 2be 4gotten". She felt very grown, and of course clever, as she inscribed it.

That night as Grace lay in bed, struggling to settle down to sleep, she heard Mare tiptoeing into the bedroom. She quickly realized her mother was opening the hope chest and removing something. When Mare turned around and saw Grace sitting up in bed, she was startled. In her hand was a worn, green autograph book. "This is my memory book," she told her daughter. "I can understand your excitement today. Keep your book safe and it will reward you with many happy memories to look back upon". She kissed Grace goodnight and closed the bedroom door. Grace did not hear her return the book to the chest later on that night. She was in a deep and peaceful sleep. It would be many years before Grace would see the book again and be able to explore its contents.

CHAPTER
33

During the middle of her senior year, a most monumental encounter led to a life altering situation. Grace had recently met a new member of the group of boys she was friendly with. His name was "Joey" and she found him "cute". Her red-headed friend Katherine also found him cute. Being a loyal friend, Grace made it her mission to get these two teens together. She therefore spent time with Joey in the group hoping to convince him of Katherines charms. Conversation led to her realization that he was unlike the other boys. He was a serious, articulate and intelligent guy. He was not brash or attention seeking as young men can be. She danced with him at a party at Holly's house to a song by Elvis Presley called "Old Shep". The song was a tribute to an old and dying canine. She learned two things that night. Elvis could make her cry and Joey could not dance.

It was February 16th 1958. Hunts Point was a very hilly neigh-borhood providing wonderful sledding opportunities. On this particular snowy night all her friends gathered on Spofford Ave which offered the best conditions for this sport. Joey, ac-companied some of the teenagers to the event. With three con-secutive steep hills to conquer it promised to be an exciting if dangerous night. The first three boys down the slope, passed directly in front of a tractor trailer that, thankfully was mov-ing cautiously along the cross street at the bottom of the hills. After a noisy confrontation with the boys about their care-lessness and their disregard for everyone's safety, the trucker drove on. As they trudged back up the hill, dragging their sleds behind them, she realized Joey had been one of them. She ran to him to see if he was alright. Instead, he was laughing, exhilarated by the experience. That night he asked her to be his girlfriend and she agreed. She really had tried to match him with Catherine. Six years later, to the day, they were married.

CHAPTER
34

Throughout her junior high experience her father suffered chronic eye failure. There would be many surgeries in attempts to save his eyesight. He moved thru the progression of uveitis, cataracts, detached retina, and glaucoma. Ultimately his left eye had to be removed. This was an especially difficult time for him and put strain on her mother and their marriage. He was often sullen and despondent about his situation. He was cross at times as well. But Mare was a wonderful and constant comfort to him during this time. She spent all day and every evening with him when he was confined to a hospital bed at various intervals. Hers was a long journey from the south Bronx to upper Manhattan to the Institute of Ophthalmology at Columbia Presbyterian Hospital. She traveled alone via public transportation to be at his side. Neighbors and family stepped in to care for and feed Grace and Clare when necessary. On weekends they would accompany her to the hospital and spend all day confined to the facility. While Grace sat doing homework or studying, Clare would troll the ward and the nurse's station talking to the staff. Mare would always convince Grace to do Clara's homework as well. The delicious little chocolate candy sabots from Holland she bought her daughters on the way home from visiting Daddy was sufficient incentive for Grace. They also reminded her of the little wooden shoes brought from France by him that had been returned to the hope chest. Unfortunately, her sister had yet to develop the delight in school that Grace experienced. Grace doubted she ever would. However, her hopeful sibling decided during this time she wanted to become a nurse when she was older. A hard career to pursue without an education but her sweet sister Clare had things to learn as we all did.

CHAPTER
35

A joyful graduation, replete with caps and gowns in blue with gold-colored tassels and a yellow rose corsage from Dad defined this event for her, as it would forever. Her scholarship was duly noted which elated her parents. She, however, did not receive an award for citizenship. She totally understood that decision. The symbolism of the yellow roses was known to her. Her father had received his basic training for the army at Camp Maxey, in of all places, Paris, Texas. The song "Yellow Rose of Texas" became a standard tune in their home. You knew he was in good form when you heard him humming or singing this ditty. Perhaps this was why, when he gave any of his "ladies" flowers, they could expect yellow roses. It became a tradition in the family that would endure. Grace felt very mature that day and more loved than she could ever remember. Clare was only 3years from entering the school and

Grace walked her around and introduced her to some of her teachers. The size of the facility and the number in the graduating class seemed to stun the child. She was always reticent of anything school related. Grace hoped that response would improve before she became a student at her, now, alma mater. She would learn, regrettably, that she had left a legacy for her little sister to overcome.

Grace was excited about entering high school at the close of the summer. She would be attending Walton High School in the west Bronx. She was saddened, however, by the fact that many of the close friends she had made would now be dispersed throughout other high schools in the city. Walton had a superb academic reputation. She did not delude herself by thinking that this was the only, even primary reason, her parents had insisted on her attendance there. The fact that it was, at the time an all-girl school, once again made it that much more attractive to her very protective parents. It certainly tampered her enthusiasm for this impending new beginning!

CHAPTER
36

Her social life was beginning to supplant her emphasis on her studies. Fortunately for her though, she was innately a very capable student. In addition to the prescribed curriculum, she continued with her French language studies. She would become quite competent in this subject before she left high school. Only the introduction into new areas of math (geometry, trigonometry, advanced algebra) proved challenging. Not unexpected, since the "old" areas of math had always given her difficulty. However, by the end of each semester she would master the discipline and earn her Regents credits.

Grace loved to swim. The fact that this school had an Olympic swimming pool, that she would have access to, exhilarated her. It actually eased the initial disappointment of attending Walton. However, that would end in her junior year. One cold and snowy day in January, only Grace and a smattering of other girls chose to swim. She was alone in her cramped little locker donning her swimsuit, when the curtain to the shower was thrown back to reveal a very 'underdressed' male facing her. He growled, "Don't say a word or I'll hurt you". Grace began screaming, of course, and exited her locker, running around the pool to the teacher's office. In pursuit was the intruder. Fortunately he gave up the chase and disappeared. Unfortunately, the teacher was not at her station choosing instead to have hot coffee on such a blustery day with colleagues in the lounge. By the time she appeared she encountered Grace and several other girls shivering in a state of panic. The first statement from her was, "Girls I'll handle this. Let's just keep it between us". Grace left her pleading as she sought out the principal. The principal also tried to keep the issue within the school, opting not to call the police, and suggesting Grace not upset her parents. Grace asked for the phone, called her father, and he called the police. When they arrived, they seem convinced on getting her to admit to letting a boy into the pool for a "rendez-vous". She had noticed the intruder had not been wearing a jacket (among other things) and deduced that perhaps he worked on the large custodial staff of the building. She requested they line up the men that were working at the time since she was sure she could identify him. They refused her request. That was the end of the story as far as anyone in authority was concerned. Grace knew her parents would accept this outcome rather than be interrogated as she had been. Her mom, who had lost all her teeth, over the last five years had stopped coming to school due to embarrassment. Of course, there were no financial resources to restore her confidence in her appearance, although she was always beautiful to her husband and children. Grace never felt safe in the shower again. Her anxiety in that situation, though she knew it to be irrational, would persist forever.

CHAPTER
37

Never having difficulty making friendships, these years would be replete with many such alliances, some more enduring and significant than others. Her most important relationship, of course, was with Joey. When she introduced him to her parents that first winter they met, she witnessed how intuitive he was.

He arrived on Ash Wednesday with the residue of ashes on his forehead, identifying himself as Catholic. While her parents were impressed by his display of religiosity, Grace would soon learn he was the first atheist she had ever met. She continued to go to church, and Joey continued his charade for the benefit of her parents. Eventually the truth would come out but by then they had developed a fondness for him. They seemed to have decided that in a neighborhood of dwindling prospects he was at least an industrious youth and very protective of their daughter in an often dangerous and unpredictable milieu. She was happy to learn that her safety, if not her happiness, held more value than his religious affiliation or lack thereof. By the time her high school years had passed they would still be dating.

On the surface theirs was a typical teenage romance of the era. They did things alone as well as with other couples. Most evenings during her sophomore and junior years would be spent in her apartment in the company of her parents and sister, playing cards and boardgames. There would be long walks to the Hunts Point Cemetery. Though macabre as this sounds it was a wonderful historic park name for Joseph Rodman Drake, an influential New York City poet who died at only 25 years of age. The park had benches, grassy knolls and lawns encircled by a walking path around the perimeter. Right in the middle, in an area encircled by a wrought iron fence were the gravesites of Drake and other influential deceased Bronxites. It was a popular haunt for dating, trysts and clandestine meetings of all kinds. Grace loved reading the inscriptions on these aged but enduring relics. She loved to learn about local history and culture. It lifted her spirit above the bleak and hope bereft atmosphere of a rapidly declining neighborhood.

Her only bad memory of the "cemetery" as it was called did not involve haunting by interred entities or harassment by local thugs. It involved young Clare and a careless bicyclist. Enjoying a harmless game of tag with her sister, Clare stepped in front of a swiftly moving bike. She was actually thrown into the air and landed loudly and painfully on the cement path. Instead of stopping to see if the child was okay, the rider increased his speed and sped away shouting obscenities at his stunned and bruised little victim. Joe carried the sobbing child home where Grace would be upbraided for not properly watching her little sister. The guilt she felt already was only compounded. It would be years before Clare would attempt to learn to ride a bike due to the trauma of the afternoon. It would be only two days before Grace faced her judgement in the confessional.

On weekends Grace and Joey would take public transportation to pools and beaches located not far from home. Orchard Beach and Pelham Bay Park were frequent haunts. Subway rides to Coney Island were tackled occasionally. Grace, who was disinclined to risk taking, had her first rides on the Cyclone roller coaster and the Wonder Wheel with Joey. Unlike her, he courted danger and would take steps to scare her, rocking the swinging cage of the wheel or lifting his arms above his head on the coaster. He mocked her for not following his lead. He had a taunting and somewhat sadistic nature that was beginning to emerge and this concerned her. His mood would change swiftly, however, and he would again be the amusing witty boyfriend whose company she enjoyed.

Joey struggled with school, played hooky often and finally dropped out. He joined the Marines at 17 and after not completing bootcamp, dropped out. She was led to believe it was because he had developed asthma which became debilitating during training in the excessive heat and humidity of South Carolina. She, however, had always believed his father, who was a card carrying communist and greatly displeased by his son's decision to enter the military, had worked to undermine his success. Working with a relative who was a surgeon he was able to present medical rationale to facilitate his son's departure from the Marines. Joey then began an apprenticeship in the painter's union, where his father, an émigré from Scotland, had been a founder and activist for many years He worked hard, earned a good salary and only one year later, he was able to purchase his first car. At eighteen he showed up one night in a big, flashy, turquoise Oldsmobile that was very impressive, indeed, especially given his age. Her parents, at first reluctant, finally allowed her to go in the car with him. She was 16 years old by then.

Their options for entertainment immediately broadened. They would drive now to Jones Beach on Long Island and venture even further east exploring the gorgeous coastline of Nassau and Suffolk counties. They could enjoy the many lakes and beautiful state parks of the upstate as they explored areas north and west of the city. They were frequent patrons of the Whitestone Drive-in outdoor movie theater. Grace, succumbing to teenage male pressure, had her first sessions with "necking", as teenagers of the time called their first forays into a developing sexuality. At this time, struggling with Church expectations and her parents trust in her, she enjoyed what was happening in the snack bar more. In truth the pizza stunk! The evening was a success for Joey if he was able to drive out without dragging an outdoor speaker, hung on the car window, with him. His temper was becoming an issue with Grace. It would flare up, subside and ignite again for seemingly no valid reason. He could be loud and bullying with her. On one occasion he yelled at Clare at the drive-in. There was a movie she was looking forward to seeing and Grace offered to take her along.

This did not please Joey. He made Clare sit alone in the front seat and threatened her not to turn around. Grace could not wait to get home and share the incident with her mother. Mare verbally chastised Joey and expressed her disappointment in him. Later she would caution Grace about being too obedient or submissive to his whims. Grace had not yet learned of the various forms of abuse women mistake for love. She would learn that lesson eventually. She had learned, however, that she would never again allow anyone to intimidate her sister again.

At home life droned on during these high school years. She would continue with her religious instruction, courtesy of release time, once a week. At the completion, during her senior year, she received her Certificate of Christian Doctrine. She felt by now it should more rightly be called a certificate of indoctrination. This document, emblazed with seals and signatures, meant very little to Grace. She actually believed it to be an indictment, a mockery of her grasp of Catholicism. Not having attended parochial school she knew it meant her cousins and some friends had relegated her to second-class citizenry in the world of the devout. She was happy, however, that it made her parents, who had both attended parochial school in their youth, extraordinarily pleased. She would eventually learn it was more a vindication than a victory.

The nomination of John F. Kennedy for President of the USA brought overt political energy to the Church. The pastor of her own church, in his most insistent voice, spent many a sermon imploring his sheep to vote and help elect the first Catholic president. That any rich man, no matter what his religion, could relate to her family and community, was a concern but not the real issue, for Grace. It was what she personally experienced as a blatant violation of church and state's rights in her local parish that troubled her. Grace had long stopped worrying about the implicit threat of hell attached to issues. She began to follow the race closely in the newspapers to make an informed decision about who she would endorse. That November 8th, 1960, she would be voting age. She ultimately would cast her first vote for Kennedy but not because she was pressured to. And she would mourn with her nation and her Church when he was assassinated in 1963. Her approach to political paradoxes, formed then, would foreshadow her decisions during the turbulent times of the late sixties thru the mid-seventies. She would learn much and lose more during that time.

CHAPTER
38

One vignette from this part of her life would simultaneously amuse and confuse her for years. Arriving home from school one day she found Mare, prone on the kitchen floor, with an open oven door nearby. The kitchen definitely had the odor of gas escaping into the room. When Grace ran to her mother, terrified and already in tears, Mare began to become aware but in a very dazed and confused way. She chided Grace for "saving" her from her futile suicide attempt. She was depressed she said. No one seemed to need her anymore. She might as well be dead. It was then that Grace realized the kitchen window was wide open. The oven that never worked, because of the missing knob, was mysteriously serving up a deadly repast. And her mother who believed in all things Catholic had just tried to kill herself, a dire if not deadly, mortal sin. The timing too seemed inconvenient. Afterall, Grace was always home just about the same time and surely would have intervened in the plan, as she did just then. Grace knew her mother to use drama and guilt to make a point but did not dare be accusatory. Her mother made her swear not to tell anybody and she promised never to try such a thing again. Thank God she did not. Grace could never be sure if this had been a cry for help or another creative performance by her parent. She did, however, begin immediately to give her mother more of her time and attention.

Grace was acutely aware of her mother's ability to get her way with her dad. It didn't even require a high degree of sulking or brooding. Her father was never at home in NYC and always talked of moving the family up to New England. The job he had in the post office gave him the opportunity to request a work relocation. When he suggested considering a transfer to Connecticut, Mare became apoplectic. Declaring, she would never leave her siblings, she became almost theatrical in her protestations. To Grace such a move seemed sensible. It certainly would be safer than their current neighborhood. Also, all her aunts and uncles owned autos and could visit them. She began to dream of the possibilities of a new place to live. Unfortunately, Mare was not a dreamer, nor did she adapt easily to new situations. Despite the fact that her dad had more siblings than her mother and never got to see them, Mare held her ground. Naturally he would succumb to her tearful outbursts. Unfortunately, growing up, there had been only two trips to Massachusetts to visit her extended paternal family. One when she was too young to remember and once again when she was 8 and Clare was 4.

She remembered the trip to Grand Central Station to board the train to their destination. Mare had dressed them identically as she often did for such special occasions. Often Grace would be dressed in clothes not best suited for her age but which looked adorable on a younger Clare. She rarely complained since new clothes were an expensive commodity in her household and she realized the sacrifice her parents were making. Besides, they were always more comfortably fitting than the hand-me downs of her obese older cousin imposed on Gracie's skinny frame.

She was emotionally engulfed by the enormity of this great terminus. The kinetic energy created by so many hurried travelers was palpable. They boarded the mighty beast that would be their chariot on the rails to her father's first home. Grace was throbbing with anticipation at the idea of meeting all her relatives. To tamper her enthusiasm, she immersed herself in the beautiful vistas of New England they were passing and spent time entertaining Clare.

She would be happily rewarded with the warm, enthusiastic welcome they received from her aunts and uncles and the sightseeing they had planned for them. She would remember Cogsall Park and the shimmering koi in the beautiful lake it encircled. With her cousin, Paul, the beneficiary of all her blue baby clothes, she enjoyed Whelan Amusement Park and the rides and amusements if offered. Her much-anticipated trip to visit the grandmother she yearned for, but had never remembered meeting, was a disaster. She did not seem affected by Grace's presence at all. She did not smile at her or embrace her as Grace had envisioned. What Grace had hoped would be a memorable encounter became a poignant one, evoking a sense of sadness and sorrow in the young girl. It would be more than 50 years, and long after her grandmother's death, that Grace would visit her dad's hometown again.

CHAPTER
39

As graduation approached, Grace realized, with disappointment, that she was beginning to feel detached from the hope chest. Distractions of the classroom and her education, combined with her active social life, competed with her continued curiosity about her favorite item in the world. As she aged, she was learning to respect, if not understand, her parent's reticence to reveal the complete contents of the chest to their children. At times it would become a contentious situation, with no better result for Grace. Eventually, that year she would put the enigma of the hope chest to rest indefinitely, she thought. Someday, she believed, all things would fall into place, all secrets would be revealed and a long-awaited enlightenment would occur. She knew this to be true.

She was acutely aware, also, that this phase of her life would be over soon and adulthood, with all its expectations and promise, would begin. Friendships she had made at school, already seemed tenuous. From the onset of high school most of the girls she met lived much closer to Walton. In fact, she lived the greatest distance away and therefore traveled the furthest to reach school every day. Grace had to ride a bus and two trains to get there. (Amazingly she would receive recognition at her graduation ceremony for perfect attendance.) Her lack of proximity was the reason that she made only a few lasting relationships during this period. She did not have her parent's approval to visit classmates after school The idea of any young lady traveling alone, back home to her neighborhood in the evening, had become unwise.

Her non-attendance at senior activities such as the prom or the senior trip further dampened her ability to form many happy high school memories. Not that she did not yearn to participate in these coming-of-age rituals. She truly did. She loved both music and dancing. Unfortunately, Joey did not and he refused to take her. It was unthinkable for Grace, given the dating mores of the era, to attend without him. The senior trip, on the other hand, was expensive and deemed too exorbitant for her parents. She would concede on both counts, to Joey out of fear and to her parents out of guilt.

Graduation day was neither auspicious nor gratifying. The venue, however, was awe inspiring to a young woman who had never been able to take music lessons. Graduation took place at Carnegie Hall! The history and ornate appearance of the auditorium was inspiring. Only her academic placement in the senior class and her perfect attendance award provided any satisfaction beyond that setting. Mom had been able to buy

Grace a lovely yellow dress in the basement of Alexander's department store to wear under her blue graduation gown. Dad, never failing, presented her with a beautiful yellow rose corsage. They were both proud of her and it was apparent to Grace. Neither of them had graduated high school and this was a vindication of sorts.

What troubled Grace however, was that even though she was accepted to attend Hunter College and had turned down the opportunity, they did not seem at all disappointed. She had expected them to try and convince her to change her mind. Afterall, she had always said since she began school that she would be going to college. Mare, in fact had confided to her that they didn't know how they would have been able to pay for college and support her at home for four more years. They agreed her getting a job, as she intended, was a better plan for the moment. It was Joey of course that had convinced her to bypass college and find a job. They could both then be saving for their future together was his rationale. She would learn this was more evidence of his need to control her and maintain what he saw as his superior position in their relationship. This of course, was beyond her sensibilities at the time.

Instead, as many young Irish Catholic lasses before her, she accepted a job with the New York Telephone Company. The woman who administered the test to Grace for a position with the monolith, surprised Grace by telling her that, since she received a 100% on the exam, she could not in good conscience recommend Grace for a position as an operator, stenographer, file clerk or any number of other mind numbing and sexist jobs that the company offered. Grace expressed, obviously with conviction, how important this job would be for her and her family. The woman asked her to wait while she explored other opportunities. She was able to secure a place for Grace ultimately with the training center for new male management trainees just out of college. Grace would be responsible to three male supervisors who ran the training program. After only one month Grace new that she and New York Telephone would be better served if she, herself, was a management trainee rather than performing the clerical work it entailed. Unfortunately, this was still 1961 and the feminist revolution had not yet occurred! She would make $43.10 a week for the next two and a half years. The most valuable truth that she learned during this spate was that she would never work in an office again! It was the symbolism of the chest and what it promised Grace that convinced her with certainty of this. Her curiosity surrounding the chest, she had come to believe, was just a projection of her aspirations and dreams for her future. She never doubted, however, in its very real purpose in her life in some still, unrevealed, way.

If Grace believed that life at home would change much, now that she was a working girl, she was wrong. If she assumed an elevation in her standing in the family was going to follow, she was wrong again. No way was this more obvious than the night she came home from work with her first paycheck. She had stopped at Woolworths after cashing it to purchase small gifts for the family in celebration of her new life. She was eager to present her mother with the lovely embroidered handkerchief she had decided on for her. Her father would receive a 5 pack of his favorite White Owl cigars. She splurged a little more on

Clare and bought her an adorable baby doll that wet her diaper when given water through a tiny plastic bottle. She hurried home in anticipation of the excitement of this momentous evening. She felt very grownup and proud when she handed her mother her agreed upon $15 contribution to the family coffers. This left her, before the acquisition of the presents, $28.10. She arrived to learn that dinner had been eaten already because of her tardiness. She sat eating bacon and eggs for her supper while the family dog, Sugar, sat chomping down on baby lamb chops her mom had cooked for her. Mare was quick to explain that the chops had a slight odor and she felt they might not be suitable for Grace. Sugar seemed not to mind. Oh, and everyone loved their presents.

CHAPTER
40

Mare was renowned in the family for her love of dogs. She would spare no expense of time or money to feed and walk them. Not so with other pets, however. She absolutely detested cats after being viciously attacked in a neighbor's apartment by her feline friend. Birds fared no better with Mare. In the years to come, her goddaughter and beloved niece, would ask Mare to "bird sit" their colorful finches while she took a vacation with her husband. Mare was aware already that her niece despised these birds. They arrived in Mare's home in a beautiful, well-maintained cage, with a dozen graceful warblers, perched on a fabricated tree in the cage. On the first day in Mare's care, she found one of the tiny birds at the bottom of the cage, dead. This situation repeated itself daily until all the finches were resting eternally in bird paradise. Perhaps they had arrived to Mare carrying a bird flu of some kind. Undeterred Mare remedied the situation in her own way. She went to a local variety store and purchased a dozen, life-looking, stuffed but colorful bird replacements. Using the tiny wires that formed their feet Mare affixed them to the tree limbs. There they remained in all their muted and motionless glory until the niece and her husband returned from their holiday. Though the niece's husband was horrified at the situation and clearly in distress about the loss of his birds, Mare's niece thanked her aunt for her help with the birds. She was even heard to remark to her husband, "They really will be less trouble this way", as they departed with their new brood.

Life actually changed very little for Grace on completion of high school. She had anticipated more freedom since attaining adulthood. She had created friendships at work and was planning a trip to an upstate dude ranch with some female co-workers. Her dad would not entertain such a possibility for his daughter. Grace was told, "As long as you live under my roof you will not stay out overnight." He also added that he knew all about these dude ranches and what went on there. Grace was appalled that her father would question her intentions. She honestly felt she was back in the confessional and being accused again of impure thoughts. The difference being she now knew what the term meant. It made her angry that her father would even suggest that she would involve herself in anything beyond riding horses and bonding with her workmates. He went so far as to threaten not to walk her down the aisle at her wedding if she disobeyed him. More threats and inuendoes courtesy of his parochial mindset. It was clear that Grace was not being given the opportunity to properly evaluate her relationship with Joey by putting some space and time between them. Her parents now seemed complicit in guiding her to accept a very traditional path for their daughter. There was simply no basis of comparison available to her and to seek it out was to somehow show disrespect to her father and his Church. In December of that year, she accepted Joey's offering of an engagement ring. She was only able to show it to his mother at the bus stop on the way home from work one evening. She had yet to be invited to formally meet his parents. Additionally, they had ignored her parents request to come for dinner. Clearly her family had been adjudged too conservative and religious for his certified card-carrying Communist, atheistic, parents. Obviously, Joey had his problems at home as well. Nevertheless, a wedding date was set for their marriage.

CHAPTER

41

During the ensuing two years Grace was consumed with her plans for the future and her impending union with Joey. There were other weddings being planned for friends they were both close with. There were births occurring to cousins on her side of the family. Naturally all this led to engagement parties, wedding and baby showers, christenings, sacrament rehearsals and some funerals thrown in to maintain levity. With holidays, birthday parties and sundry occasions both religious and secular it was a busy time for Grace. These events showcased the Irish American ability to celebrate life's events heartily. Every funeral became a celebration of a person's life. Stories were told and anecdotes shared about the deceased. It was often overlooked that the guest of honor was not present for the festivities. Then they would be remembered by a parent, spouse, or child and the keening would commence.

A fitting and well-fortified bereavement party would follow to ease the pain of the suffering.

Finding a place to live and leave Hunts Point behind them concerned the betrothed couple in the months leading to the wedding. At that time virtually all apartments were secured through a grapevine of friends and family who knew "some-one". It was uncommon in her social circuit to answer an ad or pay an agent for assistance when looking for a new residence, particularly in a "safe" and "stable" parish neighborhood. It was Aunt Marge who found them a 3 room, 5th floor, walk-up on her block in St. Helena's parish. The building was old and elegant to Grace with an outdoor court, guarded by 2 impres-sive stone lions, leading to the entrance doors of the building. A big, though sparse inner foyer greeted the residents, with staircases ascending on each side of the structure. Grace could imagine that at another time there might have been a chande-lier overhead, carpeting on the marble floors and several velvet couches to sit and chat with neighbors on. Thinking of her first one-room home in a boarding house and her current address in an underprivileged and under-served community, she felt blessed to have an opportunity to live here. She stood gazing up at this monument to her brighter future as though it was the Taj Mahal. However, the happiness she anticipated here with Joey would not last forever. Much like the real Taj Mahal, constructed out of love, as a tomb for his deceased wife, this edifice would become the birthplace of the two greatest loves of her life. It would also become the tomb of her marriage.

The closer it got to her wedding day, the more Grace hoped her mother would surprise her with a sentimental heirloom hidden all these years, for this occasion, in the hope chest. Perhaps a personal item from her own wedding that Grace could treasure forever. Even a memento from the marriages of her grandparents that would be no less prized. She had hoped to be given it at her bridal shower in front of her family and friends who could fawn over its nostalgic symbolism with her. That did not happen. "She must be waiting for my wedding day," reasoned Grace. That, too, did not happen. Nothing borrowed, nothing blue emerged from the hope chest to Grace's great disappointment.

CHAPTER

42

The disappointments were adding up. Joey had decided he did not want a big wedding. In fact, given his choice he would have settled for a quick trip to city hall. This would have been an anathema for Grace and her entire family. Afterall, she had been a bridesmaid in several of her cousins' weddings and was eager to return the honor. She didn't need the glitz and glamour of an event such as one of her Italian friend's family had paid for. Grace was certainly not expecting her own parents to be able to afford that. She had saved her money and knew she could arrange a tasteful, gracious affair in a nice facility without burdening her family. This was the vision she had held onto throughout her engagement. Joey was relentlessly disparaging of her desire for such an event. He would only agree to a small event, with very ordinary food and no music but a record player. Grace scaled down her aspirations and once more compromised to his advantage. In desperation Grace beseeched her uncle to allow her to rent out his social club for the day. She hoped to eliminate the smell of stale cigars with some air spray. Since there were no real kitchen banquet facilities, she had to settle for what was labeled at the time a "football" wedding. This consisted of cold cuts, rolls condiments and some salads that were passed or "thrown" from guest to guest. She selected a good, reputable delicatessen for the wedding fare. She would not compromise on the cake which she ordered from an hispanic, Hunts Point bakery, famous for their decorative occasion cakes. Being a social club, liquor and beer were not a problem and at discount prices. Her uncle took care of this task.

Finally, the music would be provided by a three-piece band that performed at all the club's socials. She took their experience and the recommendation of her uncle, as an augur for success. Wrong! Their introduction, and first dance, was performed to the playing of "Let Me Call You Sweetheart", a 1910 song, recorded by Bing Crosby in 1934. It was not long before a record player was located and dancing to "The Twist" by Chubby Checker was in order. Ironically, the newest musical sensation, The Beatles, were performing on the Ed Sullivan show that same night. While the entire country of young people awaited this event, she was dancing to music that pre-dated her own parents! When she reflected over the years on her disappointment of this day, she would realize it had been her fault to cede to Joey's badgering, aggressive personality. And it was his fault for always selfishly considering his own needs and wants before anyone else's. It would be sometime however, before she could turn the light of clarity on her lingering disappointment and embarrassment of this important event.

One final responsibility had been undertaken before the actual sacrament of marriage could be administered. It required that the couple meet with the pastor of the church in advance of the actual ceremony. In their case it was with Monsignor Fogarty, a well-respected and seemingly kind member of the church higher order. Locally, though, he was known as Father Fatso Fogarty, a reference to his considerable girth and the skills of the cook at the rectory. After running through some preliminaries about the sanctity of marriage and the permanence of the sacrament, he addressed Joey, unfortunately, not being a believer. He explained why this would not permit the couple to be married on the altar proper. They could, however, take their vows at the railing separating the congregation from the altar. This made very little difference to Grace who had been prepared for this stand on the part of the monsignor. When they both agreed to abide by his position, he assumed a more jocular countenance. He jokingly made Joey promise not to lock Grace in the closet when she had to be at mass. "Of course," he continued jovially, "all children born of this union you commit to baptizing, and raising, in the Catholic faith". So, there it was. In exchange for the "privilege" of being treated like two pagans at the altar rail in the house of God, the Church would reap the bounty of all the little souls born of their marriage. Odds were clearly stacked in favor of the Church like their bingos and bazaars. She would follow through with the christening of her children for the sake of her parents and their deep commitment to their Church but, she knew that day, that the rest would be open for further evaluation.

After the typical honeymoon in the Pocono mountains of Pennsylvania, life settled into a regular pattern. Work, dinner and what seemed like long boring nights. No need to cruise in the car every night now that they were married. She began to concentrate on her wifely "duties" of creating a nice home environment for her husband. The very first meal she cooked for her new spouse, was a meatloaf. She was sure it would be "nutritious and delicious" as the recipe taken from a cookbook she received at her bridal shower purported. Imagine her surprise when Joe, walked to the fifth-floor kitchen window, opened it and hurled her tasty creation out the window. He turned snarling at her that the meal was a failure This was followed by hours of crying and arguing that would leave a lasting impact on Grace. It highlighted again his insensitivity and selfishness but again Grace moved past this. She believed things would get better. They did for a while.

CHAPTER
43

One night, several months later, Joe returned home to find a little plastic piggy bank sitting next to his dinner plate. When he asked the reason for its presence his glowing, young bride announced it was to save money for the baby that was due later that year. In a frightening display of his temper, he removed his work shoe and flung it past her head where it stuck in the wall. Through his rage he berated her for ruining his plan that she would work for two years to save money for a home. At clearly her happiest moment to date in her life, he proceeded to try and ruin it with his temper tantrum. He would have, had it not been for a very joyful conversation later with Mare, who was overwhelmed and grateful that she would be a grandmother. Even when she said she was hoping it would be a boy, Grace found it within herself to forgive her. What made the conversation even more special was Mare's excitement about sharing something from the hope chest with Grace to make this moment even more noteworthy. Grace could not wait to see her mom again. As for Joey, he calmed down but he was beginning to display a very unpredictable, Jekyll and Hyde dimension to his personality. This troubled Grace for the future of the child growing inside her.

Eventually an incident would occur in Mare's home that would finally get her parents to move from their ever growing more dangerous environment in Hunts Point. In early 1964 Grace's parents left their apartment to go and get their annual taxes done. Clare, now 16, was left alone sleeping. When her parents returned, Eddie witnessed a man entering the bedroom through the fire escape window. With the speed and agility of an alarmed father he sprinted toward the bedroom. He grappled with, and subdued the invader. It was clear his intentions were not good. When Mare entered the room, she realized the interloper was a neighbor's son, a husband and father here illegally from Cuba.

While Eddie detained the intruder, Mare went to summons his mother. The frightened woman accompanied Mare back to the apartment. There she found her son, shameful and sullen about his motives that morning. The woman fell to her knees at Mare's feet begging that the police not be involved because of his questionable immigration status. Mare knew the irony that Clare had occasionally babysat for the family to earn a little spending money. She thought not only of this terrified woman, but of the wife and children downstairs. The children her own child, Clare, loved. The mother continued imploring Mare, as a mother also, to spare her son. She promised she would have him and his family removed that day, to a relative's home in another borough. Eddie, who by now had taken some liberties with the man's face, conferred with Mare.

When the story was related to Grace later that day, she would learn of her parents' decision to spare the young man. He was never seen in the vicinity of their tenement again. Clare never discussed the incident, and the potential seriousness of it, with Grace. Grace would often wonder if the incident evoked the memory of her mother's own possible abduction as a child. Had she been too frightened to confront the realities of what could have happened here, to her daughter? What was the full story? Grace was acquiring a suspicious disposition molded by the secrets she knew existed in her life but had not yet been revealed to her.

Expecting her first child, and worrying about her first family, she contacted her landlord to secure an apartment for them in her building. Eddie and Mare signed a lease for a one-bedroom apartment, purchased a convertible couch, and moved into their new home. Mare was ecstatic to have her family close again and Grace was relieved. Clare would become the most caring aunt to the two nephews Grace would provide her with. They loved her deeply and she returned that love, in many ways, every day.

CHAPTER
44

What followed for the next years were some of the happiest of her life. Grace's decision to give her a new mother's handbook she claimed had been given to her by hospital staff when she was born, and a pair of old, wrinkled baby shoes from the hope chest, was exhilarating to her. She gave birth to her first child and to Mare's delight a beautiful, healthy boy. Just 19 months later she enriched the world further by the birth of her second child, again a healthy, adorable baby boy. Her life was complete and centered around her little family. Her children were bright, curious, active toddlers that gave love freely and made friends quickly. There were outings everyday with them to the playground. Mare would accompany them since her parents had by now secured an apartment in the same building. On the weekends there were excursions to the beach, the city, the museums, the zoo and the aquarium.

There were family vacations to the Adirondack Mountains and Lake George, Montauk Point and the ocean, and Washington D.C. Joey seemed to enjoy the boys and loved them she believed, as much as Grace. He spent all his time with her and his sons. He forbade any visits from her parents or teenage sister Clare after 3:30 every day, the time he would usually return home. Friends and family visited only if he was at work because his icy demeanor to being disturbed was legendary. He made an exception for his own mother who was also living in the same building after the death of Grace's father-in-law. Jane joined them every night for dinner and her usual consumption of a pint of vodka. Obviously, she had no trouble with Grace's cooking.

Grace greatly respected Joe's obsession with the news and the events happening in the world. He held strong political views obviously from exposure to his own father's political beliefs. He could speak with authority on most topics of international significance. The war in Viet Nam was an especially difficult time in this country and at home. It contributed to divided loyalties in families. Protests and reactions against the war demoralized our troops fighting in the Asian arena. Grace always sympathized with these young men, and believed our government was not always taking the necessary steps to resolve the conflict and bring our troops safely home. She was disturbed also about a new weapon of the war, Agent Orange, being used to defoliate the countryside but bringing harm, as well, to the Vietnamese people and our young men. She agreed with the protests against chemical companies such as Dow Chemicals who were amassing huge fortunes at the expense of their safety. As the years passed and the fighting lingered on, she joined a group called Another Mother for Peace. While not a militant organization, it gave mothers of the next generation of soldiers a voice in the present situation. On a bright Sunday morning she drove to Washington D.C. with her children and husband to protest the war. It was endorsed by many groups, among them Another Mother for Peace. The need to take action in opposition to this conflict was one of the few things she and her husband could agree upon at this stage of their marriage.

Grace took the boys that day and went to Sunday mass at the local parish. She prayed for our troops and for healing in our country. She prayed also that her little family would return safely from this demonstration. When they reached the mall, they sat on the grass to witness the speakers who were expected to address the throngs sitting there. Looking to her right she observed, behind a high fence cloaked in camouflage cloth, a tank right at the gate. Clearly it had been placed there should it become needed during the event. A young soldier dismounted his station on the armored vehicle and approached Grace who was sitting with a fussy little son in her lap. The young man asked if he could get her water for the baby. In that beautiful moment, witnessing an example of our common humanity, Grace felt hope for us all. She would seek out, and find, many such instances in her life.

While Grace may have had no doubt that Joe loved his children, his parenting was a paradox and greatly concerned her. While he could be warm and physically affectionate with the boys his usual approach with them was to ridicule and demean them. He was quick to be physical with his sons when they would have benefitted more from positive guidance and correction. Tyranny increasingly became his preferred form of punishment. This is not to blame him totally. Grace, who had lived a life of conforming to the traditional expectations of home and church, was now doing the same in her marriage. Though troubled by his behavior she felt it was her duty to support him as head of the household. But she was going through profound internal changes of her own, reflecting the new norms and mores driven by the emergence of feminist doctrine. She adopted the belief in the popular women's rights philosophy of the day.

While she was not extreme in her expectations of course, she did believe its dogma provided her with a solid platform from which to defend, even to herself, her rights to achieve her own destiny. These ideas would change her forever. Her expectations for herself and those she loved would evolve greatly for the betterment of her sons' lives and her own.

CHAPTER

45

One afternoon she found herself alone ironing tiny sun-suits and socks. She realized in that instant how mundane her life had become. She was actually trying to fill her time with some tedious, unnecessary chores to pass the time. Where had her dreams for herself of a college education and a chance to see the world gone to? She also feared what would happen to her and the boys if their parents divorced. The possibility of that was becoming a reality to her. She grabbed the wall phone next to her ironing board and immediately called her mother. In near hysteria she asked Mare if it was possible for her and Eddie to babysit during the day while she attended college classes. Before Mare could answer she would have to ask her husband but promised to call back. She did with alacrity and the great news that they would be delighted not only to watch the children but to assist Mare in anyway, to get the degree they had been unable to assist her with financially. Grace, full of trepidation, began to create a rationale that would convince Joey of the validity of her plan. As expected, there was the usual emotional outburst and the vehement condemnation of her proposal. Yet, he knew she had wanted to be a teacher since they began dating. She stressed how safe and happy the children would be for only a few hours a week in her parents' care. She would never have considered such a decision if it meant putting her boys in someone else's care or, God forbid, a daycare situation. She implored Joe to look ahead to the additional income they would benefit from if she acquired a teaching degree. She even thanked him for raising her political consciousness since that, also, inspired this desire of hers to pursue her education. Appealing to the selfish side of her husband, and pointing out how he would gain from her efforts, was the catalyst for change he needed. However, he insisted her degree would be in home economics. This way, he reasoned, she would learn at the same time, how to better handle their home and finances. Grace showed great appreciation for this opportunity he was allowing her to pursue. "Frank" was becoming, sadly a deceptive person, for the first time in her life. She knew she would get her degree but in no world would it be in home economics! Her excitement was enhanced by the knowledge that she would be the first in her extended family to attend college.

There were times during the beginning of her college career that Joe would seem to be genuinely invested in her success. He seemed to be earnestly trying to be helpful to her. He would take the boys on little excursions to give her time to study or work on papers she needed to complete. He would express pride in her efforts in front of her sons. She was exceedingly happy to hear this. They continued to participate in family life, even going swimming on summer evenings to a pool in nearby Yonkers. Unfortunately, this appearance of unity and happiness was a hollow stasis dependent on Grace not challenging the status quo. She did one evening as she stood in the kitchen cooking dinner and waiting for the arrival of Joe's mother who had become a regular dinner mate in their home. Joe told her to do something which she balked at. He flung a large set of keys across the kitchen where she was trapped in the corner. They struck her head right above her eye and, given the propensity for any head injury to bleed profusely, blood began streaming past her eye and down her face. Just then the doorbell rang and she answered to the shocked look of her mother-in-law. "What happened here Joseph?", she asked her son. He said he accidently hit Grace while trying to throw his keys against the wall to make a point. Indeed, the point was made, the dinner was served and Grace's decision about the future made.

The pursuit of a college education proved difficult and time consuming for a young mother. It also proved to be self-affirming and enlightening. She found she loved the world of academia and the people she found inhabited it. They were motivated, opinionated and full of hopes and dreams as she was, for a better world and a more productive life for themselves and their students. The years flew by, she earned her degree and began thinking seriously of beginning her career. When she graduated, magna cum laude, with a degree in English and education, she was eager to secure a teaching position. Though she received several invitations to teach in the most desirable and affluent areas of Westchester County, located just north of the Bronx, her desire had always been to help those children, like herself, of less societal stature and acceptance to realize their own potentials. She felt she was a perfect role model for these students who may have lacked the positive motivation and expectations that are critical to success. The city of New York, however, under yet another budget crisis, was scaling down hirings for new staff. Grace, as usual, had a plan.

Armed with her curriculum vitae, determination and evidence of her 5th place ranking on the Bd of Ed exam, she headed straight to her former elementary school in Hunts Point. The secretary in the main office advised her that the principal was not conducting interviews due to current Board of Education restrictions. Grace asked her to please advise the principal she was here to see her name in the honor roll ledger she had signed when she graduated from this school. The secretary disappeared into the principals' office and reappeared with the principal who was smiling broadly. She greeted Grace warmly and invited her into her office. There she reviewed Grace's credentials then, surprisingly to Grace, produced the tome with a young Grace's signature. After a conversation that could be termed an interview, she offered the young aspirant a teaching position. "I could never refuse someone with such chutzpah!", she declared and informed Grace she would begin the next day. Grace would research the word "chutzpah" and realize her new boss had read her correctly. Grace reestablished ties to her old neighborhood and would become Secretary of

Education on the planning board that encompassed her former schools and parish. Her career was beginning and everything looked encouraging. Not so at home though.

CHAPTER

46

As the years progressed Joe was becoming more discontented and belligerent towards her. He seemed to resent her involvement at school, her new friendships and her new found freedom. Grace had acquired a car so she could get to work. Even though she tried to pull him into her world he resisted. His old tactics of ridicule and bellicosity were not working on the new Grace. The more he tried to rein her in and determine her limits of mobility and thought, the more she resisted. She encouraged him to seek training or lessons in things that he verbally stated interested him such as playing the guitar or flight instruction. He was very vocal politically and she thought, perhaps if he became more of an activist, he would feel more relevant. At least he might do more than just complain to her. She had always been his sounding board for his opinions and erratic emotions. Grace could finally admit to herself that she was no longer sure a marriage based on teenage romance would withstand adult realities. She was right.

In college Grace had met and befriended a woman in a similar situation. She had a young son she was trying to find daycare for. They met in front of the bulletin board where these possibilities were posted. Grace was taken by her friendliness and quick humor. Although they would pursue different majors, they're ultimate goal was the same, to become teachers. They became good friends. Their subsequent conversations revealed that Ann's homelife was much like her own. She had become pregnant at 19 and agreed to marry the father of her child. He would spend the rest of their life questioning the legitimacy of his son. He was cruel, controlling and unfortunately, quite ignorant. Ann, a victim of sexual abuse at the hands of her own father, would struggle through years of physical abuse inflicted by her husband. Ann had the strong will and ability of Grace. They both performed outstandingly in their studies. Their ability to compartmentalize their experiences at home and not let them interfere with their success was truly amazing. They remained friends through both their divorces, long and illustrious careers and the growth of their children to manhood. They comforted each other through several tragic deaths and celebrated together the births of grandchildren. They traveled to Paris together later in life and remained friends for 52 years, until Ann died suddenly one evening. It was among the greatest losses of Grace's life. She would never forget how Joe hated her and treated even Ann's mother rudely when she came to visit one day. Their friendship would outlast her marriage to Joe by 40 years.

CHAPTER
47

After their divorce Joe would find his political outlet in his union. He became president of his union and a driving force behind its direction. He also remarried. She was a woman who apparently accepted his need to be the overtly dominant person in their relationship nor did she have the educational background that, contrary to what he said, clearly threatened him. Grace wished them well and was able to separate herself from any form of dependency on him. This was not true for their sons. What would follow would be years of continued humiliation, control and abuse that had become a hallmark of his fathering skills. For this Grace would always share the guilt. The important thing, however, was the unconditional love and pride that was mutual between Grace and her boys. Their life moved forward as well.

Her intense love for her children was something Grace marveled at! To her they had always seemed perfect in every way. They had always been surrounded by the love of her family as well. Joseph in elementary school was starring in school plays, writing and illustrating a thirteen chapter book on a space odyssey at age eight, and having the adventures of a normal, healthy young boy. During middle school he began taking guitar lessons and he displayed amazing facility with this instrument. Ultimately, he began having issues at school generated by the pressures at home during and after the divorce of his parents. Jimmy, who could assemble fifty-piece puzzles without trial and error at age 2, began writing poetry. By middle school he had been named "poet laureate" of his school district and had received an award from the New York Times. When she went to the ceremony at the main library in NYC at which his Times award for his poetry would be presented, she was surprised how nonplused he was by the honor. He thought, given his youthful lack of conceit, that he was being rewarded for being a monitor at school who delivered the newspaper to teachers in the morning. Outwardly he appeared well adjusted, even complaisant. As in the case of his brother, Grace became aware how his home life was affecting him as well. While Joe was often singled out for physical punishment by his father, Jimmy was exposed to a torrent of ridicule that began to affect him. Things would not get easier in the years ahead for Grace's children. Only now Grace would be, unintentionally, complicit in their unhappiness.

CHAPTER
48

Their divorce occurred during the infamous "disco era". Grace had always loved dancing. She had a passion for music as well. While still married she had often asked Joe to take her out dancing. They had done this occasionally before the marriage and she had enjoyed it. Instead, Joe declared, "you will only dance over my dead body". He seemed to her to be joyless. Now though, while not wanting to create a self-fulfilling prophecy, she was free to "boogie". Both Mare and Clare were eager to babysit the boys so that Grace could begin to enjoy more of her life. On the nights she would go out and venture into the dazzling clubs of NYC at that time, she was, of course, in the company of Ann. These ironies were not lost on Grace. They were like a musical epithet on a dead marriage.

Her two sons continued to provide her with purpose and great pleasure in her life. Jimmy, who wanted to be an Indian when he grew up, cried every time the Indians lost in a cowboy and Indian movie. He virtually lived in a teepee in the living room. It had been purchased by his Aunt Clare at FAO Schwartz in Manhattan, decidedly the most famous and amazing toy store in the world! He maintained a chief's headdress which he insisted his grandfather wear when he was in the apartment. The day his teacher told him he could not be an Indian when he grew up was devastating to him. He came home sure his own mother, a teacher herself, would debunk this idea. Sadly, she had to explain on a less than sophisticated level, that he could not be an Indian because he was not born an Indian. He wanted to know why he had not been born an Indian in the first place. He seemed to be holding Grace accountable for this new found misery in his young life. Eventually she believes he forgave her. As an adult he traveled to South Dakota to stand as best man at his best friend's wedding. He visited a reservation at that time. He came home sadly disillusioned at the life of the American Indian of the day. He was no longer disappointed he was an Irish American and not a Cherokee.

Joe, who was greatly affected by the daily reports of the Viet Nam war at the time, began creating huge drawings of battles as he imagined them, on large sheets of drawing paper. His combatants were portrayed as stick figures waging a violent and brutal battle. Each sheet would contain many, many figures in different stages of the conflict. What was so mesmerizing about his drawings was the expressive bodily movement of his troops as their stick bodies moved forward in engagement. This artistic style Grace saw developing in her child would become of great significance later in his life. It was the genesis, she believes, of his career as an artist.

Both boys hated structured day camp which she tried several times to engage them in. Grace sought to involve them in activities that she believed would heighten their socialization skills while offering great opportunities for physical and creative outlets. She was so wrong. They loved the generally unstructured activities of the YMCA or the Police Athletic League even attending sleepovers when given the chance. Their greatest memories involved their daily play time at the sitting park down the street from their apartment. They had many friends, learned to appreciate and respect elders, and could be with their beloved grandmother whenever Grace was not available.

They became writers and musicians without the help of any serious formal training. They were athletic, both enjoying little league and informal group sports with their neighborhood pals. Joe became an extremely competent swimmer, even saving his brother from drowning when they were away with their father one weekend. He would eventually become a master diver and scuba instructor in keeping with his life long love of the water. In moments reminiscent of Grace's own life, Jimmy, tutored by grandpa, would become a Red Sox fan. Joe of course, guided by his Aunt Clare, would become one of the Bronx Bombers' legions. History repeats itself they say.

Grace was most proud of the fact that they both evolved into prolific readers. They would recommend and discuss books with their mother throughout their lives. She would think back often to those nights before bed, when they were young boys, and how they would listen enraptured by the many books and stories she read to them. Their scores on reading exams at school always reflected this love of literature and the skills they developed during their early childhoods.

Humor was another strength they shared. Their sharp intelligence and creativity shined through in their hilarious take on many of life's situations even the most painful ones. They combined their love of music and their love of teasing their mom on many occasions when they would make up, on the spot, hilarious ditties that would find her begging for them to stop because of the side-splitting laughter they created.

When she tried to instill in them an awareness of the effects of poverty on people, she would tell them of her own experiences living in the one room early in her life. Grace would describe the hardship of sleeping four in the one bed and eating on a sled instead of at a kitchen table. Being teenagers, and with their gift of wordplay and wit, she became "Sled Zeppelin" for a while. Each time she told them about these earlier life experiences, and she did often, she saw not mocking humor but sympathy and compassion. It was this compassion, developed slowly over time, that made them the beautiful human beings they became as men. They could speak to, and respect, all groups of people with no regard for age, race, religion or social status. They were Grace's greatest accomplishment.

CHAPTER
49

Throughout the most difficult times they were always building memories. These stories would remain in their collective oral history forever. They would be told and retold in the most dramatic and eloquent way as bespoke their Irish American culture. The most humorous ones always seemed to center around Mare. Aging people often find new interests or hobbies to develop as they grow older. They may play golf, become omnivorous readers, knit or do volunteer work. Mare, however, bought herself a police scanner/radio to fill her time. Between her husband, family, dog and police scanner Mare was beyond content. What "10-10 WINS News" couldn't provide for Mare, her police scanner did. She in turn could keep everyone she interacted with "up" on the daily happenings in their precinct. Her reports were riveting. Although Mare was undoubtedly the most pure-hearted, compassionate person she would ever know, Grace did discern a macabre streak in her. To add to her tales of beheadings and mutilations previously noted, she now was consumed with accident reports as she followed the scanners endless emergency calls for police assistance at vehicle crash sites. Grace's boys, often in her care, became her audience for the re-telling of these reports.

Grace learned that on one particular day the children stood with Mare at the fire escape window of her 4th floor apartment, looking out through the big gate affixed to the frame to kept out potential Bronx marauders. The risk of burning alive during a fire if unable to escape due to a locked gate seemed less important somehow. Their grandmother would often position them here and point out the accidents on the Cross Bronx Expressway which she so conveniently overlooked. On this day, she directed their gaze to a particularly devastating crash. One of the cars involved was the same make and color as Grace's. Mare, who was irrationally afraid of automobile rides, had convinced herself that her daughter was in that pile-up. She instructed the boys to begin praying. Knowing no other prayers, they began reciting the Lord's Prayer, "Now I lay me down to sleep, I pray my soul the Lord to keep". Who can know the terror that may have engulfed them at that moment! Well, clearly their innocent incantations were effective because just then there was a knock on the door. When the door was opened Mare was besieged by two sobbing, nearly hysterical, boys relieved to see their mother alive. The incident offered opportunities for endless and hilarious retelling which, thankfully, her boys eventually saw the humor in.

Then there is the creationist story by Mare as shared with Grace's children. This one is less dark and sinister than the one she created for her own daughter. For this Grace is thankful. In this version Mare takes the children on a field trip to the local hardware and variety store, K&F. This is soon after Joseph began asking his grandma for information on his own beginnings. In the store she directs their attention to a bin holding replacement Christmas tree bulbs. She explains that we all begin life as small lights such as these. She tells them that their incarnation was no different. She postulates that they both began as small blue Christmas lights and were sent to our family so they could be the two little boys she was so disappointed she had never had. Since Grace's birthday was in December, Mare reasoned they were each a holiday present from God to celebrate their mother's and Jesus' birthday. This seemed to satisfy the children at the moment. At the least they did not develop a phobia about bulbs or Christmas. Moments like these propelled her towards thoughts of the hope chest. She knew she had not yet been given the true story of her birth even though she herself was a mother now. She recommitted herself to finding her answer. It was, she felt ever more strongly, hidden in the suppository of all good things and untold secrets, the omnipresent, beckoning hope chest.

The words funny and sad seemed irrevocably intertwined in the Irish culture. They constitute a paradox that follows you through all of life's events. They form the symbiosis that enables you to survive grief and appreciate absurdities. To truly understand the Irish Americans, you must understand the interdependence of this dichotomy. To do so is to realize, and appreciate, how it impacts the Irish American spirit. It will illuminate, for you, the essence of the soul of these descendants of a strong Celtic people.

CHAPTER
50

One evening Grace and Ann ventured into Manhattan. Besides the disco scene in New York at the time there was a proliferation of venues that attracted a more folk music, politically oriented crowd. Protest music, poetry readings and the appreciation of seasoned folk music performers such as the recently deceased, Woody Guthrie, was growing. They were joined by the likes of Richie Havens, James Taylor, Joan Baez, Pete Seeger, Bob Dylan, Arlo Guthrie, Jr. and others during this period of national discontent. The atmosphere of these clubs was welcoming, the music was mellow and the conversation socially relevant. It was here that Grace and Ann would find a comfortable, safe, niche in the places along second avenue on the upper eastside. It was also here that Grace would meet her second husband.

Walter was a denizen of the 1970's music scene in Manhattan. His taste in genres was varied but he leaned towards rhythm & blues and folk. He would name Pete Seeger, Richie Havens and James Taylor among his friends. His social circle included lawyers, movie directors, politicians, social workers and civil servants. A handsome, personable man he worked in the Dept. of Corrections. He had been married before as well and was the father of two children, a boy and a girl. He lived on the west side in an apartment in a townhouse off of West End Avenue. An army veteran, he had served in the Korean conflict. With a generous smile and a gift for easy conversation and shared values, he gradually became a fixture in Grace's life. A dreamer herself, she was beguiled by his dreams for the future. In a year they would marry. It would be the first inter-racial marriage in both their families.

Though, at first, she had been somewhat trepidatious about bringing this news to her parents, Grace was greeted with the unconditional love and acceptance she needed. Clare was ecstatic for her as Grace knew she would be. Grace needed all their love and support as she moved forward with having her children meet the potentially new man in their lives. Society's mores and taboos would be a major factor in her decision to proceed. As a realist Grace knew what horrors this could portend for her children. There would be three things that would lift the veil of fear from this young woman. First, she was a deeply loving mother, and intelligent woman, that could recognize, and counter any negative impact her children might experience from ignorant people. She was in fact a teacher trained in child psychology and development. Secondly, they had the profound love and support of a loving and protective extended family. Thirdly, they had suffered too long under an abusive father and deserved another role model, a more accepting soul, to rely on. She could only hope she was right. Their collective future sat in her hands and lived in her mind everyday thereafter. She believed in the adage that only a happy mother could raise happy children.

Unfortunately, it was the "sainted" scoundrels of her own family, the religious phonies, that caused the most sorrow to her newly reconstituted family. Her own godparents, refused to acknowledge the union at all. Mare's beloved brother, Barney and his wife assumed the same stance. Her cousins, their husbands and wives, all claimed to be too busy to attend her wedding. The same people, who learned the same catechism of the same faith as Grace, who had said the same prayers and attended the same Church now looked aside. The teachings of their faith discarded and replaced by the racism and bigotry so pervasive at the time. However, the example of this marriage she hoped would bring changes to their attitude ultimately, if not the acceptance she craved.

Grace and Walter's wedding was a beautiful event. They were married in the chapel of Columbia University where Grace was an alumnus. The couple arrived there in a Rolls Royce driven by an Afro-American doctor Clare new from her work at a methadone clinic. He was accompanied by his wife, of thirty years, a white woman. They had invited themselves to the event to show support for the union. Their own story was one of rejection that love sustained and rose above. The Methodist minister who performed the service was completely on board with their hopes and visions for their future. He knew too their apprehensions and fears. He realized this would be a very special event for the couple, their four children and their families. It was planned and performed as a celebration of their commitment to each other in the most joyous, yet serious, manner. In keeping with the theme of acceptance, love and unity the minister suggested the inclusion of butterflies and turtle doves in the event. To his disappointment, the couple rejected the theatrics of such a move. He was permitted, however, to conduct the service in a Mexican wedding shirt. An original musical piece was played during the service written by a music teacher from Grace's school. Ann stood and read the treatise "On Marriage" from the Prophet Khalil Gibran.

"But let there be spaces in your togetherness,
And let the winds of the heavens dance between you.
Love one another but make not a bond of love:
Let it rather be a moving sea between the shores of
your souls.
Fill each other's cup but drink not from the same cup.
Give one another of your bread but eat not from the
same loaf.
Sing and dance together and be joyous, but let each
one of you be alone
Even as the strings of the lute are alone though they
quiver with the same music
Give your hearts, but not into each other's keeping.
For only the hand of Life can contain your hearts.
And stand together yet not too near together:

For the pillars of the temple stand apart,
And the oak tree and the cypress grow not in each
other's shadow

Their wedding rings were circulated among their guests during the ceremony to have each person add an individual blessing to the union. A folk guitarist played and sang, "The Wedding Song" by Noel Paul Stookey, of Peter, Paul and Mary fame. Grace had even traveled to Woodstock to purchase her white wedding dress, hand-made in Czechoslovakia. Clare went with her and bought a beautiful Afghani silk dress to wear as matron of honor. The children in beautiful ethnic clothing, reflecting their different and distinct heritages, stood beside their parents at the altar. The entire wedding, Grace now felt, should have been preserved in a snow globe, as an example of the naivete, hope and guilelessness of the era.

CHAPTER
51

After purchasing a beautiful brick tudor-style home, in a semi-integrated neighborhood in Queens, the marriage moved forward. The boys were enrolled in their new school which they seemed to enjoy. Joe was recruited for the basketball team. Jimmy continued writing poetry with the encouragement of his new teacher. He even starred in the school production of Oliver Twist. Grace transferred to a position in a school closer to her new home so that she could teach in the same school district her sons were enrolled in. Walter was ultimately promoted to the rank of captain in the DOC and looked forward to an early retirement. He was very interested in his stepsons' progress, attending Open School Week and going to school performances. He enrolled them in the local Little League and brought them to and from games. He courted team coaches to get Jimmy the catcher position he coveted.

He visited the homes of boys he felt were bullying Grace's children and spoke directly to their parents. Invariably the boys would end up friends because of his intervention.

A particularly hilarious story highlights the depth of his devotion to the boys. Jimmy had been complaining about a particularly aggressive boy who was not only hurling racial insults at him but was threatening to get an older brother to beat him up. Walter made an unscheduled visit to the school about the matter. The school secretary advised him he could not see the principal without an appointment. When, in frustration, he finally bellowed, "I do not send my son to school to be called a honkey", he was rushed into the principal's office. The specter of a dark-skinned black man saying he didn't want his son to be called a honkey, was beyond the scope of the secretary's understanding. Jimmy was summoned from class and his appearance in the front office brought clarity to the situation immediately. The complaint made by Walter was acknowledged and dealt with quickly.

Walter was supportive of the boys' interests and talents at all times. A young Jimmy would stage poetry readings, under the direction of his "manager" Walt, when adult friends came for dinner. Since his own father had been a drummer with the Count Basie band, he was very supportive of Joe's musical ability. He encouraged both of the boys to be involved with music, often driving them to concerts in Manhattan or on Long Island. There was always some genre of music playing in the house from blues, to soul, to jazz, to Motown, to hard rock. It was a lively home where everyone's friends and family were accepted, even Joe and his second wife, Joan.

Grace knew that the healthy development of a boy's ego was inextricably connected to his biological father. For this reason, he was welcome in their home. She also chose not to involve family court in the issue of child support. Joe, unfortunately, was not generous in the least with any support for his children. As a result, the financial support of her children fell on Grace's shoulders. She and Walter would pay also for the things their father would not indulge such as rock t-shirts, leather jackets, music lessons, spending money, etc. Her parents and Clare would do much for them as well.

As she reflected back on this time, she realized how much they all learned from Walter. For instance, he had stood next to Martin Luther King during his famed "I Have a Dream" speech in Washington, D.C. He had been recruited as one of the law enforcement members to guard the great orator on this important day. He could recount with passion the impact of this day on his own life. It is still bittersweet for her to see his visage at MLKs left side on the podium during annual observances of the great leader's impact on the national conscience. Walt had much to share of his own personal history as a black man growing up in this country he loved and fought for. Watching "Roots" as a family was another opportunity for spiritual and social growth. By now they had all been victims of the racial and socio-economic antipathy of the country. These were lessons they had learned and internalized long before the marriage began its descent.

CHAPTER
52

Unfortunately, Walter was an alcoholic. Unaware of this, Grace was not quick to recognize the signs of his dependency when presented. The culture she grew up in shielded her from seeing the destructive facets of addiction, by always making excuses and blaming other factors for the problem the alcoholic was dealing with. After all, she drank, her friends drank, most of her family drank. Hell, most of the country drank. He was not physically or verbally abusive to her or the kids. Eventually it did become obvious how he was damaging himself and as an extension, everyone around him. He agreed to seek counseling and was successful in eliminating alcohol from his life. Life moved on.

One day, her car in for repairs, she was driven home from school by a colleague. Though generous to offer her assistance, the woman was a cynical woman, in self-denial about her own racism. As they approached Grace's lovely corner home, the woman grabbed Grace's arm and said to her, "Be careful there's a schvartze sitting on the wall near your backdoor." Grace replied, "Oh, that's my husband. Thank you for the ride!". Grace knew she would be the topic of conversation in the teacher's lunchroom the next day. What concerned her more at the moment was the marijuana cigarette hanging from Walter's lip.

Walter retired from the department after 20 years of service. He had dreamed of becoming an entrepreneur his whole life. Over the years as an employee in the penal system, he felt he, too, was in lock-up. The many necessary rules and regulations of his occupation combined with the noise, smells and general savagery of the prison setting had him yearning to begin the next stage of his life. Grace offered him her support and encouragement in every way. He was free to follow his destiny as it were.

Though he dreamed big, his follow through was weak. He would jump from one "million-dollar idea", as he called them, to another. It was becoming a moment of hilarity between her and the kids every time he used this phrase. He was becoming impatient and discouraged and his occasional use of marijuana had become his occasional use of cocaine to cope with his disappointment. The multiple failed attempts he made at self-employment were exhausting to everyone.

He tried selling and installing brick facing on homes, with absolutely no experience in construction. Immediately he purchased a warehouse to store his "product" and equipment. He decided to open a laundromat which never materialized after countless weeks of shopping for machinery and storefronts.

His idea of opening a reading institute/summer program for inner city youth led to the purchase of property in the beautiful Shenandoah Valley of Virginia. Walter's grandparents had been slaves in Virginia and he conceived this as the perfect project and location for a tribute to his own roots.

Grace gave all her time to this project, designing a program and writing proposals for its implementation. Ann, too, a fellow educator, became fully committed to the success of this undertaking as did Walter's friend, Joe, a NYC social worker. Pete Seeger gifted a reading device he had designed to the endeavor. The Fashion Institute of Technology in NYC donated an elaborate playground facility for the campers use designed by a prominent New York artist. Howard University, a black university in DC became involved on the funding level with a grant to assist with construction. Walter was attempting, at one point, to organize a benefit concert with several music headliners.

His behavior was becoming increasingly erratic though. His mood swings and chronic agitation were becoming an impediment to a stable home environment. Grace was exhausted teaching full time and coming home to countless hours of research and proposal writing. The boys complained to her about the burdens it was creating for them as well. Her attention diverted by so many things she was not focusing enough on their needs as young teenagers in the way that she should have. Her full and unconditional support of Walter's ventures was waning. Financially, they were suffering. Finally, Grace would insist he seek medical treatment or she would seek the services of a lawyer to end the marriage. All projects ceased as he would begin treatment for what was ultimately diagnosed as manic depression and bipolarism. Grace made the decision to stay and help him through this struggle but never fully re-committed herself to the marriage.

CHAPTER
53

While coping with this adversity, another shock befell Grace and her boys. Her father was diagnosed with congestive heart failure, the result of a previous heart attack, and the onset of dementia. Her parents lived in a four-story tenement walk up, still in the Bronx where the boys had grown up. The doctor declared that if he was to survive, he could never make those stairs again. Grace, with Walter, picked up her father and mother (and the dog) and moved them into their home immediately. Clare and her husband cleaned out her parent's apartment bringing anything of value or importance to Clare's. And that was the way the hope chest found its way back into Grace's life.

Walter agreed to give up the use of the master bedroom and its bathroom, for his wife's parent's convenience. The couple relocated to the basement. Within days they had a mechanical staircase installed to ferry her father between the first and second floors. The boys were thrilled to have their very generous grandparents and their favorite animal under the same roof as themselves. Walter stepped up and looked after her father's needs and went shopping for whatever her mother wanted, usually sweets of some kind which she shared with him. Grace now incorporated everyone's needs (medical and otherwise) into an already compressed schedule. Although this period was emotionally draining and physically demanding, the opportunity it offered to shift focus from her own marriage to the needs of her parents was far less daunting. She could never have suspected it would serve as the threshold to the final revelation of the secrets she always knew existed in her life.

PART II

REVELATIONS
AND
REDEMPTION

CHAPTER

54

Several months after moving in with his daughter's family, Eddie suffered a stroke. He was sitting in the dining room with Grace and Mary when it occurred. After an examination at the hospital, he was discharged to return home. Grace's meeting with his physician that day made it clear Eddie's time with the family was limited. He suggested that Grace and Clare begin to get their parent's affairs in order. With their father back home and safely ensconced in his bedroom, Grace met with Mare and Clare downstairs. Sitting around the dining room table she, as compassionately and calmly as possible, shared the doctor's diagnosis and advice with her mother and sister. Then, in an attempt to shift focus from the very sad events pending in the near future, she addressed her mom's need for security and continuity after the fact. Grace suggested, to her overwrought mother, that the girls contact social security and the government pension office to be ready with the necessary documents they would certainly need. Of course, all this investigation and research would require her parent's official wedding certificate. She asked her mother her wedding date since she had offered several different dates in November in the past. Her mother replied that she was quite sure it was November 12th. Clare who had been quiet until this moment, said "No problem mom. I will have one of the lawyers from my agency look it up for you. What county were you married in?" When Mare replied that she could not remember, Grace could literally hear the lid blowing off her beloved hope chest! There it was. Both girls knew a woman could never forget where she was married or even the date for that matter. Incredulous Grace could only utter, "Mom, you were never married to Dad, were you? Clare and I are bastards, aren't we? Am I an adopted bastard on top of it?".

Mary began crying convulsively and Clare began swooning, almost passing out. Grace, however, felt a strange relief. She had always only wanted to know the truth. Therefore, she was prepared to hear it. Her premonitions were confirmed. There was no anger or disappointment. She was filled with an overwhelmingly sense of love for these two people who had been together for almost 40 years. Clare on the other hand, admitted she had never questioned anything about her own birth or her parent's marriage. It grew even worse for poor Clare when she heard her adoring father was a divorced man! Clare recalled proposing to her parents in the late 1960s that she move-in with her boyfriend since she was not ready to commit to a marriage just yet. Her parents were shocked that she, a good Catholic girl raised in a good Catholic family, could consider such a vulgar and blasphemous idea. Even though the culture was changing and it was no longer considered lewd or lascivious to live together as a committed couple, Clare quickly changed her plans and a wedding was planned. Grace and her sister would laugh later in life that Clare was the first one in the family that "had to get married" (from pressure, not pregnancy) and Grace was the first to be divorced.

How little they had known of the family secrets. How heavily, unbeknownst to them, they had carried the stigma of illegitimacy. The greatest sadness for both girls was the fact that, being Catholic, their parents believed themselves excommunicated from their beloved Church and unable to ever marry, even civilly. Such a marriage could not be sanctioned by Catholicism. The birth of a child outside of marriage was viewed as an actual sign of depravity. The children born of such a union carried the sin of this depravity. At one time in the history of the Church even a male born under such circumstances could not enter the priesthood. Quite a condemnation formatted and enforced by a male dominated hierarchy. In a culture that celebrated the birth of a boy and his potential elevation to the clergy, this was unthinkable. This truth was more demeaning to Grace and her sister than the story of Helen Kilroy she had been horrified by. So it was, that their dedication to their faith, combined with their ignorance of the law, condemned her parents and their offspring to a life as outcasts, as though they were, indeed, religious lepers. Grace's one relief in the matter was that she definitely had not been adopted nor had she been found in a trash receptacle!

CHAPTER
55

While still absorbing this one, but most important, fact of her life, Grace recalled, with amusement now, the beautiful 25th anniversary celebration Clare and she had hosted for their parents. Mare and Eddie never made the fuss about their own anniversary that her two sisters did. This she explained to her girls was mainly due to their father's reserved and very private ways. He did not participate in outward displays of emotion and referred to his sister-in-law's propensity to do this as "theatrical". He called their marriages the "hon and dearie" variety. Grace's own parents was anything but. It was strong without being showy, their commitment to each other deep without seeming pretentious. As a result, there were never any splashy soirees to celebrate this annual event. The upcoming 25th anniversary, as they had computed it, they felt could not go unnoticed. Grace and Clare had put their plan for a low key, but lovely event into motion. Ironically, at that time when questioned, Mare had given them November 11th as the wedding date. She claimed Eddie had chosen this date at the time. "Veteran's Day November, 11th," Mare stressed. The entire family was invited to celebrate with them.

It was a brilliant affair culminating with Eddie presenting Mare with the lovely zirconia ring his daughters had purchased for the occasion on his behalf. Mare had never had an engagement ring. From time to time, she would splurge on a fake engagement ring and matching wedding band at Woolworth's. It turned out to be a very poignant moment when Eddie presented the ring to Mare, his hands actually shaking as he placed it on her finger. They kissed, presents were opened, jokes and colorful stories were shared and the guests departed. Their very grateful parents assured the girls their party had been wonderful and very much appreciated. If they did not ever celebrate another anniversary Grace knew her mother was grateful for this one. That made it all the more worthwhile for the two sisters who had always shared a deep love and respect for their parents. There had always been, however, a sadness that permeated the relationship that they were both aware of as well. Grace felt it now as she mused on the irony of arranging a 25th anniversary for parents who, still yet, had not been married.

CHAPTER
56

As they had once prepared their parent's 25th anniversary celebration, Grace and Clare now set about planning their parents' wedding. There was no question who would be the two witnesses at the ceremony. Grace knew the next hurdle she had to confront - The Holy Roman Catholic Church! This church she had been raised to love, and she now knew to be her adversary, she would confront with every weapon in her emotional and mental arsenal. She would see her parents married in the presence of a priest with the blessing of their Church. Clare and Grace would receive the respect and vindication they deserved.

Grace was now free to rummage through the hope chest to locate the facts and documents she needed. She would find among the lovely treasures that had already been revealed to her the documents and certifications she needed now. The chest, having given up its biggest secret, produced her father's civil divorce decree granted in 1946. Mare had already confessed that it was the fear of Grace, who was a precocious reader as a child, finding this document that had caused her to purchase a lock and key to prevent this. Both daughters' birth certificates had been stowed in there as well. Their births had been registered long before his divorce but clearly named him as their father. The divorce papers included the name of his former wife.

Questioning her mother, she learned that even though her parents had been dating, he went to a party with some co-workers one night and met this woman there. Shortly after she announced her pregnancy naming Eddie as the likely father of her child. Grace's mother, with the purest part of her strict, but broken, Irish-Catholic heart insisted her love marry the other woman as it was "the right thing to do". Not long after the marriage, on a visit to the doctor, and in the presence of Grace's father, it was confirmed that she was not "with child". She was instead, an immigrant from Ireland seeking marriage as a way to legitimately remain in America. Eddie called a cab, drove to Grace's grandmother's house, and picked up Mare. They lived together every day thereafter but not necessarily with the blessing of everyone on either side of the family.

Grace could now understand why her paternal grandmother had always been a distant and unforgiving entity. She would absolve her in the future but never forget the pain her rejection inflicted on Eddie's first child, Grace. The revelation brought Grace to tears. She grieved for the loss of so much of her parents' happiness and dignity. She grieved for the fact that those who knew may have viewed her and her sister with aversion or worse, sympathy. At some point in the future Grace did try to locate her father's first wife to confirm this account but was not successful. She realized then that it was no longer an important factor in her life. The story that had been uncovered would be established as fact by the loving relatives on both sides of the family that had known, but concealed the truth, hoping to protect the children. Grace wished that it had all been different.

One evening, armed with a portfolio of documents, and several glasses of wine, Grace headed to the local church. This would be her first visit there, ever. She knocked on the rectory door hoping it was not too late to see a priest. She was greeted by a genteel looking, heavily bearded, middle-aged man who introduced himself as Father Ted. When she advised him, she was seeking his counsel and wisdom, he immediately ushered her into his study. He had the visage of a confessor in the best possible sense and she found her story gushing forth in a stream of consciousness that surprised even her. He sat and listened carefully letting her speak, and cry, as she felt necessary. She displayed all her documents, divorce papers, birth certificates, including her certificate of graduation in Christian Confraternity that took 12 years of release time class to complete. This too had been stored in the hope chest. In that instant she knew why she had never been able to attend parochial school. It was not a question of money or even intelligence, as her irritable parochial school cousins had speculated. It was simply that she had not been acceptable, an illegitimate child of licentious parentage. She looked now, carefully at her attentive listener. His face revealed not judgment or condemnation. It shone with compassion and acceptance. He was clearly reflecting on her words and responding with his own non-verbal cues. His need to articulate these emotions with words, totally unnecessary. Finally, she tiredly completed telling her story after providing countless reasons and rationales for why her parents should be married, at this late date, by a priest. He assured her he thoroughly would support such an application especially considering the state of Grace's father's health and the damage already endured by the family. He explained it would require the granting of an annulment of Eddie's first marriage, releasing him to marry again as a Catholic. It all depended on knowing if the first wife was still alive, a very possible scenario Grace had to admit to herself. Father Ted was anxious to start that night on the paperwork he needed to submit to the Chancellor's office. He would also have to begin a reasonable search for the first woman. He then asked Grace if he could pray with her for her family and the wisdom and leniency of his Church to grant this request. It was the first time Grace had consciously and vocally prayed in many years. Grace left the rectory that night confident she had done all that was in her power to help her parents. She had confidence as well in a new friend, Father Ted, and his ability to assist her in achieving this. So it was that she was not fully surprised when Father Ted called her at 8:00 am the next day to say the paperwork had been completed, a reasonable search had been conducted, and the Diocese, with the permission of the Papacy had offered her father a special dispensation to marry Grace's mother. Father Ted asked if he could be permitted to conduct the ceremony in her home at their earliest convenience. She was sure she could hear bells ringing!!

CHAPTER

57

Walter, who had always respected her parents, arranged for a representative of the court to come to the house and certify Eddie as mentally competent. He then escorted Mare to the court and stood in as proxy for Eddie while the judge performed the wedding ceremony and issued the wedding certificate. We would always joke that Mare was almost the second woman in the family to marry a black man!

The Catholic marriage ceremony was set for the following Wednesday in the bedroom her parents now shared in Grace's home. Aside from the solemnity of the upstairs ceremony, a festive party was planned downstairs to celebrate the long overdue event. When the good news erupted throughout the extended family, Uncle Barney and Aunt Marge called to claim what they thought were their rightful places as formal witnesses to the wedding. Grace offered them second billing, each one standing beside her sister or herself as they witnessed and signed off on their parents' wedding. Understanding the true propriety of the girls' decision to take their places, but still acknowledge them, was accepted as fair. The four of them witnessed the marriage performed by Father Ted but only Clare and Grace attested to its veracity. In the room as well were Grace's two sons. She had told the boys of the circumstances surrounding the marriage of their grandparents lest they too fall victim to the secrecy of the past. She vowed to break this cycle of deception that had tainted her own life before it could affect theirs. Even though she protested the idea at first, the girls convinced their mom to wear a white dress for the service as it was her first marriage. Her daughters did as well to symbolize their innocence in the matter and their complete love of, and devotion to, their parents. When Eddie, seated in a wheelchair, took Mare's hand and asked her commitment that they would never break up, there was an audible hush in the room. With the wedding documents ensconced safely in her hope chest, Grace, Clare, the boys, Uncle Barney, Aunt Bridget and Father Ted went downstairs to join the others for a good old-fashioned Irish-American 'craic'.

And so began the celebration! Grandchildren, aunts, uncles and cousins, friends and neighbors joined the festivities. There was good food, hearty laughter, ample storytelling, ribald reverie and a wee bit of drunkenness. A typical Irish wedding! The bigots who had shunned her own marriage, now had the opportunity to meet Walter and witness his commitment to Mare and Eddie. They verbally stumbled over each other, each one giving a detailed account of their one black friend or co-worker. They felt vindicated, Grace was sure, telling how they contributed to the United Negro College Fund at work. It truly was amusing to Grace though she would never feel the same love for any of them. The only true pall over the day was the absence of Eddie's family. Attempts to reach them had not been successful. Grace hoped this too would change someday. She also knew, sadly, it would be too late for her father.

Three weeks later, his continued failing health took Eddie, the new groom, from the marital bed to the hospital. He would never return. Mare's joy had quickly turned to grief. Her daughters now had a funeral to arrange. Grace went back to the hope chest to see if there was any insurance policy to offset expenses. From the very bottom of the chest, she extracted one more secret offered up to her now. Yes, there was a small policy issued upon Eddie's retirement from his job at the post office. It was not the amount that was stunning in its paucity but the fact that he had named Mare, his beneficiary, as his "friend". How sad it all seemed now to Grace. Had there been more honesty and trust in the family Grace could have resolved this problem years ago. Had there been more time they could have reveled in their marital joy longer. She stood now besides the monument to the past, her beloved hope chest, and vowed that in her family at least, history would not be allowed to repeat itself. Overall, it was a wonderful day. In the end it was Clare and Grace that had facilitated the marriage of their parents. Those crazy kids! Not many offspring can say that. It wasn't "On Golden Pond" but it was close! It was a story of love, and ultimately, marriage, family bonds, close relationships and intergenerational conflict. Mare and Eddie, unfortunately, also had the darker side of the Church dictates against them from the inception of their love for each other.

Eddie's funeral was typical of so many Irish American wakes and burials. It was like the gathering of the clans, sad but lively, tears and laughter, with the unending sharing of photos of children, grandchildren, christenings and weddings. In spite of the respectful and somber tone there was always levity at these funerals.

Grace approached a distant cousin who was crying inconsolable at the coffin. She was surprised to see the woman's extreme reaction to this particular death. As she comforted the woman, her arm around her, the woman began telling her of her little dog that she had left leashed on the back porch of her home. Her daughter, who had just arrived at the funeral parlor, had just informed her the dog had jumped off the porch. She shared that her puppy was dead, ostensibly, having hung himself with his own leash. When the woman tried to relate her grief over the doggie's demise to Grace's sorrow over the death of her father, Grace just walked away. That's when she encountered Ida Horowitz, a colleague from the school at which she taught.

Ida was a 60s-ish middle class, Long Islander that taught sex education to junior high school students in the inner city. She arrived in her polka-dotted capri pants and cat's eyed bejeweled sunglasses as though she had just left the cabana at her beach club, which ironically enough, she had. She was carrying a bottle of vodka and offered it to Grace as some might give a mass card or send some flowers. Ida wanted it placed, as she said, "On the table in the funeral parlor where all the liquor is kept at an Irish funeral". Grace accepted her generosity, rather than embarrass her, and went immediately outside and put it in the trunk of her car. It would reappear for the bereavement "party" following Eddie's internment at the national military cemetery. There it was placed on the table reserved for such accoutrements at this very traditional Irish-American ritual of passing. Slainte Eddie!

CHAPTER
58

After such a sad and busy period, it was time to look forward. Mare continued to live in Grace's home. As was feared, she had no further income since her husband's passing. The government was not obligated to continue to send his pension to his widow as they had not been married during his period of employment. She was not eligible for social security under his name as postal workers at the time did not contribute to the social security system. Mare was left with no cash, no house, no investments, no survivor's pension. She could claim social security under her own name for her employment at Woolworth's for a time in the early 1940s that totaled $118 a month. When Grace inquired if she had ever considered having a plan for the future she simply replied, "I knew my two daughters would take care of me or your father when necessary". She smiled proudly knowing she had raised two girls that would indeed do just that.

Ironically, the facilitation of her parent's marriage rang the death knoll for Grace's. She had been distracted for too long from the problems in her own relationship and could not continue to be so. Things were not getting better at home. During this time Walter's delusions went unchecked from lack of consistent medication. Bills went unpaid as he purchased things he liked or that simply amused him. She found herself continuously monitoring his actions and addictions. Dealing with her career, the medical needs of her father and the ensuing emotional needs of her mother was becoming debilitating for her. These combined with the growing rebelliousness of her teenage sons was, at times, overwhelming.

Grace was considering returning to graduate school. She had sought this same kind of distraction during her first marriage. Walter returned to Virginia, now selling timeshares at a ski and golf resort in the Shenandoah Valley. This kept him away, to everyone's relief, from home for much of the time. Clearly not a solution but a much-needed respite. When his ambitions in Virginia inevitably began to disintegrate, he returned home permanently. His newest idea, generated by his manic state, was to sell jewelry at street fairs and on street corners primarily in Manhattan. He selfishly expected Grace to participate in his newest venture, dismissing the fact that she was a full-time middle school teacher. At first, she agreed but when she eventually realized the toll on her she refused to continue. Walter had become irascible. His behavior at home was increasingly unpredictable and erratic. He was irrationally accusatory, charging Grace with everything from infidelity to stealing from him.

The boys, now young men, had found their own elixirs to deal with their reality at home. Joe, sadly, began drinking, mirroring a common coping mechanism in the Irish community. Jimmy, on the other hand, found solace in marijuana and mushrooms, no doubt an homage to his American Indian spirit guide. This behavior, of course, was concealed from Grace who continued to view them as her "little boys".

Their pain, however, became increasingly visible. It manifested first in their deteriorating attention to their schoolwork. Joe got deeper into his music spending hours mastering his techniques. Thus, his proficiency on the guitar grew. Jimmy, meanwhile, learned to play the bass guitar nourished by his love of the blues. Even though they had good neighborhood friends, many of which would become life-long friends, they were forming new friendships in their high school communities. Having endured many instances of racial bullying or menacing over the years they seemed comfortable in the more integrated venue it provided. Their friendships now included young people from different races, cultures and religious affiliations. Grace was exceedingly proud of her sons and their ability to accept and mingle with all people. It was a blessing their homelife had nurtured. Their friends would always be welcomed in Grace's home. They knew they had the freedom to eventually choose partners knowing they would not be subject to the frequent pressures, biases and prejudices of other households. What Grace truly missed was the presence of her sons in the house as much.

Mare began spending weekends at Clare's home. Eventually she moved in with Clare's family full time. She claimed Clare needed her to watch her youngest child who was just beginning kindergarten part-time. Grace rightfully thought it had more to do with Grace's situation than the needs of Clare's. She could not blame anyone but herself for this. She was happy her mother had this opportunity to spend with Clare. No one knew then this would not last forever.

Her decision made about her own future, Grace began her studies to obtain a degree in School Supervision and Administration. Grace's responsibilities at school and college became a welcome diversion from her home life. Grace had always loved teaching, enjoyed her students, and worked hard to ensure their success. She would often share stories of her own life and education hoping to motivate them to positively approach obstacles and learn to overcome them. When she taught elementary school, very early in her career, she would bring her own sons on school trips with her class. They became friends frequently with her students. With their parents' permission Grace would sometimes come home with several students in tow. Her boys especially liked these afternoons of sports and games they shared with Mom's students. At Thanksgiving she would have a class committee come to her home to cook an entire feast that she would bring to school for a celebration the following day that included their parents as well. Many years later she would run into former students

who immediately asked about her sons and shared their remembrances of those times. Grace would always cherish these
memories.

Most of her career, however, was spent on the junior high
level teaching reading and then language arts to teenagers.
Here too she enjoyed tremendous success with her students,
respect from their parents and peer recognition in her field.
She piloted and received funding for novel ways of teaching.
Her selection by the Board of Education as a teacher/mentor
was testament to her ability to inspire and lead.

Responding to the turmoil in her present situation she would
seek respite in her professional life. Eventually she would go
on to earn the training and credentials she would need to become an administrator, first as a dean, then an assistant principal and finally a principal. Her personal educational journey
and her career as an educator, culminating in her role as an
administrator, was one of her greatest triumphs in life.

CHAPTER
59

Over the course of her career Grace began to notice how much she emulated Mare in her interaction with youngsters. She was kind and patient with them. Grace believed in her students' ability to succeed and achieve in their studies. That was very much in the mode of Mare when educating her own children. What she gradually detected also was the frequency with which she told stories or fabricated reasons the children should be compliant in her classroom. Recently she had them believing that she held a black belt in karate and her son was Axel Rose of Guns 'n Roses music fame. The kids loved her stories! She was a colorful "blarney" spinner and a descendent of the most prolific yarn tellers and story writers this world had ever witnessed. Probably the reason she sought her first degree, a BA, in literature. It might have been genetic she speculated at times. Exemplary of such creativity were the following two sketches.

One day she noticed a student who was chewing on the top of a BIC pen. He ignored her first two requests to stop. She was able to get his cooperation by reading out loud from the newspaper from her desk the report of a youngster, who just the day before, choked to death by inhaling his pen top. He was at home doing his homework when this tragedy befell him. Of course, Grace was making up the account as she held the New York Times dramatically in front of her. She reassured the student that if it happened here, in the classroom, she would just use the Heimlich maneuver to revive him followed by CPR if necessary. This was followed by a general warning to the class to be quiet while she performed this life-saving exercise lest their friend and classmate expire. His pen top quickly went in the classroom receptacle accompanied by several others. This dangerous habit never manifested in her classroom again.

Each year, during the preparation for the first fire drill of the semester, she explained the necessity for their complete compliance and silence once the fire bell rings. Children respond well when given believable and reasonable cause for cooperation. Grace would explain why such efforts, on everyone's part, are mandatory in school. She would then petrify them with actual accounts of children who had died in school fires because of refusing to follow these life-saving directions. Of course, she may have embellished the accounts somewhat but it was, in her mind, to protect her students. When descending the stairs to evacuate the building, she could hear the shushes of peer pressure, behind her. Grace's classes always, understandably, were positively cited for their amazing conduct during these drills.

CHAPTER
60

It was important to Grace that all these memories, good and bad from this stage of her life, be shared. Her marriage to Walter had been declining for a while. However, to ignore the good would not reflect the entirety of their marriage or the relationship they shared. It saddened her that the marriage would inevitably need to end. Grace was not sad for her sons this time. They were adults now and had suffered or prospered from the journey by then. She hoped they would look back as she was doing and see the goodness that had existed in a damaged human being that had truly loved them. For herself, her spirit and resolve were in jeopardy. When she felt the necessity of the intervention of the police, knowing he kept a gun in the house, Grace knew this could not go on. She began in earnest to develop a plan to end the chaos.

It was arranged that Joe and her mother would move in temporarily with Clare. Jimmy had already left the house months before moving in with friends. Grace had arranged to housesit for a month for another student she knew from her college studies. She would use this month's reprieve to sort things out in earnest. The morning she decided to execute her plan, Walter followed her out of the front door, hurling invectives and insults at her as she drove away. When he left for the city to go peddle his wares, Clare would pick up Mare and Joe, and the treasured hope chest. Grace packed nothing and took nothing with her. As she drove away, she felt the freest she had in many years. She would not return to her home until the court settled the matter in her divorce litigation. The ensuing years would be some of her happiest, and also, her saddest.

Grace moved into a luxury condominium in Queens. The view of Little Neck Bay and the Throggs Neck Bridge from her 12th floor window was spectacular. There was a deli, beauty parlor, cleaners and impressive pool and health club on the first floor. With a concierge in the lobby to screen visitors and a guard station at the underground parking garage, which could only be accessed with a swipe card, she felt quite safe. More importantly she was out of Walter's reach. Her decision, also to obtain an order of protection against him, amplified her feeling of security.

Grace continued with her graduate studies at night after teaching during the day. Although one might think this to be a heavy load, especially in the midst of a contentious divorce, it was not. Grace enjoyed the relaxation her new environment afforded her. She was no longer stressed and tense as she had been. It was, in fact, the first time in her adult life that she was focused almost totally on herself. Eventually she would begin growing her social life. Adding to her weekly Friday afternoon happy hour with her professional colleagues, she began gradually to re-enter the dating scene.

She would count among her admirers a Sri Chinmoy adherent, a Yemenese Jew, an Irish writer, a Polish newspaper reporter, an Italian lawyer, and a Puerto Rican civil engineer. But as they say, "there was no love connection". She was not looking for one, thankfully. Her three friends, Ann, who she knew from undergraduate school, and Maria and Betty who were her neighbors during her second marriage, were all the friendships she needed. They were, all three professional women who possessed intelligence, incredible loyalty and boundless senses of humor. Ann and Maria were fellow educators and Betty was a registered nurse. Like Grace they were strong woman. Grace actually began to feel she was being given a second chance to live the teenage years and young adulthood she knew she had missed. However, she could do so now as a responsible and competent adult. Her personal recognition in her field was growing and her love of her profession grew right along with it. Then came the first blow to her status quo. Mare, now 67, was hit by a car on a rainy day in April.

CHAPTER
61

To understand the full horror of this story, we must first understand that Mare was known by the very dramatic silvery wig she wore. Since her mid 40's Mare had longed to have white hair. Her own mousy, salt and pepper hair would just not cooperate with this desire she harbored. Mare eventually purchased a very dramatic, and glamorous, silver wig that she wore daily. The hairpiece was very aptly promoted as the Zsa Zsa Gabor model.

One day, April 1st ironically, she headed out in a rainstorm to place a small bet at the Off-Track Betting parlor. Mare, who had loved to gamble her whole life at church bazaars and church run raffle drives, was down to her weekly lottery bets and a few small horse bets. This was the extent of her entertainment. Well, that and her gentleman friend, named Eddie ironically, who she was going to visit after placing her wagers.

As she stepped off the curb, in the crosswalk, and with the Stop sign in her favor, she was hit by a vehicle and hurled into the air. When the police arrived, she was unconscious and they could not revive her. Her wig was still sitting in the road 20 or 30 feet in front of the car's bumper. An ambulance was called and she was taken to the hospital.

As the officers gathered information about the incident, and interviewed a witness, a policewoman sat with the 86 year old driver, who feared he had just beheaded Mare. Ironically, he lived in the neighborhood and was just returning from the betting parlor Mare was headed to. Must have been an Ichabod Crane moment for the old gent, the relentless weather, a headless woman and horses, colluding against him. When Eddie came outside to see why Mare was late with her visit, he was confronted by neighbors who told him what had occurred. Since he did not have either daughter's phone number, he was clever enough to go to the local elementary school that Clare's daughter attended and was given Clare's work number from the emergency contact card. He called her and she in turn contacted Grace. They agreed to meet at the hospital.

When they arrived, Mare was still unconscious, and in a coma, having suffered an obvious concussion. She had several broken ribs and sustained extensive contusions to her hip and pelvic area. She woke up later in the day, and found her daughters keeping vigil at her bedside. In true Mare style she first asked what had happened to her wig. When advised of the decapitation scare, she began laughing. That's when she realized the scope of her injuries as her ribs were unforgiving and causing immense pain. It would be months of therapy before Mare would be mobile again and then only with the aid of a cane that would be with her indefinitely. Grace and Clare were grateful for this prognosis, but not so much Mare. When she had recovered enough, she returned home to Clare's house and began her rehabilitation. There would be other problems for Mare during the following year.

CHAPTER
62

In a telephone conversation one afternoon, Claire was complaining about a terrible odor in her house whose origin she could not determine. Ironically, Joe had complained of the same thing to Grace. She decided to visit and help them sort out this situation. When no one else was in the parlor but Grace and her mother, Mare took her shoe off and revealed to her daughter a horrifying, putrid smelling, blackened, big toe. The doctor's diagnosis was gangrene, and he immediately scheduled Mare for surgery the following morning. During the night Grace was contacted by the supervising nurse on Mare's floor advising that Mare was inconsolable and had asked her to call. Grace was well aware of her mother's fear of surgery. Due to her terror of doctors, she was always prophesying that she would die "on the table" if she ever had to go "under the knife". Thinking this call would require her to only appease and comfort her mom on the eve of her procedure she of course agreed to talk to Mare. How shocked to learn she had been visited by Clare and Clare's husband who advised her she could not return to their home after her hospital discharge. Mare was not only frightened but feeling deeply hurt and rejected now.

Grace was able to console her by expressing her delight that Mare could now move in with her again. Her mother able to sleep now, Grace knew she must talk to her sister in the morning. She would learn from that conversation that things had not been going well for a while. Mare had always overstepped her bounds with her daughters especially when it came to her grandchildren. Grace knew this could not be well received in Clare's home. She also, childishly Grace thought, did not approve of their mother's relationship with the "new Eddie". Remember Clare and the "old Eddie" had been "a mutual admiration society" as the old saying went. Finally, it was her concealment of her gangrenous appendage even though Clare had become more and more concerned of its origins, that led to the eviction. Grace listened but knew this could not be the real reason for such an apparently heartless move by her sister. Clare had always been an incredibly loving and attentive daughter, doing anything she could for them. She had been her strongest supporter, on every level, as she struggled through two waning marriages. The love of her own children seemed to be matched by the love and emotional support she had provided to Grace's children since their births. Grace, though the older one, often believed Clare had adopted the stance of the older more stable sibling over the years. She admired her strength, her resiliency, her patience and her seriousness.

Grace could not now relate to the stridency in Clare's voice, nor her refusal to examine her position on the matter of their mother. Although happy to shelter Mare again, Grace was aware of the sadness, even fear she detected in Clare's voice. Too soon she would learn the reason for this.

CHAPTER
63

Mare had always been jealous of her daughters' time and attention. It was not unusual for her to pout if they were not available to her. At times she would even cast aspersions on their friends and associates, hoping to create suspicion and division in these relationships. Both Grace and Clare knew this had more to do with their mother's low self -esteem, under-nourished by years of rejection and secrecy, then her innate good-natured kindness to everyone. With her mother firmly ensconced in the condominium with Grace, it became clear that her job and night classes at college, would create stress on Mare and their relationship. It was often a lonely existence for Mare with Grace gone from early morning until after 9 pm in the evening. Even though the deli in the building delivered to the tenants, Mare insisted on waiting for Grace to return home so that they could eat together.

Grace was, once again, in the position of caretaker to a parent. Her mother had never cultivated friendships, given the veil of shame and secrecy she had lived under with Eddie. Besides her daughters, her sisters were her only strong relationships. They were aging as well, dealing, one with a stroke, and the other a heart problem. Neither one drove and public transportation for any of the three women was not an option. Therefore, she relied on Grace for all her needs, including companionship. Grace's social life suffered a serious curtailment.

Her mother took to bemoaning the fact she was no longer at Clare's where she would be less lonely. She grew quite irascible and suffered bouts of moodiness and sullenness. Grace was growing more and more disappointed that Clare had almost fully withdrawn from interaction with Mare or herself which contributed, undoubtedly, to her mother's sadness. She fully accepted that she, and the deli deliveryman, were now Mare's only connection to the world. A horrible phone call from Clare would change this forever.

Late in the evening, just before Christmas in 1988, Clare's husband called to speak with Mare. In that brief call he advised her that Clare had been admitted to the hospital and diagnosed with an extremely aggressive and advanced form of breast cancer. He had been advised she was terminal. Left untreated she would succumb in 3 to 4 months. With treatment, perhaps, that window could be expanded, though a cure was not possible. At first Grace refused to accept this, even calling her sister dramatic. She was looking to deflect concern about Clare to herself. She was looking for her mother's sympathy to divert attention from the coldness Clare had shown her mother recently. Mare's hysterical squealing brought Grace back to the hideousness of the moment. She was stunned at how swiftly denial had seized her and how rapidly she had actually grown angry at her little sister. Now, flooded with feelings of fear and remorse, she remembered that she had felt things had not been the same with Clare in the last year. The actions of this once loving daughter did not match her treatment of their mother or her attitude towards Grace. This dreadful disease, while not acknowledged by Clare, had been devouring her body and soul for a time.

The knowledge of her prognosis was causing her sister to mourn immediately the future she would not share with her husband and her two children. She would not resign herself to a life of "waiting". With her inherent strength and an unbelievable exhibition of courage she began planning for the future they would share together. She firmly believed that projects and positivity would prolong her life. She set about completing the projects in her home she had planned to do one day.

A new kitchen and laundry room were installed. A new car for her ease and enjoyment was purchased. Travel plans, long held in abeyance, were planned for the immediate future. On these family trips, she would include Grace and the boys so that as much time together as possible could be shared. There would be wonderful jaunts to nearby destinations such as Cape May or the Amish country and more extended trips to New Orleans, Orlando and Niagara Falls. Every opportunity to travel together created opportunities for treasured memories to be imbedded in Grace's mind forever. With shame she would note how it was that this scourge, that afflicted Clare, had brought them closer as sisters than ever before.

When her nephew, Robbie, was granted admission into the National Honors Society, Grace was invited to attend her godson's installation with his parents. This was the proudest moment of Clare's life. How ironic for poor Clare who did not receive her own high school diploma because she never presented the school with a completed dental treatment certificate. Mare had passed her well documented phobias of doctors and dentists on to susceptible little Clare. Grace could remember her suffering through childhood with many toothaches that went untreated except for a little whisky rubbed on the offending tooth and surrounding gum. So, although she was a highly intelligent young student who had completed all her coursework in a most exemplary manner, she was denied this final parchment of validation. Grace remained angry for years at the school system who withheld this prize from a child victimized by the fears and financial situation of her family. But, finally, here she sat with Grace and her family, congratulating the next generation's success. Grace sat teary eyed reveling in the accolades her sister's first born was receiving. Well done, Clare!

CHAPTER
64

G race, on the other hand, had no fear of the dentist. Her earliest dental care was administered in her first public school. They had a dental chair and visiting dentist right in the building. What a wonderful opportunity it provided her with to combat the fears of her mother. Through her young years she was a habitual client at the NYC Dept. of Health dental clinics. When, as a teenager, she needed braces to fix the terrible misalignment of her teeth, she eventually received them through a program geared to the underprivileged of the city. She could thank a school nurse for arranging this.

During high school, a wonderful guidance counselor intervened to help Grace get the treatment she required. She had been called to the general office, in her senior year, about her failure to submit a dental note. A proud girl, aware of her family's inability to pay for treatment and having aged out of her ability to use the services of the public dental clinic, she became loud and profane, stomping out of the office. Her behavior was referred to her guidance counselor. After a revealing talk with Grace, the compassionate counselor referred Grace's case to the Women's Clubs of New York City. They selected her as one of five girls that they would give a monthly stipend to that was to be used only for routine dental care. In this way she was able to present the dreaded dental completion note to the school and receive her diploma. Every month, a chauffeur driven limousine would pull up in front of Grace's tenement building in the Bronx. Grace would hurry down five flights of stairs to greet and thank her sponsor, a very wealthy woman from Long Island, for the ten dollars she would be given.

At the end of her senior year in high school she was requested to speak at the organization's annual luncheon at the Biltmore Hotel in Manhattan. She sat at the same table as the mayor's wife with the other four award recipients. When it was her turn to speak she rose and delivered the speech Mare had written for her thanking her sponsor profusely for the opportunity she had been given. Grace had been unable to write anything, struggling with the idea of the self-praise and accolades she knew this meeting was about at its core. Grace knew in her heart she had given her sponsor an opportunity as well. The chance to be socially relevant and help the generations of women who would come behind her. Well done, Grace!

CHAPTER
65

At long last, Mare and Grace, spent time now, together, examining items in the hope chest. Mare had a small packet holding both her own and Eddie's birth certificates. Grace perusing her father's, noticed his mother's name was Julia Margaret. This immediately captivated her interest. She had always been told she was named after her paternal grandmother. Her name, however, was neither Julia nor Margaret. The fact that she, clearly, did not bear the name of this ghostly and icy presence in her life did not unsettle Grace. It did, though, create another mystery. Who was she named after, if anybody? Mare could now openly fill in these gaps. It seems, not surprisingly, that "Grandma" Julia had rejected her viability from the onset. This pillar of the church in her hometown, who sang at mass with the voice of an angel, who Grace was sure condemned the idea of abortion per Catholic canon law as a murderous, destructive procedure, had rejected the idea of Grace's existence! The law states "human life must be respected and protected absolutely from the moment of conception". Mare had lived her faith and given birth to Grace. Miss Julia had clearly failed as a Catholic in this instance, and failed abominably as a grandmother. Grace said a prayer for her soul as she sat alone with her mother. The mystery remained and Mare was about to reveal the answer.

Grace's father had a younger sister named Anna, who she had heard very little about over the years. Her mother did tell her Anna was actually his favorite sibling. She had, however, been exiled from the family by Julia Margaret, the reigning matriarch. It was revealed by Mare that young Miss Anna had become an outcast because her sexual predilections (i.e. promiscuity and prostitution) obviously disgraced the good family name in Julia's mind. How crude and cruel this woman had been to her daughter, and yes, her granddaughter as well. In juxtaposition it revealed again her father's humanity. The love of his sister had inspired him to name his own daughter after Anna Grace. It surely was a defiant tribute to a beloved sister. Grace would never meet her namesake or learn, her ultimate fate. She did however, now more than ever, love the name she had been given, to honor her aunt and a sister her father had adored.

On another occasion, Grace brought to Mare's attention a picture of a handsome young soldier she had previously thought to be that of her dad. Mare was able to put a name to the photograph as Grace had hoped. It was her Uncle Phil who Mare had thought mostly closely resembled her dad of all his siblings.

The Uncle Phil she found so warm and kind when he had visited the family in her younger years. Mare went back to the chest and returned with a faded yellow paper Grace, of course, had never seen. It was a telegram sent by her uncle to her father when Pearl Harbor was attacked. Grace did not even know until that moment that her uncle had been among the brave fighting men that had survived the Japanese attack on our forces that fateful December 7th. As the story was told, a young Phil had been out with some base buddies on the previous night. In the morning, Phil a very devout person, rose that Sunday to attend mass. Unable to fully rouse his earlier rowdy roommates, he let them continue to sleep and went off to church. At some point during the mass, the roar of planes overhead and bombs dropping alerted the parishioners to the attack being carried out on the island. Rushing back to his bunkhouse he discovered it had been bombed and there were no survivors. Thankfully Grace knew he had returned safely because she got to see him on his visits to New York. Mare then continued to tell her more about Phil's family. She knew of course that her Uncles Phil and Paul had married two sisters. She remembered that Phil and Kay had a lovely, little child they named Cherie. What she didn't know, however, was that Cherie was actually the biological daughter of a third sister. That young woman, overwhelmed and facing many problems, had suggested that Phil and Kay adopt her child, knowing that they had been unable to conceive a child themselves. What a beautiful gift of a precious child from one sister to another. What an act of love from her aunt to offer her sister acceptance, love and a way to confront the decision she felt forced to make. What a wonderful story for a woman who had just discovered the worst stories of rejection and religious hypocrisy in the same family. It was the local priest at their parish who, in fact, facilitated the process of adoption. He would remain in Cheryl's life forever Grace would eventually learn. Grace prayed that she would someday have the opportunity to meet her now, beloved cousin Cherie, again. She would make it happen she knew.

Life continued for Mare and Grace, although now their roles were reversed. It was Grace who comforted a distressed and loving Mare who had already begun to mourn the imminent passing of her baby girl. Grace who administered to all her needs, cooked her meals, took her to doctor appointments and sat with her in the evenings as they watched her favorite game shows together or just reminisced about life. They had not been as physically close in many years. Grace realized that beneath all the heartache they endured, she was being given a blessing to have this time with her mother. Together, with Clare and her grandkids, they had shared the sorrow of Eddie's passing. Now, the family rallied around Clare, and the strength she demonstrated in confronting her deadly nemesis. This time would be recalled as replete with beautiful times together. It would also be remembered by Grace for the thrashing of her spirit when she was alone. The shroud of fear they lived under, especially Clare and her family, was implacable. "Could she, and her boys who adored their aunt, endure more?" she often worried.

CHAPTER
66

In Spring of 1989 Mare, along with Grace's oldest son, attended Grace's graduation as her daughter received her second masters. Grace had not attended the ceremony awarding her the Bachelor of Arts degree, in protest against the war in Viet Nam. Her first master's degree was awarded in absentia for a reason she could no longer remember but it most certainly was a social or political statement! Unfortunately, now, Grace realized how she had deprived her parents of celebrating such a huge achievement in an extended family in which she was the only college graduate, indeed, the only non-parochial school attendee. Her achievement had filled her mother, a first- generation Irish American, with pride and vindication. The fact that she did not afford her parents the opportunity to attend the actual ceremony has since been relegated to a list of things she would come to regret. There would be more to add, unfortunately.

That Christmas, 1989, would mark the first year of Clare's survival. It was acknowledged more as a quiet observance than a victory. The holidays, once the most joyous time of the year, assumed a somber tone for everyone in the family. Still, they were together and celebrated as always with tree trimming, beautiful gifts, delicious food and even laughter. Clare invited Mare to spend the winter break with her family since the children were home from school. Grace welcomed the reprieve this would grant her from her caregiving responsibilities. She looked forward to the opportunity to celebrate the upcoming 1990 New Year in a more festive mood. Unfortunately, a new year would bring more sorrow for Grace. It came in the form of a phone call from Clare.

Apparently, Mare had come down from upstairs, sat on the bottom steps of the staircase, and could not get up. As much as Clare tried to coax or assist her, she was unable to rise from this position. Grace advised Clare to call an ambulance and met them at the hospital. Mare was admitted and scheduled to undergo a battery of tests to determine the reason for her weakened condition. After interviewing her, it was suggested to the sisters that their mother be seen by a psychiatrist, as well for a bedside consultation. They then agreed to be interviewed first by the doctor themselves.

Both daughters were candid in their revelations about their mother's actions and antics over the course of their lives. Though many of these produced real fodder for some very humorous anecdotes, they had both felt, and shared openly, their real concerns for their mother's mental state. They expressed their concerns as well for her inability to perceive real threats to her own health as in the case of the gangrenous toe.

His subsequent in-depth conversations with Mare over the next several days led to the diagnosis he shared with her daughters. Mare was suffering from clinical depression. Although he understood the sadness and anguish of the last year she had been experiencing while coming to terms with the inevitable death of her daughter, he believed she had suffered from this condition her entire life. Grace was not surprised. There is, she had long felt, a melancholia distinct to the Irish people. She had met too many troubled souls in her own Celtic journey to consider their torment an aberration. Hence, she postulated, the reliance on spirits, both liquid and mystical, in the lives of her Irish-American cohorts. Just as other groups suffered from, and passed to their progeny, genetic deficiencies such as sickle cell anemia, thalassemia, or tay sachs disease, the Irish passed on hemochromatosis, a disease caused by the absorption of too much iron into the blood. Even more treacherous, and in Grace's opinion the true curse of her people, is the culture bound syndrome of melancholia. This condition is darkly and deeply rooted in Irish society, with its origins grounded in the bleak history of its past. Many, wrongly, have romanticized this trait among the Irish. Institutions like the Church condoned the destructive indulgences of the Irish, a manifestation of such depression, in an attempt to keep the status quo of Irish historical politics. This curried more favor for them with the oppressors and furthered their power over the oppressed, her people. She sat alone now, silently, in the hospital waiting room, having just heard this diagnosis. She was concerned for her mother, her loving and anguished mother. In that same moment she experienced an instant of recognition and clarity of her own capacity for misery and self-loathing.

Unfortunately, the revelation of Mare's chronic depression, was not the end of the story, nor its worse aspect. In a straightforward, but compassionate manner, the hospital resident shared with her daughter's the confirmation of the detection of ovarian cancer in their mother's body. Grace was stunned by this news. She could only imagine the impact on her own sister who was dealing with a hopeless case of breast cancer. Surgery was recommended, and immediately at that. First Mare would have to be told. Grace offered to tell Mare alone, as Clare, understandably, could not. She approached her mother's room already grieving the possible loss of her mother and the conversation ahead of her. Grace was not prepared for the ebullient, almost joyous, reaction of Mare. She would repeat, over and over, "Thank you Jesus for not letting me experience the death of my baby!". I could not, then, understand such a reaction. Surely, she would want to live on for the sake of her older daughter and her grandchildren. Mare insisted on speaking alone with her physician. When Grace was invited back into the room it was decided that Mare would have the surgery but under no conditions would she undergo chemotherapy. She rejected, also, any measures to prolong her life beyond what God was granting her. She made it clear that she was undergoing surgery only to be given more time to spend with Clare. She would be praying, however, to die first. Grace overwhelmed by the sorrow in her life at the moment, and trying not to think of her own needs, consented to her mother's terms. The surgery would prove to be a success but the power of prayer would serve to be omnipotent.

CHAPTER
67

G race's second divorce was meandering its way through an already overcrowded court schedule. With Mare's comfort and physical needs to consider, Grace petitioned the court to work more quickly on her behalf in the hope of returning soon to her home with her mother. Grace, a great believer in signs and omens, was not surprised that a decision in her favor for possession of the home, came on Valentine's Day 1990. Surely it was an act of love and a gift for her and Mare. Several weeks later with Mare ensconced once more in Grace's home, arrangements were made for daily home assistance and regular monitoring of Mare's health.

Although she quickly became home bound and confined to her bed, Mare's social schedule was full of loving family visits and pleasant evenings in conversation with Grace. Mare had always followed Grace's teaching career closely and loved her daily, often humorous, stories of her life in the classroom. Visits and daily phone calls kept her close to Clare as well. Unfortunately, it became obvious quickly that Mare was not fully cooperating with her recovery. She left the bed less and less.

One morning when Grace discovered Mare bleeding, she called a private ambulance on the advice of Mare's oncologist and accompanied her to his office. There, after a thorough exam, he determined her cancer had spread to her bladder. He admitted he had not expected this, and certainly not so soon. Privately he concurred with Grace that her mother was willing herself to die. Not surprisingly, Mare was not fazed by this grim news. Grace, on the other hand, reeled under the force of such a deadly blow. With her sister and mother dying simultaneously before her eyes, she feared it was impossible to go on. She found her strength within the realization that there were too many in her family handling their own pain and looking to her for consolation and direction. She was beginning to assume, what she knew would soon be, the mantel of matriarchy for this weary, grieving family.

During the summer of the same year, Clare, recognizing Grace's need for a respite, arranged for her nephews, now in their 20's, to stay at home with their grandmother while their mother traveled to a friend's summer refuge in South Carolina. Clare and her husband promised to stop by daily to monitor her mother's condition. It was to be a short visit for Grace of four days offered as a belated graduation present to her by Clare, so that she might rest and enjoy some time away from the pressures of her life.

Two days later she was called home by her now hysterical sister, advising her their mother had been taken to the hospital again. After driving through the night on a twelve- hour return trip to New York, she went directly to the hospital to see her mother. Mare, was prohibited from visiting the hospital due to the risks posed by her chemotherapy treatments. She had Mare's doctor paged. This would be, of course, the inevitable final consult as it was confirmed Mare was dying. Now began the vigil Mare believed was part of every culture, waiting for the end.

The call came at 6am on August 18th. The kind doctor who had guided her and her family through this terrible, frightening experience advised her that Mare had only hours to live. As it was so early, she chose to call and notify everyone after she arrived at the hospital. She contacted her good friend Betty, the nurse, loved by Mare for the help she rendered to Eddie during his illness and together, with a bottle of rum and some Pepsi, they headed to their final "party with Mom". Grace knew this was the only way she good possibly face this day.

She made her calls and one by one the family arrived; Mare's three adored grandsons, Mare's only remaining sibling, Marge and her daughter, Joan, Mare's much beloved niece. They all joined Betty and Grace in the hospital room. The sadness was amplified by the absence of Mare's beautiful daughter Clare, stopped from being at her mother's bedside by her own deadly adversary.

The nurses requested everyone leave the room as they prepared Mare for her last visitation. Returning to the room

Grace was presented with a vision of her mother she would keep in her heart forever. Mare laying there on her pillow, her long white hair splayed around her like a halo, resembling in the flesh those beautiful, ethereal angels she had learned about long ago. Grace sobbed, for Clare as well, who missed the beautiful blessing Grace was given of holding her mother while quietly thanking her for her love. Then they locked gazes and as Grace loving looked into her mother's beautiful blue eyes she slipped away.

The peace and beauty that filled the room surrounding Mare was unimaginable to describe. Grace knew with certainty, if there was indeed a Heaven, her mother was already in transit. She would be waiting there as she planned to be for her lovely Clare. Grace, however, would be seeing Clare shortly, bringing the unbearable news of their mother's death to her little sister.

There would be a somber wake in the same funeral parlor where her husband of three weeks had been laid out eight years earlier. The mass that would follow was an emotionally challenging experience for all in attendance. As the priest conducted the liturgical part of the service, Grace sat beside her sister, both numbed by the events of the past few days. The knowledge that this would not be the last tragedy in this small family went unspoken. Grace sat silently with a feed-back loop running through her depleted mind. On this vicious memory cycle her mother is staging one of her typical, theatrical, tongue-lashings directed at her first born when she was being recalcitrant in her youth. She sees Mare on this loop as she encourages Grace to "bring a banner to my funeral that says,

I killed my mother!" How terrorized and frightened she had been when Mare would yell this at her. Well, now a mother herself, she fully understood the frustration that had generated this reaction by Mare. She turned off the loop in her mind and put it to sleep forever while she gazed at the beautiful blanket of red roses draping the coffin of her mother. This is the banner she had brought with her to honor her mom and declare her unending sorrow at her loss.

When Father Ted called her to the pulpit to eulogize her mother, Grace was not hesitant but she was trepidatious. As she had sat writing an outline of her speech the night before, she had found it difficult to summarize the essence of her mother in mere words. She was a complicated, compassionate, often despondent woman, loved by all but rejected by her church and cultural milieu. In spite of this, she had presented a serene countenance to the world and a deferential, compliant exterior. She had been deeply cherished by those who truly knew and loved her. The words came freely now for Grace as she stood before family and friends. She knew she had the words and composure to accomplish this final tribute because of the love of her mother and her belief in her girls. "Thank you, Mom", she silently whispered. She then removed a single rose from the floral blanket. She would take it home, allow it to dry out and place it beside her growing memories and treasures in the hope chest that had been bequeathed to her.

Once in the limousine, headed for the long drive to the national cemetery for burial rites, an amusing incident occurred that only Mare could have appreciated. Among the group of mourners accompanying them to the cemetery was young Jimbo's best buddy, David. He chose to ride his Harley in the procession of cars escorting Mare to her final resting place. At some point the motorcycle broke down. The line of vehicles moved to the shoulder of the road as they awaited the reappearance of the bike. When this did not happen, the hearse left the line and took the next overpass to circle back for David. Grace would never forget the site of the hearse crossing the highway and entering on the other side to go back and retrieve David. It seemed so typically Mare, going to get one of her lost lamb's and bringing him safely back. Mare had always loved and indulged her grandchildren's friends. They in turn all loved her. The hearse, now also carrying David, passed the limo with Grace and Clare inside laughing at this strange interruption. They both knew Mare would approve and the mourners continued their journey.

The bereavement dinner that followed at Grace's was unlike the usual Irish Catholic sendoff. The aura of impending doom the family was still engulfed by would not permit it. While the abundance of food and alcohol, for some important drinking, was there, it lacked the boisterous celebration of the departed's life. While there was the expected effusive display of tears, the hilarity and jocularity were missing. The only real consolation afforded Clare and Grace was the solace of being able to inter their mother with their father in a military cemetery where their marriage was acknowledged. They would now be together for eternity safe in the sacrament of marriage that had been deprived from them for so long in life. Both daughters could be proud of the love, respect and shelter they had afforded their parents in their later years.

The following two years would be tumultuous for Grace on many levels. Her career and professional esteem would flourish. She would be involved with her son in a car-jacking incident. There would be wonderful plans for Robbie's graduation and college entrance. Her home would be burglarized. And the gift of the claddagh would presage sorrow. She would also receive the greatest gift of all, love, in the form of a NYC detective named Jim.

CHAPTER
68

O ne morning her younger son, who had again returned home, had an unusual request. Could he drive her to school since he would be boarding the subway at the station near her building? Two blocks from home, and riding in Grace's car that had plastic replacing a broken passenger side window, they observed a man running up the middle of the street. Jimmy slowed down to avoid hitting him.

The jogger seized the opportunity he was clearly looking for, ripped through the plastic, flung open the car door, and pushed his way into the front seat beside Grace. Being a tall individual, his legs became jammed under the dashboard of Grace's small car and he was trapped. As Grace leaned forward, Jimmy driving with one hand, began pulverizing the man's face with the other. As he did so he kept repeating the phrase, "you are going to die today m----------r!". Their attacker was now pleading with them to stop the car and allow him to leave. He was in the most awkward position, hanging half in and half out of the speeding vehicle facing a young long-haired blonde guy with the visage of Conan the Barbarian. We would always laugh that perhaps that morning he thought we were easy prey, two blond women just driving along. Instead, he encountered Conan and his ferocious mother, Queen Maeve, who was now caught in a struggle to protect her child. Grace managed to turn sideways on a highway overpass and ram her four-inch heels into his torso. He went tumbling from the car, on a turn, and was catapulted down the slope along the highway, never to be seen again- neither by the victims turned victors of the attack, nor the police that searched the area he had landed in. As they embraced in the car after the incident, secure in their safety, Grace would think of her cousin Gerry in Hell's Kitchen, her grandfather's brother Peter, shot and killed in that same horrible area and her own many close calls with danger in the South Bronx. She was glad they were part of the fighting Irish that day! Her son had emerged a warrior in the tradition of Finn MacCool!

CHAPTER

69

G race shared her successes after finishing her master's in Supervision and Administration. With things static for a while, she could focus on the career she prepared tirelessly for and the happiness it brought her. She had moved from the classroom into the position of dean of discipline. This was a wonderful fit for Grace who now could interact with a broader spectrum of students, not just those in her English classes. A firm, but fair, educator she enjoyed the opportunity to guide and counsel students towards a more successful school experience. There were those of course whose lives were shattered already by drugs, neighborhood violence and dysfunctional family life. To these students she could offer compassion and direction improving their already diminished options for success. She knew of life on the fringes for the disenfranchised. She had lived there. She also demanded they put forth their best efforts and follow the rules for everyone's safety and achievement. She knew they were capable of this she assured them. Grace impressed upon the staff, also, during the teacher training seminars she conducted, the adoption and maintenance of a safety culture. She quickly gained the respect of the students in this role as well as the school administration. It was not long before she was offered the position of assistant principal in her middle school. She would now supervise and evaluate teachers and be responsible for the overall safety of staff and students. In addition, she would supervise several subject areas. It was a challenge she knew she was prepared for, and competent of meeting. She threw herself completely into her new role and was rewarded by being named Supervisor of the Year in her school district. Unfortunately, Mare would not be there to see her receive this prestigious accolade at the ceremony where it was presented.

Once upon a time, as a school supervisor sat in her office, a handsome detective entered her realm. And so, the story would begin. As good as he looked to Grace, his business was indeed "bad". He had come to arrest one of Grace's students for robbery. Grace would summon the student to her office. She explained the nature of the detective's business and assured the teenager she was attempting to reach his parents. As other staff members circled in and out of the office, the men striking their best macho poses for the benefit of the detective and his partner, Grace observed his demeanor. He was tall, silent and thoughtful. His deep-set eyes took in everything as he leaned against a tall file cabinet. He looked around without ever moving. She was acutely aware of his presence. He had an intensity about him that drew Grace in. His demeanor was one of professionalism and authority but he did not try to intimidate or frighten the boy. He just observed. Grace admired that.

Unable to contact either parent, she arranged for a school representative to escort the student to the precinct in the company of the detective. He thanked her for her assistance and left. Grace hoped they would meet again. In September, 1991, as the new school semester was just beginning, he walked into her office again. This time it was to check out the details provided by a young female complainant, who attended the school and had been robbed. Before leaving he asked Grace if she would like to accompany him to court and give testimony about the character of the girl to fortify her allegations. Grace readily agreed as she was happy to be of assistance to the girl. She had her own motives as well she would admit to herself. This time she asked for his business card.

They say three's the charm. When he came striding into her office for the third time, in October, she could tell he was there on personal business. He explained he was on his way back to the precinct after given testimony in court. Within only a few minutes of idle banter, obviously uncomfortable for him, he asked her out for drinks after school. She agreed and their romance began.

On their first date, she found him very forthcoming. She learned of his service as a marine in Viet Nam where he had been wounded and received a purple heart attempting to disarm a mine. He shared with her that his father, also a NYC detective, had been shot and killed during an armed robbery of a taxicab in Harlem. That occurred in the 1970's when rioting and a distrust of the police was rampant. He seemed eager to learn about her life as well and, happily for Grace, expressed a sincere interest in her career. Grace found it easy to share the stress she was shouldering with such an attentive listener. They sat together for some time. "My mother died last year and my sister is dying soon," she blurted out. "I've just survived a second divorce. I need to know right now if you are an alcoholic. I have two grown sons who I will always be there for on every level and an insatiable need for trust and personal freedom." Obviously taken aback for a moment, he began smiling and added, "I am also divorced, with three sons, who I will always be there for as well. I'm actually a very trustworthy guy who would never deny another human being their personal freedom unless I had them under arrest. Now what can we look forward to that will make us both happy?" The recognition of his sense of humor in dealing with serious subjects was reassuring She agreed to accompany him to a "racket" the next week. Jim explained that it was what the police force called a celebration or party. He used this opportunity to introduce her to his friends and co-workers. She would do the same at an upcoming school shindig. They would soon be seen by everyone as a "couple". With the growth of their relationship, and the corrosive, continuous decline of Clare's health, Grace felt an urgency to have him meet her family. She had avoided such an overt commitment to their future but knew the time was due.

CHAPTER
70

Her first step was to introduce Jim to her sons. Her sons had contradictory reactions to this suggestion. Jimmy did not like the police. This was not a decision made from any social or political vantage. It was personal because he was treated poorly and sarcastically, by one policeman, one time. She had supported him them and supported him now in his reluctance to meet Jim. She knew of his deep concerns for her and knew how much he had endured in her two marriages. Joe, on the contrary, was eager to evaluate this guy's "worthiness to be dating his mother," as he put it. He had always been the more "up front" of her children. She understood each son's reaction as she understood each son. Basically, they were taking the same protective stance. They had always been loving, loyal sons. Jimmy relented and a meeting was arranged. They were both tall, well-built men by now and Grace hoped the encounter would be productive. Football, bar-b-que and beer was on the menu. He had them at Giants and Coors. There was an easiness and acceptance about the day that elated Grace. Jim shared stories of his career and the boys were totaled engaged. He listened with real interest to their tastes in music, fishing and women and laughed easily at their jokes. Their relationship was cemented quickly. It would continue well into the future.

The harder part for Grace, ironically, was introducing him to Clare. Clare, though the younger sister, had always been her anchor. Grace valued Clare's opinions and required her acceptance of Jim, now, to move forward. The family, at this point was in a critical emotional state. She did not want to upset Clare in particular but knew she would be hurt more if Grace malingered any longer with an introduction. She knew also that Clare would be generous with her feed-back. She would hope for her approval as well.

Jim was invited for Thanksgiving dinner to meet, not only Clare's family, but the small extended family of one aunt, her daughter, her grandchildren and a great-grandson. Jim grabbed an apron, carved the turkey, and coddled Aunt Marge who was now into her 80's. It was a good Irish American holiday dinner. Jim's humor and attention again won the family over.

Clare would call the next day and ask Grace to meet her at a local pub Grace and her friends frequented. Knowing Clare was not a drinker, she found this unusual and quite unexpected. Relieved, she learned Clare had arranged the meeting to confirm her blessing of Grace's new relationship. She asked Grace to be careful but not to be afraid to get close to Jim because of her past. What went unsaid was the need for Grace to position herself to assume leadership of this broken brood they both adored. She knew she would with Jim by her side. The sisters then shared a toast to the future they hoped they would continue to share.

Shortly after the new year, and a Christmas celebrated in New Orleans rather than spend their first Christmas without Mare at home, Clare would again wind up in the hospital. On their visit to her bedside, Clare pointed to the foot of her bed and told Jim that Jesus had stood there that day and comforted her. A strange, unshakeable declaration from her very secular sister. Like the little shepherd children of Portugal, to whom the Virgin Mary had appeared, she was steadfast in the authenticity of this visit. Reverting to that tiny appendage of Catholic faith that still lived on in Grace, she was comforted to share Clare's belief in this apparition.

CHAPTER
71

I n February of 1992 Jim surprised Grace with plans for a cruise to Bermuda. They would sail in July. He had envisioned it as an engagement or "commitment" sailing. More importantly at the time, he intended it also as a way to remove Grace from the immediacy and futility of her sister's illness. After a week at sea, and the visually beautiful, and fragrant, ambiance of Bermuda, they returned to horrifying news.

The home they now shared together had been burglarized and ransacked. Then Grace's brother-in-law, out of earshot of Clare, administered the coup de grace. Clare's oncologist had determined Clare was approaching the end of her courageous struggle. He did not expect her to last through the summer.

Time spent planning for her sons graduation and visiting Robbie's choice for school, the University of Buffalo, would consume much of the spring for Clare after her discharge from the hospital. In late July they planned a visit to Niagara Falls as a delightful respite for Clare, her husband, and Grace, who was invited to join them. The trip was lovely until the moment they were to leave. Now in a wheelchair, clutching the handrail of the promenade from which to view the spectacular sight of, and pounding fury of the falls, Clare refused to let go of the guardrail. She had loved this spot always and it was poignantly clear she knew she would never return. They would all drive home in an abject state of surrender to the capriciousness of life.

Grace would now spend every day of that summer, from early morning until evening, in the company of her sister, caring for her and catering to her needs. They had long conversations, watched television together and reminisced about family and friends. Clare did not speak of the future at all.

Together, in her bedroom, the sisters would celebrate Clare's 44th birthday on August 10th. As a gift for her sister Grace had selected a beautiful claddagh pendant to give to her. The meaning of the claddagh in Irish history, a recognition of enduring love, loyalty and friendship, had always been important to both women. It represents the fundamental commitment of the Irish soul to another entity, be it spouse, family, friend or country. In this especially poignant moment, Grace was affirming her love of, and loyalty to her sister in a symbolically significant way. They sat, talking nostalgically, but not without humor, of the life they had shared and the family they would always love. Suddenly, Clare asked, "Am I dying Grace?" Grace was shocked by the revelation that neither her husband or doctor had been truthful with her sister about the imminence of her death. Grace would respond by saying, "We are all dying Clare, but no one will be missed like you." Just two weeks later, on August 25th Clare would pass away.

The evening before, in the emergency room of the hospital, and before she would sign a DNR order, she had requested to speak to Grace alone. This time when she questioned whether she was dying Grace would tell Clare the truth that she deserved to hear. She reminded her sister what a wonderful mother she had been to her children. How she had developed their character, prepared them for the future, and loved them unconditionally. Clare had aced the hardest job in the world, motherhood. Then Grace looked at the baby sister she had always been there for and pledged to do the same for the children she was leaving behind. Clare summoned the doctor and signed the DNR. The next morning, she passed away. Her husband sat beside her holding her hand, and of course, her big sister was at her side. Her son, Robbie, was attending his first day of college and her daughter had spent the weekend with her godmother. Grace was sure Clare had arranged this so that they would be spared the sight of seeing their mother leave them. She was just that selfless.

To this day Grace has trouble remembering all the details of Clare's wake, funeral or bereavement dinner so great was the sense of loss. She would recall being stunned that Clare had expressed her desire to be cremated. Her husband had selected a lovely location beneath a flowering dogwood tree in a small, intimate cemetery not far from their home in which to inter her ashes. He asked Grace's help in designing a memorial stone on which she included, of course, the claddagh. Grace had composed the eulogy but was unable to deliver it and sought the assistance of the priest. She will always remember, however, the vocalist in the choir loft singing the Ave Maria. It was a beautiful hymn they had both loved while growing up. The dinner that followed in Clare's home afterward was remembered for a crude relative putting a spatula into an unserved lasagna, pulling it out, licking it, and replacing it into the pan with the remainder. The beautiful, sure to be tasty dish Clare had prepared from scratch, while reeling from her loss, went uneaten. He was a Hungarian, wearing a pretentious ascot, she would note. Her advice to him, at the time, "stick to goulash".

CHAPTER
72

In those weeks after Clare's passing, Grace would be consumed with thoughts of her sister. An extremely intelligent woman, Clare had been exceptionally successful in the business world. Molded, as well, by the experiences of her upbringing, she sought positions offering opportunities that facilitated the care and treatment of the disabled and disenfranchised. As a compassionate person, she would find an outlet for her need to help others through her years with United Cerebral Palsy, Victims Services and the Methadone program of NYC. She eventually had two children, a boy, and four years later a girl. Each would also be highly successful in their chosen careers.

Her son Robbie, Grace's godson, was born thinking he had two older brothers named Joe and Jimmy. He informed, but confused, his teacher of this on his first day of school, since this fact did not concur with her records. This was soon corrected by Clare. Although he eventually realized these guys were really his cousins, a bond had been formed between the three of them that would endure throughout their lives. His close relationship with his grandfather fortified his membership in the Red Sox nation and his place in his grandpa's heart. It put him on the correct side of this family rivalry much to his godmother's satisfaction and the disappointment of his Yankee parents. Grace felt she had scored a major victory in this life long contest with her sister who had already secured the baseball soul of her own godson, her nephew, Joe. After completing his education at Buffalo University, Robbie would work first, in Brooklyn, as a teacher of students with emotional disabilities. He would ultimately follow his dream of becoming an executive chef.

Clare's daughter, Siobhan, was always a difficult and frequently cruel youngster. As the first granddaughter, and her with a head of fiery red hair, she was loved by all. It was easy, early on, to ignore the signs that problems lurked within that adorable, if sassy, demeanor. Grace recalled her as a youngster of only seven years old, chasing an aging Mare around the house with a knife. Later on, she would pull a chair out from under Mare as she attempted, cane in hand, to sit. It was Grace she would respond to with more compliant behavior than she showed at home. They would spend many weekends together at the request of an often frustrated, Clare. Ultimately it would be determined she was a sociopath, but not before she was married and had two sons of her own. Eventually she turned her back on her brother, his wife and her mother's entire family. Grace was secretly grateful that Clare had not lived to know this. Robbie, the little boy Grace remembered sitting on the floor with while he played with his Star Wars figurines and space crafts, followed her and Jim to South Carolina. He is still an important and well-loved member in their life.

It would be many years before the sorrow, of the last several, would begin to ease for Grace. The loss of her mother and her only sibling in such close proximity felt like a curse cast upon her. Was she being punished for something? Was it her illegitimacy? Grace often felt she was living in the shadow of events not of her doing. But she knew also that the same sins of the past had given her the determination and strength to move forward. She had to. She had promised.

PART III

RENEWAL
AND
RECONNECTIONS

CHAPTER

73

It was Jim who stood beside Grace during the days and months ahead. Grace would remember how Clare had encouraged their relationship and spoke to the need for stability in the years ahead for her sister. Is this what she had seen?

As time moved on, they would learn more about each other. He liked old, classic movies which mirrored a nostalgia in him reflected in his usage of archaic phrases such as "going to hell in a handbasket!" He was solicitous of her safety and feelings without being overly fawning. He would hold her hand in public, which she loved, because he was not afraid to display affection. Very content in his own space, he was not attempting to crowd hers.

He was a fanatical football fan and supporter of the NY Giants. She undertook to learn the game which she had never cared much about before because it was important in his life.

Secretly she admitted it was nice to finally root for a New York team. Jim was grateful for her efforts and began calling her "the fabulous sports doll". This was a high compliment and not a sexist comment he assured her.

Grace now perceived the rigid dichotomy between security and freedom. She was safe with him but had not compromised her freedom to think, to act, to grow, to learn, to love.

With regard to politics there were gradations and nuances in their beliefs and opinions. When they met Grace was a liberal, left leaning, democrat. He was a moderate, right leaning republican. Their discussions could be fiery but never without the respect for each other that they had earned in life experience. Over time they clearly adopted each other's most important principles if not always their perspectives.

Fortunately, on the bigger issues they would always be in accord. Their love of family, love of country and love of each other would be expressed through the truth, honesty and support they offered each other and their children. There were many good things to follow in the years ahead, it would be revealed.

CHAPTER

74

Predictably, but sadly, life moved on without Eddie, Mare and Clare, Grace's first nuclear family. Grace was engaged in building a long-term, loving relationship with Jim, and Joe would surprise her a year later with the news that he had met the girl he would marry. Grace remembered how he had sat with her at the kitchen table, the site of many serious talks, and delivered this news. When asked for more information about this chosen young woman, he had incidentally just met the night before, he replied, "She's as cute as a button." He was smitten Grace concluded.

Gradually she would learn more about Alison, with one "L". She was indeed a pretty young woman. She was a college graduate with her degree in speech therapy. Check and Check! With a great sense of humor, and being easy to talk to, she gave Joe the support he needed at this time. What he didn't need, unfortunately, was the painful rejection he experienced from her father.

Religious discrimination has often been a scourge on our species. Throughout history it has been the source of war and unnecessary death. Grace only had to examine her own roots and the violent time of "the troubles" in Ireland, pitting Protestant against Catholic, to see clearly the devastating impact of religious intolerance. On a smaller scale it has stood in the way, too often, of love between two people. This was the situation this young couple experienced.

Grace had raised her sons to judge no one on the basis of their religion. They both knew they were free to date anyone they cared to without regard to their race or religion. Her own life was a testament to this honesty. Now her son was being denied respect and acceptance by some in Alison's family because he was not a Jew. Grace resented this rebuff by her family and the repudiation of her first born. Such a feeling of disdain she feared would be injurious to the relationship Alison and Joe were attempting to forge. She could only pray her support and acceptance of their daughter would encourage the same on their part. It would be regrettable if her father did not cultivate the same with Joe.

Ultimately, Grace believed, it was the stance that Alison took on this issue, in the face of tremendous familial pressure, that enabled the relationship of these two young people to move forward. It would be many years, however, before her son would be afforded the respect by her father and brother that Alison hoped for.

Grace's desire that the two families would grow to know each other better waned over the years. Her dream of sharing traditions and celebrating important occasions as one extended family faded. The tragic loss of her own mother and sister was compounded by the rejection of the wonderful, large family Alison lauded and loved. Over the years Grace would accept that their motives were not overtly malicious and she would forgive them. However, their actions were shrouded in the same prejudice that their own ancestors had suffered for centuries. The abused often become the abuser it has been said.

Grace did, however get to meet and enjoy the company of Alison's wonderful maternal grandmother, Ba. As a fellow "matriarch" they had much in common, if not their age. She had accepted Joe immediately it seems. Her and Grace forged a lovely, mutually respectful and supportive relationship over the years. For this Grace will always remain thankful. A blanket Ba knitted would be placed in the hope chest of treasures she was building. It was a great loss to her family and Grace as well, when this lovely lady died at 101 years old.

CHAPTER
75

Shortly after Clare's death Joe had shared with his mother a vision he had experienced. Joe was especially close to her sister and Grace was not surprised at the trouble he was having dealing with her death. She was not surprised either at his experience, coming from a tradition of the belief in omens, signs, tea leaves and leprechauns. Therefore, she took him at his word and did not question the veracity of this apparition. In this visit Clare appears to Joe holding the hands of two children, a boy and a girl. She presents them to Joe and lets him know these are the two children that he will father. Ironically, Joe and Alison would eventually have two children, a boy and a girl. Joe would attest that these were the same children Clare had brought to him.

Joe and Alison would marry in 1994 in a civil ceremony. The celebration that followed was small, given the complexity of the situation, and hosted in their first apartment. Joe's father and his second wife attended. Jimmy acted as his brother's best man. Alison's mother and sister were there also. Food was provided, kosher and non-kosher and drinks as well. Some of Grace's family and several of her lifelong friends did attend as well as Jim's mother, Rose. Their participation was negotiated by Grace who was advised to keep it small in deference to Alison's family, most of which would not be attending. Grace was put in the awkward position of explaining to family and friends that were expecting to be invited to share in the moment, that this was not possible. These were individuals that had been there for her and her family during their most troubled times. It was embarrassing to be treating them as unwelcome guests now. She complied, however, and put the feelings of the newlyweds first, who were attempting to soothe the feelings of a few.

Things became decidedly brighter for Grace when they announced that Alison was pregnant! She could not be more exhilarated than if she had just won the NY Lottery. In truth this was so much better than a mere lottery prize. There was at last a new life to look forward to. Her first grandchild, a boy, was born in the spring of 1995. He was named Joseph Daniel, or Danny, as he was called. Though not knowing of any specific reason this name had been chosen, Grace was thrilled that her first grandchild would bear not only his father's name, but the name of his great-great grandfather as well, Daniel, from County Longford, Ireland. Her excitement was tempered by the realization that her beloved mother would never get to caress this much prayed for great grandson.

Grace was just getting accustomed to the presence of this little gift in her life, now known as "The Bink" when Alison announced she was pregnant again. Oy vey! The next little beauty, a girl this time, was born just ten months later, ushering in the spring of the following year. She would upstage Danny's entrance into the family for two reasons. First, she was delivered confronting a potentially fatal health crisis for both her mother and herself. Joe was advised she had punctured her mother's placenta with her tiny, but obviously, forceful foot. Gladly both Alison and little Sarah would survive this ordeal but it was a precarious and difficult time for both.

Secondly, to her credit, she had the good graces to be born on her great-grandfather, Eddie's birthday. In a nod to both heritages, she was named after her mother's grandmother and her own, paternal grandmother, Grace. Naturally they would forever more be referred to as Irish twins. This designation was given to babies born so closely together that they could have been twins. It also refers, in a derogatory way, to the proclivity of Irish Catholics to reproduce often in rapid succession due to the ban by the church on birth control. As with all grandchildren, the birth of these two infants promised unconditional love and the hope of a legacy. For Grace their births signaled an assurance of renewal of the soul and the strength to truly move forward once more in joy and with purpose. Comhghairdeas! and Mazel Tov!

CHAPTER
76

The birth of her grandchildren gave Grace the opportunity to reexamine her priorities for the long term while planning for the immediate future. At the time of the babies births she found herself at home on a medical sabbatical. This was granted after an unprovoked physical attack by a deranged parent with a 20- year, colorful criminal history. She was taken to the hospital and her physical wounds would heal but the feeling of safety so important to students and staff had been shattered. Worse, the support she had expected from the local school board was non-existent. After presenting an order of protection barring the parent's entrance to the building, she learned her order had been violated and the parent was again granted admission to the school grounds. This, not oddly, occurred the day before his court appearance surrounding this incident.

Things got worse unfortunately when he followed her to the bathroom in the courthouse ranting and shouting additional threats against her safety. When his behavior was reported to the judge by her union lawyer, six additional charges were imposed upon him. The assistant district attorney further complicated the matter by not redacting her address from the court record which gave access of this crucial fact to his attorney. The office of the DA actually offered to move her to a new location because of this "snafu". Grace and Jim had just bought a new home and settled in immediately prior to this assault. Grace decided to stay in her home obviously comforted by the fact that the only person who seemed capable of, or interested in, protecting her was her husband. The ADA was then moved to another office and ultimately, the perpetrator would get the proverbial "slap on the wrist". She would accept a disability retirement from the Board of Education bringing her rewarding and purposeful career to an end. Another great loss for Grace.

In the hopes of turning this unfortunate situation into a win for her family, Grace offered to babysit her two little grandchildren everyday so that Alison could pursue her career. Hadn't this been what Mare had done for her? In many ways it was one of the greatest gifts she could ever have received. She was able to pursue her dream of teaching knowing her children would receive the best care possible in the loving care of their grandparents. Grace now made this same overture to Alison. Perhaps it was the time already spent daily caring for two active and demanding babies that made Alison accept this offer. Grace was exhilarated! Her daughter-in-law could now continue to grow her experience, and make her contribution, in the field she had chosen. It would be absolutely arduous for her Grace knew but her supervisory experience recognized Alison had the inner strength, commitment and determination to do this, and do it well. Ironically, it would be Ann, Grace's life-long friend and a newly appointed principal, that would give Alison her first job with the Board of Education. In the telling of this story Grace, was proud to share that Alison had just complete 25 years of speech service to her many fortunate students.

CHAPTER
77

The next five years would be some of the best in her life. She was surrounded by laughter, love and music almost constantly it seemed. Jimbo had moved back home. He spent much time touring now, playing the bass guitar in several blues bands and didn't feel the need for his own apartment or the expenses of maintaining it. Besides, he reasoned, their home was the perfect jumping off place to launch his blues engagements.

He would often invite musicians he gigged with from out of town to sleep over at the end, or beginning of a tour. He would neglect to tell Grace, on occasion, that they had guests sleeping in the basement. Sitting having her morning tea alone in the kitchen, her thoughts would be interrupted by one of their "guests" emerging from the downstairs. The ages, races, garb and headgear were not always the same but her astonishment was. To be honest, in this way she was able to meet and befriend some important figures in the blues world. They were invariably courteous and friendly. Jimmy reasoned also he had the luxury of Grace's home-cooking, the privacy of his own room and bath, and a completely congenial environment in which to watch the Red Sox and the Giants. Best of all for him, he got to see his niece and nephew every day when he was not on the road. He was a tall, playful, very funny, and affectionate presence in their life. He would describe his life in this way, "I have my employment as a paperhanger for my body but the blues is for my soul."

He and Jim, ironically, bore the same two first names, James Edward. Jim would often say it was nice of Grace to name her son after him, twenty-five years before they ever met. Their mutual love of sports contributed to the origin of "Football Sundays" in their home. For the guys and their friends, it was a great way of sharing the game and some football banter, not to mention the beers. Here Bink would show his first indications of real intelligence. At three years old (maybe), he could fetch any guy in the basement the beer of their choice from of wide selection of different labels, glass colors and caps, simply at their request, "Get me a beer Bink". When he learned to use a bottle opener to pry off the caps, he was applauded as if he had just won a gold medal at the Olympics! He had established himself as an integral part of the Football Sunday team and would reign as a beer savant forever. Such were the mile markers in this testosterone infused Irish American family.

Grace was elated the football tradition on Sundays was creating, and sustaining, an even more important family tradition, the Sunday family dinner. A steady stream of treats and snacks would be funneled down to the basement where the men and boys, raucously entertained themselves. At the same time, an aromatic, tasty feast would be prepared upstairs by the ladies. After half-time of the second game on Sunday, dinner would be served. It would be a loud, often noisy affair with abundant sarcasm, laughter and boastfulness, and the occasional threat to an overzealous participant. For each season there would be another sport to watch or several birthdays or anniversaries to celebrate and so this maddening, wonderful, uproarious, loving tradition continued. May it be so always, Grace prayed.

CHAPTER
78

Wonderful mementoes acknowledging the uniqueness of these times found their way into her hope chest. Photo albums, team memorabilia, the grand kids found treasures such as rocks and shells, their impromptu little love "u" notes, band posters, and heartfelt signed greeting cards to name a few. They would join her own children's artwork, poetry, baby clothes, diaper pins, birth announcements and hospital bracelets. They would rest among the stained glass and woodworking projects her young boys had presented to her when they were young. Eventually it would include dance recital outfits, swim team medals, school awards and commendations. Its contents were growing, slowly but magically. Not with darkness and mystery this time. Grace would guard against that. Her "little Prince" ensconced safely inside would keep everything safe.

As with many grandparents, Grace's life now revolved around her new blessings, Bink and Cece. It was Bink who named her granddaughter, "Cece", in his toddler attempts to say "sister". The sobriquet stuck and until her teenage years she was Cece to all. In deference to her adolescence, it was shortened to "C". With no way to shorten this moniker, it clung to her with the family.

These two cherubs would provide endless entertainment for Grace. Like the time, little Danny on his first day of school, told his teacher that his name was Danny, not Joseph Daniel as was clearly indicated on his school record. In an attempt to clarify this further for the teacher he went on to add, "I'm Danny, but not Danny the bookie". This was a reference to the genial man Jim used to facilitate his wagering on sports, his bookie, Danny. He then pulled a betting slip from his new Toy Soldier backpack and inquired if she would like to place a bet. This would be the first of many times his mother was summoned to school.

Sarah Grace was born a caregiver. Within her first 2 years she assumed, even though she was the youngest, the role of caretaker for her brother. If he was put on time out at home, not an infrequent occurrence, she would plead his case with the weakest link in the chain of authority, usually his grandparents, to intercede for his release. She spoke early and often! She wasn't even one year old when she found her voice.

Her mother recalls taking her to a drive-thru for lunch. The staff apparently were to slow for Miss Sarah who began to scold them from her car-seat in the rear of the auto. "C'mon ladies", she yelled, "French fries, fast, lady!". The server who finally went to hand her the fries was shocked to see she had been reprimanded by a 2 year-old, who was now grinning broadly at the sight of her food. "WOW!" the little girl exclaimed.

Cece was an eager student and did well with her school-work. Being a people pleaser by nature it was not surprising that her teachers found her a welcome addition to their class. She was a beautiful child with round rosy cheeks and the blu-est eyes. The only complaint her parents every received was that she was very "chatty".

While the Bink would spend many afternoons in after-school detention, with his sister waiting patiently for him to be re-leased so they could ride home together on the school bus, Cece was never held after school for an infraction. In fact, she would share with her teacher often what any "troublemakers" in the class might be planning. Then came the day she was sen-tenced to serve for "excessive tattling". Her brother, the chron-ic offender, had the nerve to deride her! No one else in the family was too surprised by this allegation against poor Cece, who was just as forthcoming with storytelling at home. She meant well, of course, but her mother a teacher, intervened to stop this habit from going any further. Thankfully, she did, because little Sarah was a friendly child whose company was still very much enjoyed by the other girls in her class.

Another incident stood out from Cece's childhood. At three and four years old, the children would attend nursery school two mornings a week to insure they would have interaction with other children besides their "twin". Sarah quickly, and ob-viously, became the favorite of her group's teacher.

One day Grace was invited to attend a little songfest the instructor had arranged for the children. Of course, Sarah would be seated in the center of the students, directly in front of Miss Morrison. Grace was standing off to the side with several other parents and grandparents. When the teacher, accompanying herself on the guitar, began singing, as an introduction to the event, she was drowned out by a young child in the front, yelling, "Stop! You're hurting my feelings", as she covered her ears. To Grace's mortification it was her lovely little granddaughter expressing her displeasure, not once, but several times. Ironically, she would go on to be a member of her high school drama club appearing in many wonderful performances. She was even accepted for a special university summer camp for students with outstanding theatrical potential. But Grace would always remember most, her first shining moment in a school performance.

To say Danny was not a clever child would be to understate his abilities. He was also creative when necessary. There was the time in the second grade that Danny found himself in trouble at school, again. His teacher, as was standard procedure, sent him home with a note to be signed by a parent. When she requested to see the signed missive the next day, he proudly produced a letter signed "JOE". Assuming Danny's father to be literate she questioned why he had clearly not given the note to his parents. "Oh, my mom is so tired since she came home from the hospital last week after having my twin brothers, Eric and Tommy," he replied, "and my dad is so busy helping her with the four kids they have now that he just told me to sign it for him. I don't disobey my father, ever," he continued, "so I did." She, kindly, decided how plausible this was and what a concerned and obedient son his parents had raised. She did call his mother later in the day, though to congratulate her, a fellow teacher in the school district, on the birth of the twins. The conversation was about more than his cleverness and creativity for sure.

As a youngster Danny, while good at sports, was not good at being a team player. He would be observed filling his hat with dirt and dumping it on his head while playing 2nd base in little league. He was unphased by line drives whizzing past his head. He would unintentionally, of course, make some game winning plays due to his cat-like reflexes.

He fared no better with flag football. In all fairness to the tyke he had grown up in a maniacal football family where tackling and other forms of barbarism were celebrated. So, Bink, when the whistle blew would grab either side's flag or tackle and take down either side's players. His grandpa Jim did not find the fortitude to attend any more of his games that season realizing the boy needed much more football education which he would see to.

That same grandfather realized though, early on, Danny's athleticism and prowess when it came to swimming. He encouraged and supported all his efforts in this sport that he excelled in even traveling long distances with the family to see him compete. It was a victory celebrated by all, but especially young Daniel, now a teenager, when he won the swimming back stroke competition for his school team at the state finals. With this triumph he became a member of the South Carolina State Swim Team which was proudly covered in the local press. They

always knew you could do it Danny Boy! Danny who was emotionally, and even physically, abused by his paternal biological
grandfather, and was not afforded a close relationship with his
maternal biological grandfather, always had the unconditional
love and support of his step grandfather Jim. Sarah Grace did
as well. She would someday refer to him as "my happily ever
grandfather". They would return this love many, many times
over in the years to come. The uniqueness of the relationship
Sarah had with her grandmother Grace, could be summed up
with her excited exhortation that, "I'm gonna be just like you
when I grow up Grandma! I'm gonna gamble and travel". Thank
God, Grace thought, I no longer drink.

CHAPTER
79

The millennium was quickly approaching. The scientists worried about the resetting of computers with the change of the century and the Y2K effect on banking and economies all around the globe. Various religious sects and movements obsessed about the end of the world. Apocalypticism preached that the end of the world was imminent. The concept of the "rapture" was embraced by many fundamentalist groups. Grace only worried about her family's happiness and togetherness. In that spirit she and Jim planned a vacation for the entire family to Bermuda in July of 2020.

It would be a celebration of many things. Jim had just retired after 30 years in law enforcement and it was a celebration of his long and fruitful career of service. They had been married quietly in a very small ceremony in Myrtle Beach, South Carolina. This would be the wedding celebration they had envisioned. They would be moving to South Carolina where they had purchased a new home. Here they hoped to enjoy many wonderful visits with their children and grandchildren. They would also include the observance of several birthdays, anniversaries and life successes generally. Most of all, unspoken, was a commemoration of their survival as a family and the love that had made it possible. The destruction and spiritual devastation of "911" was still a year away.

Several days before sailing her son Jimmy made a last-minute request. He had been seeing a young woman he would like to include on this cruise by way of introduction to the family. Grace agreed given his age and that of the young woman. After the excitement of the ride to the pier on a party bus chartered by Jim, and time to settle into their cabins, everyone met for dinner.

Grace, unfortunately, did not have a good premonition about this new relationship of her youngest son. The young woman had an icy aura about her. She seemed aloof and not given to the spontaneity of this zany bunch. She seemed ungrateful for the consideration extended to her and complained openly about their cabin, its location and even its décor. Grace was perplexed by her son's previous description of her as a blues loving, warm, social individual. She seemed more of a thoughtless, smug, whiner to Grace. Then mid-cruise Jimmy revealed to her his dilemma. He had acquired 2 telephone numbers at his best friend's wedding several months before. Apparently, he had lost one of the numbers and called the one he had left. This led to his meeting with Adrianne, several dates, and an impetuous request she be included on this sailing. His description of her to his mother clearly referred to the one that got away. When he bought her a lovely ring on the island, she announced their "engagement" at dinner. Jimmy was stunned. He in no way corroborated her story and the intention of his gift. Unfortunately, he didn't say anything and reverted to what the family called his "passive panic" demeanor remaining remote and silent.

Grace had decided years before not to interfere with her sons' choices in dating and assumed the same posture now. She felt they deserved respect and trust in making their own decisions. Over the next several years it would become obvious, covertly and overtly, that Jimmy wanted to end this relationship. He was an affable, easy-going guy who did not react well to her attempts at manipulation and control of him and his space. At her best she could have joined him but never changed him. Worse, he would determine she didn't have any appreciation of his music form or its roots. To all of his family it was obvious she was also a racist and anti-Semite.

He verbalized that he wanted to end the relationship but didn't want to hurt her feelings or offend her parents. This desire of his wouldn't show of course because he hid his fears of commitment and other fearsome things beneath layers of a complaisant exterior. She was a "good girl" he would say, just not for him.

The parents, Grace would learn, had been ratcheting up the pressure on Grace's son for a commitment to marriage. When Jimmy's band was one of ten selected world-wide to compete for the title of Best Blues Band, Grace and Jim traveled to Memphis, Tenn. to cheer them on. Adrianne's parents did as well. Her mother made the mistake of soliciting Grace's help in "making this marriage happen soon". Grace clearly stated her non-interventionist position on the matter referring to her respect for her son to make his own decisions. The mother was appalled by Grace's response and any future relationship with her Grace knew would be a contentious one. She was correct.

Jimmy would finally succumb to the pressure of her family and the wedding was planned. Two things did occur that prompted Grace to discuss with Jimmy his choice of this woman. First, she would discover that a check for $5,000 that had been sent to Jimmy as a gift from his stepfather to buy new speakers for his band had been intercepted by Adrianne and deposited in her mother's account. When Jimmy confronted her, she called Grace and accused her of calling her mother a thief. Grace did not believe in stating the obvious actually. She felt the money was due her mother to put to the wedding reception they were planning. Grace reminded her that tradition would say it is the parent of the bride that pays for the wedding and she felt no such obligation in the matter.

More disturbingly, it had been told to Grace that this "good girl" had been married before and not shared this fact with her son. Jimmy denied any knowledge of this allegation. When it was announced that they had decided to marry in a protestant church instead of a Catholic one, Grace was convinced the rumor was true. Adrianne came from a strict Polish-Italian American, Catholic family. She lived at home until she met Jimmy at 28 years old. Grace could not believe this would be the choice of her and her family. She recalled one of the first conversations she had with Adrianne when they returned from the cruise. She had said to Grace, "If Jimmy and I get married you'll get to see at least one of your sons get married properly before God in a Catholic church." Her words exposed her presumptuousness and her prejudice. Grace only wanted to see them happy in their marriage. For her youngest son she knew this would be impossible. She knew it did not portend well for this union when her son dropped his wedding ring during the marital service and then knocked over the lit unity candle to the floor causing a minor panic before it was extinguished.

In late July of 2000 with the memories of their beautiful cruise behind them Grace and Jim returned to South Carolina. The mementoes and photos of their trip were placed lovingly in her hope chest. The remainder of the year would be uneventful, consumed mostly with settling into their new home, hosting visitors, both friends and family. There would be trips back home to New York City for both business and social events.

CHAPTER
80

I n the summer of 2001 Grace scheduled a long overdue
mammography. She had avoided such a decision for years
probably due to her fear that something would be detected.
She knew that her mother and sister having had cancer would
greatly increase her chances for a less than successful outcome
to testing. Yet she knew what had to be done.

On the morning of September 11th 2001 she sat in the office
of the doctor waiting to be called inside for her 9:15 appointment. The office had accommodated their waiting patients
with the morning news on CNN cable news. It was there that
Grace would witness the attack on the World Trade Center
in NYC live on television. From that vantage point she would
watch the twin towers, she had taken numerous students to,
collapse into piles of rubbish.

The event triggered a flashback of the attack on the north tower in 1993. She had been at school that day, heard of the attack and immediately called home. She was able to reach Jimmy but could not locate Joe who she knew had left to go to work at the trade center that morning. With the phone service interrupted in Manhattan she could not confirm his safety. Finally, after a day of excruciating waiting, he walked through the door, his clothes covered in ash and his face so covered in soot he looked like a refugee from a racist minstrel show. To Grace, however, he never looked so beautiful.

Now she hoped good luck would find her again. Jimmy, a union paperhanger, often worked at the trade center. She knew he was not currently touring and believed he might be working at the doomed site. Thankfully she was only partly correct. He was supposed to be there that day but his assignment was changed the day before and a fellow worker was sent in his place. That young man perished that day. Grace gave thanks that her both sons had been spared such a horrible end, years apart. Maybe her luck was truly turning for the better. But for now, she had trouble expressing the fear and horror that consumed her as she sat quietly, alone, sobbing, in that waiting room. Eventually the doctor would join her after realizing Grace was from NYC.

The impact of that attack and tragedy would last for many years in the world, in the country and in the innermost core of Grace. It reinforced for her the tenuousness of life and our responsibility to each other in a very real and profound way. In recent years, as she had shared, she had lost too many loved ones and several friends. Betty, who suffered from Grave's disease, died suddenly of a massive heart attack. Just as suddenly, a dear friend Pam, had died in an automobile crash on a country road in Maine going to the home of a patient. Now Grace felt as if she had almost lost her country! Certainly, young children everywhere in this nation lost their innocence and sense of security. Within weeks the country was again at war. When President G.W. Bush implored citizens to travel to show defiance in the face of this enemy and to keep the economy healthy, Grace and Jim responded to his call.

CHAPTER
81

Since childhood she had dreamed of traveling. Life, of course, would always intervene with her plans. Motherhood, the responsibilities of her profession, caring for loved ones, divorce and of course the availability of the necessary funds, would define her priorities and postpone her dreams of adventure. Now the moment had arrived.

Jim and Grace loaded up the car and set out on their first of many road trips across the nation. Before departing Grace went to her hope chest and removed the "little Prince". He would be coming with her, not only as a talisman of good luck on the road, but as a symbol of the beginning of the fulfillment of many dreams her heart had harbored since her youngest years. It also spoke to her of her father's service to his nation when the call had come in WWII. In the only way forward for her she would also answer the call of her nation. Her dreams were on the threshold of becoming reality although Grace would not be aware of this yet, as they set out, that morning in October 2001.

With the beauty of South Carolina left behind temporarily they would head south and west visiting Georgia, Florida, Alabama, Mississippi, and Texas as far as San Antonio. They would marvel at the topography of the nation, passing through wetlands and forests, past seashores and across rivers. The abundance of the natural gifts we share as a nation was overwhelming in its beauty. Grace was most moved by the Alamo in San Antonio, a national heritage site. This fort remains of the famous battle during the Texas revolution between Americans, their Mexican rebel allies and the Mexican Army of Santa Ana. Though the outcome was disastrous for the Alamo defenders, including patriots Davey Crockett and Jim Bowie, the shrine remains as a symbol of their bravery and loyalty to their cause. This hallowed place could not have been a more appropriate and inspiring place to visit following the 911 terrorist ambush.

There would be many more beautiful journeys across America in the years ahead. In 2002 Grace and Jim traveled across the northern tier of the country from their home in the south to Alaska. This route would take them through North Carolina, Tennessee, Kentucky, Illinois, Iowa, South Dakota, Wyoming, Idaho, Montana and Washington. Now it was the absolute vastness of the nation and the rugged beauty of the mountains, The Appalachians, The Rockies and the Cascades that inspired Grace.

Yet nothing prepared her for the splendor and magnificence of Alaska. They reached Alaska via cruise ship boarded in

Vancouver. The beauty of the terrain was glorious, with small islands and waterfalls dotting the coast. The icy blue color of spectacular glaciers dazzled the eyes and mind. Trips off the ship into the coastal towns and cities revealed the hardiness and resilience of these proud Americans, indigenous and locals alike. The successful co-existence of different cultures dependent on each other for nothing less than survival was inspiring.

They traveled home through Vancouver, Canada and then Washington, Oregon, Idaho, Utah, Colorado, Kansas, Missouri, Tennessee, and North Carolina. They had been gone for six amazing weeks. Grace had her little Prince with her and would photograph him at various locations and with people willing to be in his company. This was the beginning of a photograph collection that would have the Prince and his adventures documented for her hope chest. For Grace this melding of her past and present was essential and the Prince would become the symbol of it for her.

Unfortunately, that year Jim's mother and her brother, his favorite uncle, would pass within six months of each other. His mother had been a strong willed and strong-minded woman who had survived the murder of her husband. Unfortunately, though, she was a heavy smoker and there would be no surviving the impact of this on her health over time. She would suffer a heart attack at age 73 before moving to South Carolina at the request of her son. Five years later there would be another, fatal one, that would take her to the "dirt bath" she always claimed to be looking forward to. Grace found her to be, in many ways, a role model. She was extremely generous to her children and grandchildren. Clearly Jim would replicate this in his own life. What Grace admired most about her though was her advice to also be good to yourself. She indulged herself as she found necessary and never was ashamed to cater to herself. This had always been a problem for Grace who was raised to never put herself first. Rose helped release her from that cultural bondage. She suggested that she see to her own needs first so that she could better accommodate others without resentment or guilt. Rose did have a somewhat haughty presence and would not indulge self-pity or whining. Her sense of humor could be wry but she was quick to share a good story or a funny quip which made it easy to spend time with her. When she passed Grace would embrace Jim as yet another orphan of the world.

Uncle Donald, unlike his only sister, was generous to everyone also but extremely frugal towards himself. He was also cheerful, always, and lived without artifice or pretense. He appreciated the smallest things done for him. He always did for others. Jim recounted how impactful his uncle had been in his life as a youngster. He managed baseball teams for the local boys and there would be many trips to baseball or football games alongside him. He also invited Jim to spend weekends often when he was younger to give him some relief from his strict father. Grace was sure this worked to everyone's advantage since there is no doubt Jim had ADHD as a child! By the time Grace met Uncle Don he was already showing the signs of age and dementia. He was now being described as eccentric by his loved ones for he told the same stories repeatedly to the same people. Most were WWII stories where he had had his biggest life adventure. In his desire to help Grace's grandkids, he almost drowned in the condo pool teaching them to swim when he himself did not know how to. Jim had to save him when he went under several times. Young Danny would become a lifeguard in Myrtle Beach and Grace often wondered if this incident led to that decision. He also had grown to love Uncle Don. Danny and Sarah had been recipients many times of bikes, balls, and bats from Uncle Don. These treasures he procured from the trash and were a testament to his time spent as a foreman with the NYC Sanitation Department. Gifts of string, tools and found videos were likely presents for the adults. It was obvious everyone loved this thoughtful man as was evidenced by the many people who eulogized him at this funeral service.

CHAPTER
82

In August 2004, having just purchased a beautiful home, situated on the wetlands of South Carolina, Grace stood on her back porch admiring the beauty of the natural world around her. It was, in fact, moving day and she was anticipating the arrival of the truck bringing their belongings to this new refuge on the fringes of a marsh. When the phone rang Grace anticipated the driver of the truck was calling because of a delay.

Instead, it was her doctor's nurse advising her she had an appointment with an oncologist. It seems some aberration had been detected in Grace's recent mammography and her physician felt it merited further investigation. A feeling never before felt by Grace encompassed her whole being. It was as though she was adrift in the dank and musty cypress forest before her, without knowing how to get home. Grace was lost in the mist for the moment. She could sense the slithering and hissing of snakes, the trilling of insects and the throbbing of amphibians. All that was ugly and menacing engulfed her, forecasting her demise. She remembered saying, "Why now? Why again?" but there was no answer. She never asked, "Why me?", though. The grasp of this vicious opponent had no favorites or feelings. It had taken down her mother and sister and had come back for her. For a moment she thought how pleasant it would be to see them both again and this would be only the means to an end. Grace however, was not ready for the end. She emerged from the miasma with profound determination.

As the matriarch of this family, she would fight not only for herself but for them. They were not ready for more tragedy. Grace refused to tell anyone of the lethal possibilities confronting her. Only when subsequent tests revealed that she had a malignant tumor of the breast, and her surgery was set, did she confide in her immediate family. She would not tell her grandchildren until they were adults. She reasoned that growing up is a difficult process itself. It did not need to be complicated by the worry or concern, perhaps prematurely, for a grandparent's health. Also, she had by now pretty much convinced them she was invincible!

Fortunately, early detection saved her life. It was obvious to her, the loss of her sister and mother to cancer, contributed to her vigilance and good fortune. Had it not been for their deaths she had no doubt she would have had a lackadaisical approach to monitoring her own health. She believed the intervention of her two guardian angels had saved her life for she had a purpose to fulfill. It was becoming clearer what it was. But first two months of radiation and five years of oral chemotherapeutic treatment ensued before she was confident about the future again. Now, symbolic of her victory over the illness that had vanquished her mother and sister, she placed her medical file, with the reports of its most fortunate outcome, beside the other positive and joyful remembrances nestled in her hope chest.

CHAPTER
83

Shortly before Grace's life altering discovery, her son Jimmy's wife gave birth to a baby girl. In April 2004 they welcomed little Sophia. The poor child was born with a mutation inherited from her maternal grandfather which had been passed on to her mother and now her. Thankfully, this genetic anomaly would not affect her intellect or her survival. She did however, have an elongated cranium and a noticeable distancing and slope downward between her eyes which, as she grew, became a not unpleasant exotic demeanor. Her father adored her and Grace still feels today that his acceptance and indulgence of her in her formative years contributed to the bright, attractive, self-confident young woman she became. After divorce became inevitable, she would remain the focus of his life.

Her mother did everything to verbally degrade him before her daughter. She worked relentlessly to make frequent productive visitation almost unfeasible. But Jimmy persevered and became the light and the love of his Sophia's life to the consternation of her mother and maternal grandmother. He taught the child to play guitar and she quickly adopted his taste in music, counting Janis Joplin and BB King among her favorite musicians. In retaliation Adrianne prevented her from visiting South Carolina and her father's family as frequently as they would have hoped. Jim's court papers did not prevent these visits as long as it was on his time with his child. Yet every time he traveled south with his daughter, Grace would get harassing calls from her former daughter-in-law threatening to send the local police to her door and report her for kidnapping. This situation never changed. The damage it caused her daughter by limiting her opportunities to know and embrace both her extended families and heritage was probably incalculable. For the sake of the child everyone only spoke well of her mother, at least in her presence. The day would come when she would rue her selfish, spiteful, self-centered strategy. In the meantime, Grace continued to find joy in her relationship with her granddaughter and pride in the child's loving father she had raised. Small trinkets of Sophia's childlike affection were placed lovingly in her hope chest beside those of her other grandchildren. Grace hoped one day they would sit together and reminisce about the chest's contents and their place in this young woman's life.

CHAPTER

84

In the Spring of 2005, with Grace recovering from a hard several months of the struggle, Jim received a call from his cousin. This successful businessman had just purchased a home on Kauai, Hawaii and was offering it to Jim and Grace as a haven, a place of solitude, an opportunity to regroup and reset the framework of their marriage. They had been tested through this ordeal but their commitment to each other had survived and been strengthened. Two weeks in Hawaii was a beautiful bonus from a most generous guy. Thus, would begin the planning of their second road trip across America.

This time the couple would follow the southern corridor. They would begin the new adventure when they entered Texas on US Route 10. With the eyes of wonder of that small girl that yearned to travel and the gratitude inspired by her survival as a woman, Grace set out on another trip of a lifetime. She was enormously grateful to all the forces of the universe, her skilled physicians and the generosity of others for making this possible.

Texas is immense! Entering its eastern border, the first thing seen is a mile marker reading close to 800 miles in width. To Grace this translated as farther than her return trips to NY from her home in SC. And, that's all in one state, not the five states you drive through heading to the Empire State. There was much to see of course. The Houston Space Center stands as a testament to our ingenuity and bravery as a Nation. It was awe-inspiring to stand among the space ships and vehicles that celebrated the achievements of our astronauts and scientists. A trip to the ballpark for a tour and the serendipitous encounter of a former Red Sox great, Roger Clemmons "the Rocket", made it all "Houston Heaven". Though there were other interesting natural sites and features on the drive west, such as Fort Davis, home of the Buffalo Soldiers of Bob Marley musical fame, Grace was happy to finally cross the western border into New Mexico.

"This state", she opined, "has a magical, even ethereal quality. Las Cruces is festive and old worldly, with color emblazoned on all building surfaces. It shouts from colorful storefronts surrounding its old town plaza. It screams from pinatas and ropes of chili pepper swaying in the yards and on the front doors of homes." The Basilica de San Albino located in the central square of old town, is an imposing edifice and heralds the Catholicism and spirituality of the mostly Mexican-American population that lives in the area. Grace visited the beautiful basilica and felt the stirrings of the faith she had abandoned years before. She still felt comfortable with the traditions and trappings of the religion if not the belief system, and hypocrisies, of too many of its members and leaders.

The ambiance of White Sands, Grace went on, is diametrically opposed to Las Cruces. Most glaringly it lacks the intensity and vibrancy of color or even a hint of the lively ambiance of the latter. It is a stark chalky environment that is eerily beautiful in its ghostly albino-like colorless state. Here great white sand dunes of gypsum have created an almost extraterrestrial landscape in New Mexico. It was one of the most beautiful sights Grace had ever seen.

Traveling further, into Arizona, they toured the amazing ecosystem of the Sonora Desert with its famous saguaro cacti, symbolic of the American west. The Sonoran Desert Museum was an ecological and zoological wonder featuring the natural habitat of animals native to the terrain. Some, such as the javelina, a small pig-like creature, related to the hippopotamus, Grace, had never known existed. The western side of Arizona she found less enticing, particularly around the area of Yuma. Its bleak and violent frontier history seemed to echo into the present and was palpable on a visit to the historic Yuma Territorial Prison. On their return journey they would visit the Grand Canyon. By far the most wondrous sight in Arizona, if not the world, the Grand Canyon was carved into existence by the Colorado River. Its beauty is spiritually uplifting. Standing on the rim of the cavern Grace experienced a connection to history and the universe not experienced by her before. This is what she had been searching for since childhood. This opportunity to embrace, even momentarily, her inner spirit of freedom and wonder. With her "Prince" in her pocket and with Jim beside her, her connection to the past and present was complete in that moment.

They continued their cross-country odyssey until they reached San Diego. Jim had always hoped to return to this area. He had spent time training here at Camp Pendleton before his service in Viet Nam. He would return home from the war with a Purple Heart and memories he hasn't shared to this day. Well, Jim also being a bit of an "old" movie buff, they stayed at the Coronado Hotel. With its imposing red domed roof and magnificent Victorian architecture, this masterpiece of construction was the setting for one of his favorite movies, Some Like it Hot. Only the need to catch a plane to reach their ultimate destination of Hawaii could have drawn Grace away from this beautiful Pacific Ocean seaside resort.

Flying into Oahu the plane flies over Pearl Harbor. Grace could only imagine the terror of those kamikaze pilots and the horror of those young US servicemen below as they entered into one of the fiercest battles of military history. Grace's uncle had been one of the lucky ones to survive but it was undoubtedly a crushing defeat for our nation. The juxtaposition of the beauty of Hawaii and its tropical majesty as a backdrop for slaughter against humanity was sobering. Grace acknowledged this as she took comfort in the presence of her two Princes. One who survived with her father as he protected his nation during WWII and the other that had been saved in combat so that one day they could meet and marry.

Their final destination in this beautiful state was the lush, tropical island of Kauai. Perched on a cliff, facing the ocean, their sanctuary of two weeks would provide many beautiful memories. They watched whales breaching, powerful great frigate birds soaring, kayakers ploughing the Pacific waters and of course the omnipresent Hawaiian goose, the nene. Nothing could have been better for Grace's need for relaxation and re-cuperation. How fortunate she felt to have people care enough about her to provide such an opportunity for her. Though ap-prehensive still from her past, she could see her blessings were mounting! She would return home, physically and emotionally renewed, with beautiful memories of this journey of a lifetime, and items to recall it at will, placed loving in her hope chest.

Grace and Jim's world travels began in earnest after they had visited 49 of the 50 states. They would venture to Europe for the first time in 2006. Of course, Ireland and England, lands of their proud Celtic heritage, would be the first chosen to ac-quaint themselves with. This would be followed, over the com-ing decade, with journeys to Ireland, Italy, the Netherlands, Germany, France, Switzerland and Austria. There would be family fun excursions to Curacao and Aruba in the Caribbean. A vacation in Canada and Niagara Falls was shared with a still young Bink and CeCe. Grace was in the midst of planning a sojourn to Portugal and Spain, alone, when she reminisced about the travels she believed she would have as a young girl. Everyone believed then she was a childish idle dreamer, or as one uncle put it "a cock-eyed professor". "You'll learn", they cautioned her and laughed at her aspirations. "In time you'll find people like us don't travel." Maybe they didn't but she would, this much she knew.

CHAPTER
85

The next decade was replete with the events of most lives. There would be births and deaths, marriages and divorces, friendships made and friendships ended, graduations, illness, and yet, adventure - always adventure! Jim's oldest son, John, would marry, and have two children with his Pakistani born wife. She was a Muslim and in the style of Grace's family, they embraced the individual and gave respect to her family and their culture. They now had Catholics and Protestants, Jews and Muslims, atheists and agnostics, in their own growing, glorious melting pot. Could Buddhists and Hindis be far behind? This familial reality enriched everyone's knowledge, gave voice to grievances and debate, fostered the family's humanity and commonality and definitely expanded, and inspired, the family menus.

Jim's middle son, Robert, married in 2003 but would divorce his wife several years later after learning a local Mexican deejay had been playing her tune. This of course hit a sour note for Robert!

Tommy, Jim's youngest son would marry and move further away to the Pittsburgh area to be closer to his wife's family. Eventually they would have two sons, Joshua and Alex. To Jim's great disappointment, and because of his rapidly diminishing mobility caused by his service-connected disability, he would see these heirs to his family name only once a year. Eventually, with the onset of Covid-19 and the limitations it imposed on everyone, these visits would cease for several impactful years. He still continues to hope his son and daughter-in-law will find ways to include him in their lives.

John and his wife eventually divorced, and like Jimmy's daughter Sophia, their son John and daughter Sara, became victims of that event. Jim did as well since he rarely saw these two grandchildren after that. Currently he has not seen or heard from them in ten years. Lest one believe this is all too bleak Grace shared other successes of this same time.

Robbie, who came to South Carolina with his wife to pursue a career in the culinary arts, was dealt a heartless and cruel blow by this woman. One morning she left for work and never returned to him. She called to announce she wanted a divorce. She was in New York again. Her mother, who Rob and the family had just entertained for the weekend, had come bearing the gift of a one-way ticket back home for her daughter. The heart-rending scheme had been hatched and executed seamlessly leaving Grace's nephew stunned and traumatized. Merciless and thankless is the best way to describe this act upon a devoted husband. It would be learned eventually that she had married Rob on the rebound after experiencing her own dose of rejection. When her former fickle fiancée divorced the woman he had married, these two wretched individuals sought comfort in each other. Trust must be a serious issue in that union!

They say that one door closes and another opens. For Grace's nephew that door opened to let in Kristy, a lovely, very attractive, intelligent and supportive woman who cherishes him in her life. Kristy has been a wonderful fit for this unusually diverse family, bringing her Mormon upbringing into the mix. She has been instrumental in his success as a highly regarded executive chef in Myrtle Beach, featured in magazine articles and on TV.

Rob has paid forward on his achievement by training Danny in the culinary arts and employing him as his sous-chef. This led to the career Danny had chosen for himself even as a teenager. He now is a kitchen manager for a lucrative corporate enterprise. Although his upward mobility seems assured, he plans to open his own restaurant in the future. Perhaps a business partnership with his cousin Rob? Keep dreaming Danny. Seems in your family dreams do come true. To emphasize this point, Grace stopped in the conversation to recount how a significant dream of hers, did come true.

CHAPTER
86

As her granddaughter, Sarah, approached her 18th birthday Grace decided that there could be no better way to celebrate this occasion than with a party in Paris, surrounded by the glitter and glamour that defines this great city. This was the city that had beckoned Grace forever with its promise of excitement and enchantment. She began the planning in earnest that would finally fulfill what she had feared would be an unattainable fantasy.

How fitting it seemed that this dream, inspired by her father's service to his country, and his fondness for the French people, should be designed to celebrate the birthday of the great-granddaughter born on his birthday. Given the importance of the experience, the plans grew to include Alison, Kristy and Ann, Grace's best friend. There would be one more important and cherished traveler accompanying them, the

Prince. Grace would be bringing him home to the place his journey began.

One could easily expound endlessly about everything her greedy senses absorbed on this journey. The renowned sights and astounding art. The aroma and taste of delectable, creative cuisine and fine French wine surrounded her. Grace was enmeshed in the sounds of the seductive yet gracious French language she began to gradually recall from her earlier student life. The allure of French perfume competed with the smells of bread and pastries for her attention. Paris revealed itself to her as a visual panoply of the old and enduring adjacent to, and competing with, the mesmerizing magnificence of modern art, architecture, and high couture.

Grace's group was ensconced in an historic hotel, aptly named Hotel d' Louvre. It had formerly been part of the many structures housing the Louvre's vast collection of art and artifacts. However, it now stood as a separate, elegant edifice beside the Louvre and facing up a wide avenue leading directly to the Paris opera house, the Palais Garnier. Directly across the Seine River stands the Musee d'Orsay and its magnificent collection of art housed in a former train station. Furthermore, their room windows opened to a view of Cardinal Richelieu's residence. The "Red Eminence" was created a cardinal under the papery of Pope Gregory XV. He was yet another authoritarian, ruthless and merciless man extolled by the church of the day. There remain very mixed reviews of his contributions to the religious, political and social life of the country at this point. To this day, however, France is a very Catholic nation famous for its basilicas, cathedrals and its eerie, underground catacombs. Arriving during the week preceding Easter, Grace's group was not prepared for the shut-down of the entire country on Easter, the holiest of all Catholic holidays. The day became a respite for these weary but enamored travelers, however, who were departing the next morning. Despite the extraordinary memories this journey provided for Grace, it was the concierge of the hotel who brought her to joyful tears of gratitude for this opportunity.

Before departing for the airport on their return to the U.S., Grace had implored Michel to take one last picture holding the small pewter Prince. He immediately recognized the sculpture used as the model for the small statuette and asked how she had acquired it. She explained to him that her father had been in France and participated in the liberation of Paris, marching with his fellow American soldiers beneath the Arc de Triomphe and down the Champs Elysees to the cheering and boisterous gratitude of the French citizenry along their route.

When she looked at Michel as her account of this day climaxed, she could see tears in his eyes. His hand held the Prince against his chest, over his heart. With a voice wracked with emotion he said simply to Grace, "I wish to thank you for your father's service to my country". They embraced and Grace disappeared into the waiting vehicle. From that day forward she would no longer tolerate the ignorant remarks frequently directed by people around her towards the French people. Grace felt overwhelming pride in her father for recognizing, and transmitting to her, the goodness of the French soul.

CHAPTER
87

During the mid-teens of 2000, a significant event would change the course of Grace's life. As a young girl, you will recall she yearned to travel and to learn more about the family so strangely absent for most of her life. Omnipresent in her mind during those early years, however, was the lurking but simple mystery of her birth. That enigma being solved, her mind and body had been released to pursue, in earnest, her two other quests. The wonders and amazement of the first, travel, had miraculously led to the acquisition of the latter, family. Her journey to Ireland's countryside had engulfed her in the breathtaking beauty of green panoramas, brooding peat fields and the timeless, unhurried routines of a warm and welcoming populace. Natural gifts such as the Burren, the Cliffs of Moher and the Giants Causeway loom beside the ancient ruins of monuments to the past, such as Newgrange and the

Hill of Tara, constructed by Ireland's early residents. Lively cities, such as Dublin and Galway, stand as testament to the arts and culture Ireland has long been renowned for. Leadership and excellence in technology has joined these ancient birthrights. It was only upon her return to the States, reflecting on the significance of her trip, did Grace realize she had been there only as a visitor. She had felt, undoubtedly, the connection with the country and her people. The roots of her being were entrenched in Irish soil. She had bathed in the beauty and history of her people on this trip. She promised herself to learn more of her story and return to Ireland as a daughter. This time she would bring her sons.

Then Grace learned of a new and amazing service for tracking your biological history, Ancestry.com. After joining and exploring its capabilities, Grace developed a working profile for herself. From this vantage point she would begin seeking the information that had too long eluded her. She searched for documents and ship records to establish her grandparents' arrival in America. How mesmerizing the sight of these records were to an illiterate techie such as Grace. It was as though she had discovered Aladdin's lamp and was beginning to claim her wishes. While her search was ponderous at first, due to her lack of computer ability, she forged forward. Soon she would learn the names of her great-grandparents on her mother's side of her family, the names of her grandfather Daniels siblings and the address of the farm they were raised on in the county of Longford. There would be more revelations thanks to the existence of secured messaging between clients.

Searching for others with the same surname as her grandfather she stumbled upon a "tree" posted by a man in eastern Australia. Her outreach to him was productive. He responded by first apprising her that, although her grandparents had the same surname as him, they were not related. He had done extensive research and knew the lineage she was indeed attached to. He sent her a copy of his findings and the email addresses of two of her family members he had spoken directly to. One in England and one in County Longford. Her excitement was boundless! She held this information in abeyance while she researched the "tree" further to verify its authenticity to her. Miraculously it did! Not much time passed before she was contacted by another Australian gentleman, this time from the western side of the continent. Apparently, he had been informed by his compatriot that, he too, was part of the same lineage as Grace. He was sadly, an orphan, and had been searching his whole life for his birthparents. Though she had not actually been an adoptee as she had long suspected, his story resounded with Grace and her own search for her identity. She provided him with the email of the Longford family hoping they could give him some relevant information. Indeed, they did! He was close to Grace's age and his story was a tragic one of the impact of the Church upon his birthright. When his father, just a teenager and brother of Grace's grandfather Daniel, made a teenage girl pregnant, they were separated by the families as was the custom of the time. Clearly this was a religious disgrace and a sin of severe consequence. The lad was sent to England and, with the assistance of the Church, the young woman was sent to Australia to give birth and surrender her child for adoption. That child, who Grace now knew as Dennis, was a second cousin of hers. He was provided with the names of his parents and the location of his father's grave in England. Knowing his father would not be there to embrace him in the flesh as he had dreamed, he still went to pay respect to his dad and forgive him for the mistake that had made Dennis' life so difficult. Grace immediately felt fortunate to be in the same family as this man. He was such an honorable and loving individual in her esteem. When Grace subsequently contacted these relatives who had assisted Dennis, she was received with the same inclusive warmth that Dennis had described.

Ironically, while Grace was busy integrating this all, and relishing the success of her search, she began to wonder again about the family right here in the US, her father's. What had happened to them? They had not responded when her father had passed away, although the telephone number she called was a random one selected by name and city from the phone book. Perhaps they had never known of his death. Now, armed with the resources of Ancestry.com., she selected a possible candidate for kinship and sent him a brief bio. Within a literal instant he rsvp'd and provided her with a telephone number and beseeched her to call him immediately. That was the call that changed the direction of her life.

CHAPTER
88

S he quickly learned her respondent was the son of her first cousin. It was that cousin, born shortly before Grace, who was the recipient of all the "boy" baby clothes amassed by her own despondent mother, and shipped to a more suitable candidate. He had already died of cancer and this news saddened Grace, hopeful of reconnecting with people she might remember. However, his brother, Grace's younger cousin Phil was alive and well. So too, was their mutual cousin Cherie, the lovely porcelain featured child she had envied in her early years. Phil's sister Tricia was still around, although their older and younger brothers were gone. From these three cousins she learned of the fate of all her father' family, his parents and his siblings.

Poor Cherie, who had been raised by the sister and brother-in-law of her biological mother, had never learned the true identity of her father. Never even told she was adopted until well into her 30's, she had ultimately relinquished her search for this individual. Both her biological and adoptive mothers, selfishly, Grace felt, had failed to share this information with her. Grace's heart broke for her still fragile cousin Cherie. She had lived a beautiful life but been deprived of the most basic of human knowledge. As the relationship with Cherie was rekindled, she often referenced the local priest who had arranged for her adoption. He stayed in her life until his death, attending all important events both religious, secular and family. She referred to him in their conversations as "Father-father". Grace, knowing as she did of the intrigue and hypocrisy of the Church, and having just learned the story of her Australian cousin Dennis, worried that the paternity of Cherie's biological father may not have been the mystery it was purported to be. She secretly hoped she was wrong.

Spurred on by 50 years of separation, and a need to quench her thirst to grow her family, she began planning for a late summer reunion with her father's family. Her immediate family, nine of them, would travel to Boston to meet these "missing links". Jim booked space in a hotel so that Grace and her entire family could meet in a neutral venue. It was a soul stirring, heartening reunion with the requisite overabundance of hugs, embraces and kisses. They stumbled over each other asking questions and giving personal updates. Grace was transcended to an exhilarating place she had only dared dream of since childhood. How beautiful, handsome, articulate, humorous, sociable and loving they all were! Their acceptance of her and hers was immediate as it must be in a family. She would learn her family was comprised of heterosexuals and lesbians, handy-capable individuals and athletes, musicians and artists, sportscasters and scientists, law enforcers and law breakers, teachers and students, healthcare workers and businessmen, and one musical savant, Cherie's son Matt. Afflicted by cerebral palsy since birth, his pure heart and love of family made him a treasure to all. What a beautiful brood, encompassing the best of human qualities, intelligence and compassion. She loved them all instantly. Grace knew she was home.

They would spend an afternoon at Fenway Park since baseball had figured prominently in all their lives, hers included of course. When she learned the Red Sox would be playing the Yankees the weekend of their reunion the purchase of tickets to the game was pre-ordained. Her son, Jimmy, and nephew, Rob and his wife were all Red Sox fans like Grace. Joe, his wife and children represented the Yankees, of course, at this "slightly," competitive outing. The surprise for Grace was to learn many of her relatives were, also Yankee fans, as were her father's late brothers. This stinging fact had been hidden from her by her very partisan father. To honor her dad, Grace had several years earlier, enrolled in the "brick program" at Fenway. She was able to purchase a brick to be installed on the walkways inside the stadium. She felt it was like a star for her father on the Hollywood Walk of Fame only much better. This visit, therefore, gave the family, especially his three grandsons, an opportunity to see and spend a few moments at the brick, paying homage to the fan who had set their rivalry in motion, their beloved "grandpa". The photograph of this moment already was ranked high priority for the hope chest.

Grace suddenly began laughing, and stopped to add an amusing anecdote that encapsulated the fierce family baseball rivalry and its impact on the next generation.

She would never forget, she began, taking her boys to Yankee Stadium to attend a Yankees vs. Red Sox came. Clare had just been to Boston on a small vacation, and in spite of her own league loyalties, had purchased a handsome child-sized, official Red Sox uniform for Grace's youngest slugger. Grace saw no reason Jimmy shouldn't wear this new, prized possession to the game. She wasn't disturbed either that he took his felt Red Sox pennant off his bedroom wall to bring with him. Joe would, of course, be sporting his omnipresent Yankee t-shirt and baseball cap.

Their seats were located in the bleachers, with the hot sunlight of summer beating down on them. By the fifth inning, they were surrounded by many exuberant and inebriated fans. When one of Jimmy's heroes hit a home run, a Boston instigator behind them yelled, "c'mon kid, raise that banner". To Grace's horror her child turned, faced the throng of New York fans behind him, and vigorously and gleefully shook his banner at them. What followed was a shame to Yankee fans, NYC and major league baseball itself.

Grace and her boys were deluged with cups full of beer, corn cobs and peanuts. She quickly ordered her sons to seek shelter under their seats. The more demented of the fans began lighting up paper and programs and these incendiary weapons started raining down on them. At that point Grace observed several security officers approaching their position. They quickly sheltered and escorted them out of the stadium.

The abusers remained and were allowed to see the rest of the game while Grace and her little band headed safely, but sadly home. It was a small comfort to learn later that the Red Sox and emerged victorious in this outing against their arch enemies. On this day in Fenway, in September 2016, the Red Sox would beat the Yankees again!

CHAPTER
89

Grace requested, of course, to visit the graves of those in the family that she would meet only in spirit if not in person on this visit. She visited the burial spots of her Uncle John, and Uncle Phil and his wife Kay. Then, her second cousin, Sean, guided her to the grave of his father, her cousin Paul, who she had met once. He had always seemed part of her life because of their close birthdates and that one encounter many, many years ago.

Next, she was taken to the grave of her grandparents. Never having met her grandfather she said a silent prayer for him. She did, however, linger longer to forgive her grandmother for so callously rejecting her as her granddaughter. This was very difficult to do for Grace because she had been psychologically injured, surely, by her ostracism. Grace then took time to share with her the achievements in her life her grandmother had missed. Finally, Grace prayed for her soul.

Her Uncles Bill and Joe were interred with their parents. She noted, with despair, that the date of her Uncle Joe's passing was omitted from the tombstone. He had died in a state mental hospital. This facility had closed many years before and a subsequent search would produce no archives or records to declare his residency on this planet. Cherie and Grace agreed to right this wrong and arranged with a local stonemason to correct the situation and complete the inscription to the best of their knowledge.

The day before their return home, her cousin Sean hosted a large family reunion on the farm he shared with his wife. It was a wonderful finale to a wonderous celebration! That last evening together was replete with food and drink, love and laughter, the obligatory family "widescreen" photo, and most importantly, vows to remain in touch and visit often. Grace was happy to share that through frequent phone calls, instant messaging, and facebook posts, that has been accomplished! Best of all, of course, are the personal visits between their two home states.

Grace's two sons were absolutely ecstatic to know and meet the family they heard frequently referred to. Their only previous connection had been through a well-worn, green album of fading photos that Mare had kept in her hope chest. Grace kept the album in her own hope chest now. It had brought her alternating moments of joy and sadness as she perused it over the years. Her children, and grandchildren as well, loved to look through its yellowed pages in search of the more extended family they had all been deprived of. That chapter was now closed.

CHAPTER

90

That December, 2016, Grace and Joe flew to NYC to attend Jimmy's daughter's recital at Carnegie Hall. The weather in NY was frightfully cold that December but not as frigid as the heart of Jimmy's ex-wife who tried, unsuccessfully, to prevent them all from attending this beautiful, significant event. To perform at Carnegie Hall in Manhattan was the dream of every musical aspirant, present and past. Sophia was a gifted young percussionist and was selected to perform there with the NYC All Student Orchestra. As a musician himself, Jimmy's pride in his daughter was on display throughout the evening.

A short walk, following Sophia's performance, to view the Christmas Tree at Rockefeller Center, in all its mesmerizing beauty, was compulsory. For Grace it conjured up visits with her two toddlers to Macy's department store decades earlier. Here they would share with Santa their fervent wishes for special toys they coveted. Of course, they would attest innocently to the excellent behavior that merited such rewards. The photos taken each Christmas, as they sat on the big elf's lap, reveal variously poignant, puzzled and pouty faces. Yet they could not conceal the hope that the jolly saint's promise to them would be fulfilled once more. These photos sat among her beautiful memories in her hope chest, to be joined with those taken on this magical evening. They concluded the evening with a visit to the Essex House Hotel where Grace's parents had met and her story had begun. The love of family had prevailed that cold winter evening and the rewards would prove to be incalculable.

This trip also became an opportunity for Grace and her sons to share a nostalgic visit together in the city they all loved and had been born in. They would indulge in all the seminal New York food they had once enjoyed together. The panoply of options was extensive in this gastronomical, multicultural capital of the world but they returned, as always to their favorite spots. This would entail lively visits to a nearby Kosher deli where they would indulge in kosher franks and knishes. They would have the quintessential Chinese take-out in Flushing, Queens and savor meals replete with fried rice dinners, wontons and dumplings. A trip to a genuine NYC pizzeria, serving genuine NYC pizza was mandatory. It confirmed the undisputed fact that NYC pizza reigned as best and always would. Homemade spinach pie and souvlaki were enjoyed at their favorite Greek restaurant. A visit to the Bronx, where the boys were born, provided the tastiest chuletas, and plaintains with rice and beans Grace had enjoyed in a long time. They even included a trip to the ultimate server of NY comfort food, White Castle. Those little skinny, square burgers, onion rings and tiny donuts were a must to fill a hunger hole late in the evening. This delectable treat was affectionately called "murder-burger" by authentic NY gourmands.

The visit here brought to mind Jim's oft told story of how he could have single handedly captured the Son of Sam. He was a police officer in the Bayside section of Queens on the night the Son of Sam struck at a dance club in his precinct. Officers were deployed to scrutinize the area. On a hunch Jim walked into the local White Castle. He scanned the late-night diners at the eatery but saw nothing he considered unusual or suspicious. Later, upon his capture, David Berkowitz stated that he thought he was about to be apprehended, only once, by a policeman who had walked into White Castle the night of the shooting at the Elephas Club in Bayside.

Grace and her sons shared a somber, reflective moment at the World Trade Center memorial recalling for these native New Yorkers, the devastation of 9-11. At the reflecting pool, bathed in the solace it evoked, they paused, to honor those who had paid the ultimate price for our freedom. They recalled the bravery of the city's first responders, many of which perished themselves in the rescue operation. Numerous colleagues that did survive went on to experience years of sickness and suffering for their efforts. It was a sad and sobering remembrance. Yet, rising as the phoenix from the ashes, before them stood a powerful, indomitable, spiteful new Trade Center. Towering over Manhattan it defiantly declares the determination and durability of our democracy. It was a moving and memorable experience to witness firsthand, this monument to man's inhumanity to man.

Returning to Jimmy's home after such a melancholy experience Grace did not expect the joy she would experience from a simple chocolate cake inscribed in white icing, "Mom". Her two wonderful boys had remembered her birthday. As they sang "Happy Birthday" to her she prayed these moments would never end. Grace could not have imagined this had been her farewell tour to her beloved city. The next morning Grace and Joe flew home, not knowing they would never again see Jimmy alive. He was only fifty years old at the time.

CHAPTER
91

In the spring of 2017 Grace received an invitation to a wedding. That invitation brought her to tears. Not because it was in anyway sad or hurtful. It was at once so normal and yet remarkable. The invitation requested her and Jim's presence at her cousin Phil's son, Adam's, wedding. Grace's tearful reaction stemmed from the realization that this is what family's do. They invite family members to join them in celebrating life's most important moments. It signified to her in a small but tangible way that she was truly, unmistakably part of her father's family. After more than 50 years of searching she had found her way back home.

Over the next several months the approaching wedding was a source of much excitement, conversation and preparation within her family. Where would they stay? For how long? What would they wear? (This one truly only concerned Grace and the other "girls".) Jimmy was particularly excited to be re-turning to Massachusetts. He had previously discussed with his mother that finding grandpa's family had filled a chasm in his heart left by the death of his grandfather. That connection had expanded his world, remarkably, both in reality and spir-itually. He felt connected to a larger universe populated with people who knew him and welcomed him and loved him as he loved them. He expressed that what Grace had accomplished had enhanced Sophia's life as well and he would reinforce that for her. His ex-wife was hard at work contriving reasons Sophia could not be part of this celebration, but Jimmy stood stead-fast in his determination to defeat these evil efforts she was contriving.

In the days prior to the wedding, Grace would speak to him often. She was full of reminders about getting his clothes to the cleaner, getting his hair trimmed, checking on his flight and transportation to the airport. She even sent him photos via the message app on her phone with shoe suggestions. Ugh! She was being a mother, an annoying one at that. But she was just reveling in this momentous occasion in their life. She was as happy as she could be!

On Monday, September 18th, the telephone rang. Grace who had just entered the house rushed to answer it, slightly breathless. A man's voice asked her if she was the mother of James Quinn. Confused she answered in the affirmative. He then introduced himself as a doctor from Methodist Hospital in Brooklyn advising her that her son had suffered a heart at-tack while walking in the street after finishing his day's work. He calmly, but with compassion, told her Jimmy was not expected to live. He was returning to the operating room to see what more could be done and would call her back shortly. She hoped the call with the worst news a mother could receive would never come, but it did, too quickly. Jim answered the phone to receive the call he knew would not be good. The heart attack had been fatal and Grace's baby boy was gone. There would no longer be a wedding celebration to attend for Grace and her family. Instead, on that day, September 22nd, her son's wake would take place in Queens.

During the planning of the funeral, any attempt to be inclusive of Adrianne was met with a growing anger and resentment towards Grace and Joe. She sought to create drama and was despicable in her attempts to shift the focus from the tragedy of Jimmy's passing to her perceived injustices. Though invited to partake in the final preparations she chose to be rude and rejected all outreach for civility. Could she not see on her own daughter's face, and hear in her touching little eulogy to her dad, the pain the child was experiencing?

Grace doubted, sadly, that she even cared. In a heartless, horrifying decision on his part Jimmy's father did not come to the funeral even though he was notified. Grace would have preferred to blame his stony, antisemitic, selfish wife for his non-appearance. She knew, however, that this man, whose lack of empathy or understanding of his children, had led to his emotional abandonment of them decades earlier, bore the burden of this choice. His wife had been instrumental over the years, though, of convincing him that he didn't need to be in their lives. Due to her bitterness surrounding her own reproductively barren state, she had successfully re-focused his attention on her nieces and nephews in Ireland as a replacement for his own sons. Shame on them both.

Fortunately, there were several hundred in attendance who did care. The visitation, though somber and respectful, reflected the beauty of her son's soul and his love of all humanity. He was a completely unjudgmental man, accepting all people without trying to change them. He had only wished for the same in return. Many rose without invitation to extemporaneously extol his goodness and speak of his love of family, friends and music. The words echoed back to him, as he lay there in his Giants cap, expressing their love and admiration for him. Grace wrote a eulogy for her son that was read by her husband, who had loved Jimmy as his own, and recognized Grace's grief would not allow her to do it herself.

The most memorable part of the service was when several of his musician friends that he had toured with over the years, spontaneously began playing music and jamming. It was a true musician's sendoff, a joyful tribute of their love and appreciation of their friend. Grace, who had visited New Orleans several times with her sons, and had witnessed a jazz musician's funeral, knew about the second line, and its part in the culture of musicians there. Growing out of the slave trade of the South, such celebratory displays at musician funerals, intended to accompany the deceased joyfully into the afterlife, now transcend musical genre. Thus it was, that Grace's son, a white blues bassist, received such a powerful affirmation of love and respect from his peers. Way to go, Jimbo!

In one of the great ironies of her life her new found cousins from Massachusetts flew to South Carolina to attend an intimate ceremony in a local funeral parlor for her son one week later. This was the father and aunt of the groom whose wedding they had all planned to attend. Now they would share together for the first time not the sacrament of marriage but the ultimate and final sacrament of death. This second service allowed friends and family, locally, to pay their respects to Jimmy and his family. Her cousin Cherie sang, upon Grace's request, a beautiful hymn that had been sung at Clare's funeral as well, the Ave Maria. A family friend sang a bluesy version of Amazing Grace. Grace hoped Jimmy was pleased.

Grieve not..
Nor speak of me with tears...
But laugh and talk of me as though I were beside you.
I loved you so...
'Twas heaven
here with you.

CHAPTER
92

As with any great personal tragedy, Jimmy's death brought both sadness and salvation to Grace. The sorrow was immediate, unrelenting and unbearable. The salvation would evolve slowly and purposefully with the passage of time. At first, it had pulled her apart, like a completed puzzle suddenly disassembled and returned in pieces, forcibly, to its darkness in a box. When taken out next it would be missing important pieces so that the puzzle could never be whole again, useless to anyone who might want to engage with it.

Gradually she found comfort in signs that she imagined her son sent to her to confirm he was still present in her lonely universe. A bright penny, the serendipitous appearance of a stunningly beautiful red cardinal, his birth date on the license plates of cars passing on the road, the image of his totem, the lion, on a t-shirt or tattooed bicep, all appeared to her as evidence of his presence with her as she hobbled, shattered through the early months of his passing. These were momentary and fanciful consolations that made her smile at her darkest times. Her behavior was consistent with the Irish American culture her soul was steeped in. The desire to believe in celestial signs and messages. To find comfort in the promise of a glorious afterlife. She tried to return to these seedlings of her Roman Catholic faith and seize the comfort it offered her. However, Grace had evolved too far away from the myths and hypocrisies of the faith of her parents. She saw things rationally, and analytically, and believed in her own power to heal this mortal wound to her body, soul and spirit. After several self-indulgent months she began the real, but arduous, healing process.

She began by reading books on the subject of grieving that validated what she was feeling and offered the hope that this anguish could be alleviated if not totally vanquished. Grace tried group grief counseling at first but could not bear the extreme sadness it engendered. Other parents who had lost their children through homicide, war, horrific vehicular accidents, and suicide were at least as broken as Grace. She could not abide looking in the mirror they offered and seeing her reflection in their pain.

Grace next sought individual counseling. This was a very gratifying, and successful, experience. Able to speak freely to a compassionate and intelligent professional was the beginning of her true recovery. The sessions, though tearful, dealing with issues of loss, guilt and recovery were difficult but productive. The self-examination they promoted as well was enlightening. Grace gradually chartered a path to regain her sense of self-purpose and self-forgiveness. As important to her was her need to create a means of continuity for Jimmy's memory. Not surprisingly she would find her path to accomplish this through his music.

One afternoon while sitting, quietly recalling beautiful memories of her son, with a CD of his music playing softly in the background, a wonderful thought occurred to her. She would reach out to the Blues Foundation in Memphis. With their assistance she hoped to create a small scholarship in his name. She hoped her contribution of $1,000 a year would fund summer music camp for a student filled with fervor for the blues but lacking the funds to fulfill his dream of learning to play an instrument.

Her initial phone call put Grace in contact with some helpful reps of the foundation dedicated to the preservation of this wonderful American music style. Her call for information led to a return call from the CEO of the organization and a spirited conversation about "the man and his music". Grace was grateful to exchange stories of, and accomplishments in, her son's musical journey. She shared how this teenage "Kiss" idolizer, became a blues artist. How this young poet became an amazing songwriter. How she, herself, had hosted many noted bluesmen in her home, friends and collaborators of Jimmy. The executive invited Grace and her family to the annual Blues Awards dinner in Memphis that May. On a follow-up call, Grace was informed that the Blues Foundation would be honoring her son, in memoriam, at this yearly industry event.

The evening was amazing! The huge banquet hall was filled with famous blues musicians of the past, the present as well as the novitiates who will define the future of the genre. Stevie Van Zandt of Bruce Springsteen's E Street Band was the master of ceremonies and one of the award presenters. When he introduced Jimbo's name, a wonderful photo of him taken onstage, playing his bass, was displayed on a giant screen on the stage. Grace was overcome with a mélange of sadness, pride and love. "If only he could see this," she thought. She secretly wished it was so. What she knew for sure was that she had devised the perfect plan to honor her child. The following year a commemorative brick was placed at the entrance to the Blues Museum in Memphis. The entire family contributed to composing the words on the brick. It read simply, yet elegantly:

JAMES 'JIMBO' QUINN

BASSIST, SONGWRITER, POET

HUMBLE, LOYAL AND WILDLY AMUSING

WE WILL LOVE YOU ALWAYS

One final homage to Jimmy is yet to come. After returning from the funeral parlor Grace found atop her son's refrigerator the words to a final song he was composing. They were written on the back of a used envelope. Clearly this was a reminder of his creativity and a nod to his meticulous filing system! She stood there smiling feeling he had left this beautiful gift for her to find, knowing that she would look in obscure places for his most important papers. Joe was equally unsurprised and laughing promised to compose the music to Jimmy's lyrics.

Grace was ecstatic to hear Joe's intentions to honor his brother this way. It would be a miraculous symbiosis of her two son's artistic proficiencies. Grace left NYC with many rekindled, beautiful memories of a beautiful son and the words of his last song, in his own handwriting, to be put in her beloved family hope chest.

CHAPTER

93

In the months ahead, and having achieved the "acceptance stage" of death, she began planning a trip to Ireland. She had dreamed for many, many years that one day she would stand in Ireland on the Cliffs of Mohr with her sons by her side. It is a dream similar to the cherished aspirations of many second-generation Irish Americans like herself. She had long envisioned this journey of escorting her offspring to the land of their ancestry to experience its stunning beauty while embracing directly the culture and history, bequeathed by their ancestors. Now, with a sense of urgency driven by the unpredictability of life they had so savagely experienced, she began to plan a healing pilgrimage to her grandparents' homeland. Grace, Jim, and her son and his wife would be taking the trip together. What solidified the spirit and significance of the journey was a request by her cousin Cherie and her husband Rick to join them on this odyssey. Whoever could have imagined that after 50 years of seemingly irretrievable separation, the two cousins that had searched for a lifetime to solve the mysteries of their births, would be making this trip together? "Meant to be" does not even approach an explanation for this vagary in their lives. It does underscore, however, that the quest for meaning in one's life remains a potent force for both believers such as Cherie and doubters such as Grace.

On this return trip in 2018 for Grace and Jim, they would begin with visits to Belfast and Derry in Northern Ireland. They stayed in the Europa Hotel in Belfast known by its moniker as the most bombed hotel in Europe, indeed the world. It sustained 36 bomb attacks since its erection in 1971, most at the hand of the Irish Republican Army during "the troubles". There was a mutually perceived iciness among the staff to their party and their driver a Southern Irish Catholic gent. Grace had earlier decided to experience Belfast through a neutral prism. Her childhood had been filled with the rhetoric of republican supporters of a free Ireland. The horror stories of the Black and Tans were frequently referred to in family discussions of an earlier time in Ireland. She knew she had developed a bias to all things English and hoped this trip would help to expunge that. Most impressive to their small group were the Peace Walls of Belfast. These murals painted on the side of many Belfast walls stood as testament to the horror of oppression and the equally radical response of an enraged citizenry. Grace knew these walls had been created and preserved, not only as a visual depiction of "the troubles" but also as an attempt to begin a healing process among the North and the

South of this small country. They were spectacular in their number, size and impact on an Irish-American such as Grace.

After visiting a museum at the docks honoring the birthplace of the Titanic and taking a beautiful stroll through the fantastic Belfast botanical gardens, they moved on to Derry, the next stop on their itinerary. Grace was aware by now that their mutual cousin, Phil, had been stationed with our military forces in Derry during the troubles. He lived there with his young wife, Mary. In fact, their first child, Tara, her second cousin, was born an Irish citizen.

Grace knew, also, that the designation "the troubles", was the name given to the conflict in a land that would be devastated by brutal religious internecine warfare between Catholics and Protestants until a tenuous truce was achieved in 1998. Here the long-standing contentious politics and religious discrimination of Irish society were still on display. This tension created wounds that festered and are still oozing today. It is manifest in the murals and street art of Derry. It is more subtly decried in the latent, almost imperceptible bullet hole impressions remaining on the facades of buildings. For her son, Joe, these visual representations of his ancestors' struggles was definitive. His own art is heavily political in nature. He was drawn viscerally into the tableaus that loomed above him, glaring defiantly down on Derry. As an artist he was captured by the color, movement and messaging in these massive artistic works. As a photographer he was engaged documenting everything he saw. Grace was detecting that this experience would have an enduring, validating effect on his own art. He exhibited increased pride in his Irish heritage on many levels.

This journey became memorable for many reasons of course. Yet the pinnacle of its importance in Clare's life was an invitation to have lunch in the home of her Irish cousin Declan whom she had found through Ancestry. It was only when they arrived at his beautiful country manor in Longford that she perceived the significance of this visit. It was as she, having embraced Declan and his wife, introduced her cousin Cherie and her husband, that Clare realized she had successfully intertwined the two roots of her existence. Here she sat, engaged in lively banter with two of the missing links she had sought throughout her lifelong odyssey. A miraculous merger of her mother and father's biological gifts to her. She was overwhelmed by the serendipity of life and the rewards of following your dreams. How thrilled she was to learn that she was sitting in a home built on the land of her great, great grandfather Bernard, a simple Irish farmer. Grace knew she was home. As she shared the beautiful photo of Jimmy, she had brought to show them, even in her sorrow she knew she had brought him home spiritually as well. At long last, a profound aura of peace and self-acceptance surrounded Grace.

Speaking of the Irish, have you heard of Murphy's law, the old saw that suggests "if anything can go wrong it will"? Well, these words can be seen in many places in Ireland and because of the name "Murphy", a righteous Irish surname, it has often been attributed to an Irish origin. Ironically, however, it was actually an Irish-American Captain Edward Murphy, an aerospace engineer, who first coined the phrase. So it was that in 2019, when the first acknowledgments of a deadly new virus were breaking world-wide, Grace applied this maxim to her own life. Things at that point of her life were beginning to brighten. She had dealt with the loss of her son and benefitted in unexpected ways from the healing process. The "little world traveler" had by now seen many countries of the world and was planning one more for the spring of 2019. This would be a special experience for Grace who would be traveling solo to Europe, accompanied only by her tiny pewter Prince, to explore Portugal and Spain. Her faith in her abilities and confidence in herself would help her to accomplish this.

The wanderlust of her childhood years, were still evident in this aging woman. Grace had been reunited with her family, on both sides of a vast ocean. Mutual visits and celebrations promised, were anticipated eagerly. Most importantly, she knew exactly who she was. The question of her origins was no longer there to persistently and savagely nettle away at her. Therefore, it was with a sense of doom that she absorbed the news of a global pandemic.

CHAPTER
94

G race could not help but make comparisons to the lethal Spanish flu of 1918 that had wantonly, capriciously claimed the life of her grandfather and millions of others around the planet. Her concerns mounted as the plague evolved in severity internationally. International travel was suspended. Understandably Grace's "bucket list", independent, trip to Portugal was canceled. This special journey through which she had sought to sate the fervor in her to see the world on her own terms, in her own time, was terminated. Her disappointment, however, was insignificant compared to the impact this world crisis had on others. Commerce transformed, too. Many employees working from home with the assistance of a new business adjunct, Zoom, became commonplace. The growth of home shopping and delivery became astronomical with companies such as Amazon and Door Dash growing their profits exponentially. We were all living in a new world order and it was frightening at times.

Grace, who always worried, did so now more than ever. The knowledge that Covid 19 was especially lethal to the elderly and those with underlying health issues fully alerted her to the potential for personal impact. She worried most for her husband, who after ten long, contentious years dealing with the Veterans' Administration had finally settled his claim for veteran benefits based on the ravages to his nervous system caused by Agent Orange. The neuropathy he was afflicted with greatly affected his mobility. The deadly chemical had created other issues for his immune system as well. The worst news was that it was a progressive condition. Therefore, he was at increased vulnerability to the disease.

It resonated in another way for her son and his wife. Joe, who had been accepted as a graduate student in fine arts at the prestigious Massachusetts College of Art and Design, learned of the cancellation of his first summer classes. They were replaced with distance learning, a handicap especially for artists dealing in concrete three dimensional products and presentations. Museum and gallery visits, vital to the furthering of his professional career were interrupted. For Alison it meant a change to remote learning. She worried daily that her speech students were not benefitting enough from this "hands off" form of instruction.

Perhaps the worst effect of the pandemic was the dissension it caused among family and friends. Grace held our government responsible for this. Politicians became involved and party loyalties, not unity, prevailed. Even as they debated the efficacy of a new vaccine created to reduce the morbidity rates upon our citizens, politicians created a social drama of darkness and division. Republicans claimed the Democrats were part of a cabal with the Chinese to disguise sanctioned lab testing of deadly viruses in China. Democrats consistently blamed Republicans and the Republican president, for waiting too long to engage with the situation, giving the deadly virus a head start with its infectious abilities. All potential social and medical remedies to deal with the escalating situation were subject to partisan attacks. The horrors, hyperbole and even misplaced humor proposed to defeat such a pernicious combatant as covid 19, spoke to the fears, lack of integrity and inertia of our leaders. Citizens were left to muddle through a torrent of misinformation and name calling looking for direction. When the President himself appeared to publicly tout the use of bleach injections as an effective means of treating the virus, Grace knew we had all entered a new phase of societal madness.

The solution to the problem, both politically and medically she chose for herself, was to patiently await the arrival of the life-saving vaccine that was purported to be in development. In the interim she would maintain ties with friends and family, here and abroad, through the phone and social media. These relationships seemed especially important now. So it was, when she received a St. Patrick's Day greeting from her newly discovered family in Australia, that she was filled with excitement and gratitude. When her Irish clan sent her a link on Viber to watch their grandchildren perform at a Christmas pageant in Longford, Ireland, Grace was thrilled by the invitation. Cherie blessed her with a reading of The Night Before Christmas, a charming, dramatic performance by her son Matthew posted on YouTube. These constant reminders by her family of their well-being and her continued presence in their lives, buoyed Grace's spirit of optimism. She hoped sincerely people all over the globe were seizing this opportunity to connect with others in a more creative and meaningful way.

Grace continued hosting Sunday family dinners throughout the epidemic. Family creativity took center stage in achieving this. On warm or balmy days dinner was enjoyed on the outside patio, with seating maintained six feet apart. On rainy or colder days, the garage was transformed into a dining area, again with chairs arranged at suitable distances from each other. The background noise generated by the dread and hysteria in the outside world, was subdued by the level of humor and beautiful aromas inside their weekly refuge. Grace was thrilled by the decision to share the burden of meal preparation among the participants. With the addition of home delivery service, expanded by more eateries to offset their losses during this lockdown, her family stayed well-fed as always on Sunday afternoons and evenings.

It took time for Grace to see the possibilities this, seemingly endless, idle time offered. Always a prolific reader, she started working her way through the many novels she had on her "to be enjoyed" list. She undertook a complete re-organization of her home concentrating on cleaning every area and eventually clearing out superfluous items that had become perpetual squatters in her domain.

Grace seized the opportunity to learn to use new venues such as Netflix and Hulu to provide opportunities to see movies since theaters were closed indefinitely. This became a life line for Jim, who, as an avid sports fan was absolutely suffering withdrawal symptoms when his sports viewing became impacted. It was a challenging, and could have been an almost cheerless time, were it not for the optimism and creativity Grace brought to her situation.

There was time now for reflection on important issues that had long been hidden behind the screen of daily life and life's other distractions, both good and bad. What hadn't been expected was a truthful examination of her relationship with her older son, Joseph.

CHAPTER

95

When she had entered the therapeutic process to assuage her grief over the death of her younger child, she had no idea the experience would heighten the awareness of her immense fear of losing yet another, her first born. Reflecting on their interaction over the years she realized finally it had been encumbered by her own guilt. First, for not removing him sooner from the tyranny of an abusive father. Then imposing on her children, the tribulations of being part of an interracial family at a decidedly less receptive time in our society. She saw all their arguments and disagreements over the years as a product of the decisions she made, or didn't make, as they grew. She had imposed this burden of guilt and non-forgiveness on herself through the prism she had chosen to view their collective lives. This vantage point had been formed, of course, by her own familial, cultural and religious experiences growing up.

She now realized, yes, these had been contributing factors to their development, but so too were the normal aches, pains and parental grievances of all progeny. Her sons had not been the product of only her decisions but a compilation of all their experiences, interactions, disappointments, successes and desires. Grace accepted that beyond the battling and the petty bickering over the years, she was blessed with a loyal and loving son in Joseph that had always respected and supported her as she did the man he had become. Her acceptance of the events in each son's life, and her understanding of their personal relationships with her, had been achieved through the process of self-examination during a dark and bleak time in our country. For this alone she was forever grateful.

Grace, not unrealistically, refers to her son Joe, as a renaissance man. He is undoubtedly the most creative man she has ever known. His metamorphosis from musician, to writer, to master/diver scuba instructor, to underwater photographer, to photo journalist, has culminated into his entrance to the world of fine arts. He is a respected member of that community and has shown his work in galleries in both Charleston, S.C. and Boston, Mass. Though not his complete portfolio of subjects, his keen interest in politics and world events is reflected in his vibrant depiction of cultural and societal issues for which he has received peer acceptance and praise. He is clearly a man who has returned to the wellspring of his joys as a youngster to create his world going forward. To accompany him on this journey he has the unfailing support of his wife Alison.

At the age of 78 Grace received the verbal vindication, that she longed for, of her commitment to her sons that could only come now from Joe. He spoke of his gratitude to her for a life filled with all styles of music and art, the warmth of friendships, the love of family and his distinct, if different, multi-cultural immersion. He attributed the veracity of his life to the experiences he had growing and maturing. He had a precocious ability to understand social issues and problems since his youth. He acknowledged now it had transformed to a ferocious fire within that defined his art. This he freely attributed to the unique world he had physically, and emotionally, been raised in. His is the work of a man who is simply reflecting the environment and experiences of his life with passion and truth.

CHAPTER
96

Even the isolation caused by Covid-19 could not protect one fully from the outside world. Nor could it stop the pain of another tragedy for Grace. In September, 1920, at the peak of the covid confinement, Joe read on Facebook, about the death of his mother's lifelong friend, Ann. Ann had been omnipresent in his, and his brother's life, since they were toddlers. Joe and Alison rushed to Grace's home so that she would not discover this herself via such an impersonal venue as Facebook. Jim immediately phoned Ann's home and when her husband answered, it was confirmed by him that she had died the previous night.

Ann, who had been an anchor in her life, was now gone from Grace. Ann who had shared the college experience with her as two young mothers defining their path in life, was dead. The amazing woman who shared the same career, at the same time, who was loved and respected by staff, students and parents had been lost. Her confidante and springboard for new ideas and problem solving had left her. The one responsible for so much humor and joy in her life had stopped laughing. For the second time in three years, she was brought to her knees in stunned silence. Then came the sobbing caused by the passing of this kindred spirit and empathetic soul. The devastation was worsened by restrictions imposed in our new covid society. The airlines could not guarantee a flight to New Jersey. The church and funeral parlor restricted attendance to only twenty mourners and hotels in the area were not accepting guests. Grace would be left to mourn the life, and loss, of her dearest friend from eight hundred miles away.

Just as Mare's death had left her an orphan, and Clare's death had left her without a sibling, Christine's death had left her friendless it could be said. Christine had been her friend for 52 years.

Maria, a fiery, fun-loving and flamboyant Puerto Rican had been her friend for 35 years when she passed away from cancer in 2010. They considered themselves "sisters" having both been raised in the South Bronx and attended the same junior high and high school. Eventually, and with no pre-arrangement, they would wind up being next door neighbors in Queens as well as colleagues teaching in the same intermediate school.

Dear Betty, a nurse who had been the victim of often vicious racism due to her bi-racial origins, had been her friend for 30 years until her demise. She had assisted Grace in the care of her father until his death. She accompanied Grace to the hospital the morning of her mother's passing. Complications from

Grave's disease finally took the life of this wonderful friend and selfless caregiver. All these women had undeniably strong influences on Grace. She accepted as her mission the telling of their stories and her thankfulness for their being, until she too, would depart this world someday.

CHAPTER
97

As Grace began to plan other projects she would tackle, she remembered how she had always promised herself to write a novel someday. The concepts of time, subject and life's many problems had intervened to prevent this, until now. She found herself blessed, in some ways, with an abundance of time to focus on such a project. Her mind, body and spirit seemed to be fairly fit at the moment and could probably even benefit by some mental gymnastics. It was at that moment that she chose to seize the opportunities in front of her to finally write a novel. The subject, she realized had been emerging over time, revealing itself fully to her now. She would document her life journey to leave as a legacy to her grandchildren. Because of the vagaries of life, they had never met many of the people she had loved over a lifetime. She would strive to introduce these unique personalities to them with her words, through her writing. Grace could only hope they would love many of them as she had and claim them as their heritage.

It is said that, "Old sins cause long shadows". Grace knew this to be true. She had been born in sin, and lived within the shadows of its uncertainty for half her life. Her struggle to expose its harmful, corrosive nature and attain acceptance and self-love, had consumed the second half of her existence. It was a difficult, frequently tearful journey, filled with fears, falsehoods and fabrications. It was a struggle rife with rejection and self-torment. Ultimately, and most importantly, it was a tale of enlightenment, wish fulfillment and gratitude. Her gratitude for being able to trace her story, her history, and leave her own child and grandchildren with a legacy of love. She wants them to be proud of their working-class Irish-American heritage. How their brave ancestors traveled here leaving their own country and loved ones behind. Grace wants them to understand how the importation of the distinctive Irish culture led ultimately to its appropriation. That it was the creative magnificence and malleability of their forefathers and mothers, that led to their ultimate acceptance and inclusion in their beloved America. How they had emerged after decades of rampant discrimination, oft times violent, as a new breed, the Irish-Americans.

Grace wanted them to be aware, as well, that the successful propaganda of the Church, these newcomers loved and feared, had been successful in having them hide whole aspects of their lives and desires from themselves. How they were trained through its doctrine and tenets to self-monitor and be ashamed, in fact report through confession, your own feelings and actions, sins venal and mortal. Grace had been the victim of this indoctrination. She was not anymore. She was an old woman now, the matriarch of her family. It had been many years since she could kneel like her younger self to contemplate the mysteries of the hope chest. But no need now because her mysteries were solved, her dreams fulfilled and her fears conquered. While others may still see a simple, unadorned, inexpensive chest of clutter and frivolities, Grace sees a trunk of treasures, indeed, a vessel of vitality and vindication. There are no secrets of others, now, to torment her. She has few of her own. Her memories and mementoes of a rewarding life are displayed brazenly on her walls for all to see. Her most cherished memorabilia tucked safely in her wooden ark. Her trunk had become a time machine, forging memories of the past with dreams for the future.

Grace stirred from an afternoon nap having dozed off as older people sometimes do. She found herself seated in her comfortable, leather recliner. She was in her bedroom, facing her hope chest. The hope chest was more battered up perhaps, not only because of its age, but from the burden of the many secrets and sins it had given sanctuary to. But it still gleamed in Grace's eyes and resonated in her heart. There would be new treasures of hope, possibilities and memories cherished, for it to harbor. There would be documents of an open past. Secrets will be disdained and denied entry. Fears would be forbidden and judgments rejected. Grace was fully aware now of how her mother had suffered from her exile and excommunication from her church, her refuge. She knew also how the ramifications of the stain of secrecy she engaged in for decades, had been destructive to them all. Finally, it was over.

This had long been her favorite spot when seeking to drift away if only for a moment. That afternoon, as she often did, she had been contemplating the one thing that had not been resolved satisfactorily for her over the years. Why was the name Grace bestowed on her? Was it a symbol of irony? Was it an act of defiance by her mother directed at the Church that had shunned her? It is true that grace is seen by that institution as a holy gift for the salvation of sinners. Maybe Mare sought to give grace to her innocent daughter in the only way left available to her. Finally, and decisively, she accepted the belief that it was an act of love. It was a lovely name conferred on her by loving parents in memory of a lost, abandoned soul, her father's sister Anna Grace. With this penultimate question settled, she had fallen asleep.

Awake now from her daytime reverie, she realized she had been dreaming but couldn't readily recall the details of the dream as it was already fading. What remained were little wisps of memories trying unsuccessfully to wrap their gossamer tentacles around her consciousness to no avail. The feeling that remained, however, was a warm one, a comforting one. The kind that makes you want to return to a place where you felt good and were surrounded by people who loved you. She realized increasingly though, that they were a populace existing only in her innermost being now. Though she had known them, and loved them, she wanted others to become aware off their existence as well. She remembered suddenly that in her dream she had been writing a book for her grandchildren. Moving as swiftly as she was still able to Grace reached her desk in the corner of the room. She retrieved a few sheets of paper and a pen, and returning to her seat facing the hope chest, she whispered, "Hi, old friend. I think I am ready to tell our story now." Upon that first clean, white page, in her still resolute, very legible handwriting she wrote, in capital letters, the word "REMEMBERANCES".

ABOUT
THE AUTHOR

Anne Yorke spent her career in education as a teacher, mentor, and administrator in New York City. A graduate of Columbia University, she holds a master's degree in literature and another in Administration and Supervision. school administration. A mother of two and grandmother of three, she recently retired to the South Carolina Lowcountry with her husband, a former New York City detective. She is currently working on her next novel. Follow her on Instagram @anneyorkeauthor